IF I WERE

'Excuse me, H...

The agent glanced up at him. His eyes were cold but not hostile. 'Yes?'

Dennis took a deep breath. 'D'you need any brickies for Düsseldorf?'

Pfister scanned his list before he answered. 'I have jobs for two only.'

Dennis and Oz exchanged concerned looks. 'You couldn't make it three, chief, could you?'

'Nein. For Düsseldorf they need now only two bricklayers. Also carpenters.'

To Oz's amazement, Dennis smiled with apparent relief. 'Aw, we're fine then,' he answered quickly. 'This lad,' he explained, turning to point out Neville nearby, 'is a carpenter.'

Neville had given up on the beer for the moment and was listening in to the conversation. He looked shocked. 'But I'm . . .'

'Just get the beers in, Neville,' Dennis barked. 'There y'are. We're your lads, Herr Pfister . . .'

'. . . Dennis, I'm not a carpenter, man,' Neville protested weakly.

'Rubbish. Didn't you take woodwork at school?' Dennis was implacable.

'Well yes, but . . .'

'Then you're a carpenter.'

Auf Wiedersehen, Pet

FRED TAYLOR

based on the Central television series
by Dick Clement and Ian La Frenais
from an original idea by Franc Roddam

SPHERE BOOKS LIMITED
London and Sydney

First published in Great Britain by
Sphere Books Ltd 1983
30–32 Gray's Inn Road, London WC1X 8JL
Reprinted 1983, 1984 (three times), 1985

TRADE
MARK

Set in Times

Printed and bound in Great Britain by
Cox & Wyman Ltd, Reading

ONE

Oz's '68 Zephyr had looked pretty down even before the three of them left Newcastle. By the time they reached the queue of traffic at the Dutch border, it was at the stage of needing terminal care. Not that Oz would admit it. Not that Oz would admit anything that didn't suit whatever his momentary view of reality demanded.

'Afraid we're losin' Radio One,' he muttered darkly, fiddling with the car's radio. The material the knobs were made of looked suspiciously like bakelite.

Dennis grunted, took a drag on his newly-lit duty-free. 'We never had it in this wreck.'

'Canny car, this, kid,' said Oz for the dozenth time.

There was no answer to that, or leastways none that didn't stray into the realms of fantasy or insult. Dennis's square, well-fleshed face creased into a frown. He decided to change the subject.

'Here,' he said. 'Why've you got a Sunderland sticker on the back? I never knew you supported them.'

'I don't. Bloke I bought it off did.' Oz stared down at the radio, gave it a final thump and treated his mates to a gap-toothed grin. 'I was goin' to scrape it off, but I was afraid I'd lose the bumper ...'

Suddenly the car in front moved forward. Oz wrenched the Zephyr back into gear, goaded it to keep up with the traffic queue, hissing curses all the while. They were getting close to the customs post at last.

'This is it,' he said, turning to the third passenger, who had been sitting quietly in the back. 'Don't panic, Neville.

We'll all stick to the same story. We're off to catch butterflies in Bavaria.'

Neville nodded miserably. He hadn't even the strength to write another card home to his Brenda, let alone indulge in backchat. The sea journey, the bumpy ride in the Zephyr, the billowing cigarette smoke produced by Dennis, had all contributed – along with simple anxiety – to making Neville feel about as low as the proverbial snake's belly.

'Your passports please!' A pink-faced Dutch customs official leaned down to peer into the car. He looked bored, a little hostile.

Dennis, who had been minding the documents, passed them over to him.

'Anything to declare?' the official asked in his fluent, if rather stiff, English as he flipped through their passports, checking the ID photos. He stopped, stared at one, looked quizzically at Oz, then shrugged. Most people's reaction to Oz ran along those lines.

Dennis had his mature, responsible face on. 'Oh, just the duty-free,' he said. 'Scotch an' ciggies.'

The Dutchman looked at Dennis, then again at Oz. He didn't seem to be taking in Neville at all, which was again most people's reaction at first meeting. He came to a decision.

'Would you open the back, please?'

Dennis sighed. 'Give us the keys, Oz.'

'It doesn't lock.'

Dennis needed two tries to get out of the door, another three to shut it again. With as much dignity as he could muster by this time, he walked round and opened the boot for the customs man, silently praying that it wouldn't come away in his hand. He knew a bit about cars, and he *believed* what Oz had said about the bumper.

In the event it was okay. The boot opened to reveal two suitcases and a canvas grip bag, three pairs of wellies and donkey jackets. And a long, metal object that immediately caught the official's eye.

'What is this?' he said, picking it up.

Dennis smiled innocently. Why was he always the bloody leader, the one in the firing line?

'A spirit level,' he said.

'What is a spirit level?'

Sod it, thought Dennis. 'I'll show you.'

He gently plucked the spirit level out of the man's hands, took a couple of paces past him and placed it on the low wall that separated the lanes of traffic passing through the customs post. Then he rocked on his heels, glancing at the Dutchman and waiting for a reaction.

A nervous smile from the official. 'What does this mean?'

Dennis, who could have good timing when he wanted it, waited for a moment, looked down at the level, carefully checked the position of the air bubble with a professional eye.

'It means,' he told the bemused official, 'that your wall's not plumb ...'

Maybe the Dutch had a sense of humour, or more likely they were turning a bit of a blind eye in the tolerant way of their nation, but within a couple of minutes the ancient saloon was on its way through the flat, green countryside of Holland. Dennis, Oz and Neville were in. They kept on for a while before the general feeling swung in favour of a cuppa and a sandwich.

In the small roadside café, the two older men fetched the goodies while young Neville finished off yet another postcard to Brenda. He seemed oblivious as Oz plonked down a cup of tea and a pile of sandwiches, then shamelessly peered over the lad's shoulder to look at what he was writing.

Dearest Brenda, Oz read. *Well, here I am in Holland. It could almost be England except that we are driving on the wrong side of the road. Dennis sends his love. The other bloke, Oz, seems a bit of a joker ... I love you and miss you. Yours till the next point of interest. Nev.*

'Christ, another postcard is it, Neville?' Oz said loudly with a wink at Dennis.

Dennis, po-faced, unwrapped his sandwich, staring with mild suspicion at the meagre cheese filling. 'Aye. He promised he'd keep in touch.'

Oz grunted and slurped his tea. 'He wrote the first one at

Darlington. At this rate he'll blow all his money on postage.'

Nothing daunted, Neville pursed his lips, fished another stamp out of his pocket and stuck it firmly on the card. Only when he had completed his duty task did he show any emotion. His good-natured, though serious, young face turned wistful.

'She didn't want me to come. She said she accepted it, though,' he announced to no one in particular. '"Whatever's best for us," she said. Then last night . . . she was a bit tearful.'

Oz made a face. 'Well,' he growled. 'Mine didn't say a word.'

'That's not like your missus,' Dennis said.

'No.' Oz seemed thoughtful. 'Mind, I didn't give her much of a chance. I slipped out the back door and made a dawn departure. I pushed the car down the hill so it wouldn't make any noise.'

'You have to push that car to start it anyway,' chipped in Dennis with wry smile.

Neville, though, was quite unperturbed. 'You did a runner on your wife?' he said, looking accusingly at Oz.

'You don't know his Margery,' said Dennis on Oz's behalf. 'She's a right ball-breaker.'

Oz nodded slow, wordless agreement.

Dennis continued: 'I've seen her break the balls of innocent bystanders.'

Oz broke his temporary silence. 'Last time I came here, I didn't tell her either. I said "I'm just goin' down the newsagents to get the racin' paper, pet."'

'How long were you gone?' Neville asked, his eyes widening.

'About three months.'

'And what did she say when you got back?'

'She said: "What won the four-thirty?"'

Oz's broad, beat-up pudding of a face cracked in a guffaw at his own joke. Dennis chuckled. Even Neville relaxed and managed a guilty smile.

'I've never worked abroad before,' he confided to Oz.

'I've *been* abroad, though. Brenda and me went to Minorca. Twice.'

There was a hint of pride in his voice that wavered when Oz said in feigned puzzlement. 'Why twice?'

'We liked it the first time.'

'Ah. An' where is Minorca?'

Neville reddened. 'I'm not sure. We flew non-stop from Newcastle.'

The bravado, the nonstop banter, hid one stark fact: these three Geordies, all of them qualified brickies, were heading for Germany because there was no work on Tyneside and precious little elsewhere in Britain; and because a loophole in EEC regulations soon, alas, to be closed meant that they could work there – barring accidents or serious illness – without paying tax, insurance, or the rest.

Dennis was the anchor of the trio, whether he liked it or not. At thirty-five he was the oldest, the most experienced – he had run his own building business, worked like a Trojan for five years before the recession had finally crushed him and thousands like him – and somehow he was the one you looked to in a crisis. His only trouble was that he had problems of his own, and no one to look to but ... himself. His missus was carrying on with a supermarket manager and the legal vultures were already gathering for the sad ritual of separation. Dennis had been to Germany before, and the situation at home had done nothing to hold him from coming again. His previous experience was also why he did the talking when they arrived in Oz's lame Zephyr at the restaurant/bar of a railway station close to the German border.

The smoke-filled room was crowded, noisy, filled mainly with men in their twenties and thirties – only a few pushing beyond that – and the voices that rose above the babble were mainly English, the rough dialects of the industrial areas. Neville stared around in wonder. He had seen some cars with Brit number plates in the station car park, but he hadn't expected to clap his eyes on such a bizarre sight so far from home.

5

Dennis noticed the lad's goggle eyes and patted him on the shoulder.

'There y'are, Nev. The cream of the British workforce,' he said. He took out some Dutch guilders and handed them to Neville. 'Here, go an' get us three beers. Heineken.'

While the boy moved off, shaking his head, Dennis stood scanning the crowd, obviously looking for familiar faces. Even Oz looked impressed.

'Where did all this lot come from?' he muttered. 'McAlpines must be laid off ...'

But Dennis had been spotted. A figure tapped him on the shoulder and addressed him in the lugubrious tones of the Black country. 'Dennis, isn't it?' he asked.

Dennis slowly turned towards him: 'Aye,' he said.

'Barry. Worked with you once, last time I was out.'

Dennis smiled: 'Oh, ar, 'course you did. How's it goin' then?'

Barry looked rueful, 'I was working back home but the bloke went bust. Came back here for the crack.' At that moment Oz swaggered up. 'This your oppo?' asked Barry.

'Aye,' said Dennis, 'This is Oz. This is Barry. We worked together once.'

Oz looked him up and down absentmindedly, 'Are you all right?'

'Nother Geordie?' asked Barry.

'Ney work up our way, is there?' said Oz.

'Nor no place,' rejoined Barry. 'I blame Thatcherism. It's a misguided policy.'

Dennis and Oz looked wearily at each other.

'I was just saying the same meself, wasn't I, Den?' said Oz.

'Who's the agent, Barry?' asked Dennis quickly.

'New bloke called Pfister over there with the bifocals.'

They all turned to look at a very correct looking German who was carefully sipping coffee and punctiliously checking a clip-board manifest.

'What's the form?' Dennis asked Barry, still eyeing the unfamiliar agent.

'Frankfurt's the best bet for brickies. Mannheim's most

chippies and plasterers.'

'What chance Düsseldorf?'

'Better get in there sharpish.'

A minute or two later, Dennis was making his way towards the bar with Oz at his heels. Neville was still trying to buy the drinks, but Dennis was too intent to be sidetracked into helping the lad. He marched straight up to Herr Pfister.

'Excuse me, Herr Pfister.'

The agent glanced up at him. His eyes were cold but not hostile. 'Yes?'

Dennis took a deep breath. 'D'you need any brickies for Düsseldorf?'

Pfister scanned his list before he answered. 'I have jobs for two only,' he said baldly.

Dennis and Oz exchanged concerned looks. 'You couldn't make it three, chief, could you?'

'Nein. For Düsseldorf they need now only two bricklayers. Also carpenters.'

To Oz's amazement, Dennis smiled with apparent relief. 'Aw, we're fine then,' he answered quickly. 'This lad,' he explained, turning to point out Neville nearby, 'is a carpenter.'

Neville had given up on the beer for the moment and was listening to the conversation. He looked shocked. 'But I'm –'

'Just get the beers in, Neville,' Dennis barked. 'There y'are. We're your lads, Herr Pfister ...'

Neville did as he was told. He even succeeded this time. The three Geordies sat in huddled conference, Heinekens in hand, two newly-hired brickies and ...

'... Dennis, I'm not a carpenter, man,' Neville protested weakly.

'Rubbish. Didn't you take woodwork at school?' Dennis was implacable.

'Well yes, but –'

'Then you're a carpenter.'

'I'll never get away with it,' Neville bleated.

Dennis became serious. 'Listen,' he hissed. 'We said we'd

stick together, right? What would your Brenda think if I'd left you on your jack in München Gladbach or somewhere?'

'Three musketeers, Nev,' agreed Oz. 'One for all and sod the rest!'

Neville looked around in wild desperation, but there was no support to be had. It was himself versus the two older, more experienced men. And he really didn't want to be left alone, particularly on the wrong side of the German border.

'We could have all gone somewhere else as brickies,' he said then. A last throw.

Dennis stared at him with mingled amusement and pity. 'No. Düsseldorf's the place, kid. Got the old town there. Full of clubs and bars.'

'I was in Mannheim last time,' said Oz. 'I've got no desire to go back to that dump.' He leered meaningfully at Neville. 'And Dennis says Düsseldorf's got the biggest brothel in Germany. I mean, think of the postcard you'll be able to send to your lass: "Dearest Brenda. The weather here is fine. Last night we went to the best knocking shop in the land . . ."'

Neville winced. He'd had a feeling Oz had been reading his postcards. The take-off of his writing style was cruelly accurate.

'It's not funny,' was all he could say. By then he knew he was lost.

'Hey, Dennis,' Neville asked as they walked back out into the station forecourt. 'Why did we have to backhand that German feller?'

'He got us the gig, man,' Dennis said shortly. 'That's his crack.'

Neville nodded as if he understood, but it was obvious he didn't. He was about to say something more when they were hailed by a cheerful cockney voice from the car park.

'What's the word, then?'

The three of them stopped. Dennis cocked his head, stared at the newcomer as if he were a fuzzy-wuzzy who'd just leapt out of the undergrowth. So far as appearances went, he had a point: the young Londoner was in his early twenties and sported an ice-hockey jacket in red, white, and blue and skin-tight jeans. The whole arrangement was topped by bushy black-and-blue streaked hair and a dangling pendant ear ring. He was certainly outlandish, but his eyes were alive with a city-dweller's sharpness.

'What's the what?' said Dennis.

'You know, how's it going?'

A non-committal shrug from Dennis, who was beginning to show the strain of the journey. 'All right.'

A knowing cockney grin. 'They said inside you was goin' to Düsseldorf.'

'Maybe.'

'Got a car?'

Dennis threw him a tight smile and jabbed a finger in the direction of the Zephyr. 'Only that.'

'Any chance of a lift?'

Oz, still smarting from the disparaging reference to his beloved motor, caught Dennis's eye and looked doubtful. This lad was alien to them; he might be all right under the weird façade, but they'd never seen anything like him up on Tyneside, and at the moment they didn't need an intruder.

''Fraid not, son,' Dennis said as convincingly as he could. 'There's three of us, you see, and we've got our gear, like.'

The cockney accepted the rejection philosophically. 'Fanks,' he said. 'Do the same for you sometime.' Then he grinned, shouldered his rucksack, and sauntered off in a way that said: life's too short to grieve, mate.

Oz watched him go, then looked balefully at Dennis. 'Spurs,' he murmured. 'You can tell.'

'C'mon,' Dennis said. 'Let's be going. Next stop Düsseldorf.'

'Aye,' commented Neville, who was already standing over by the car, hands thrust into the pockets of his jacket. He lunged at the Zephyr in a momentary, uncharacteristic burst of violence, but pulled his boot back just as it was about to make contact with the nearside wing. 'Sorry.'

His anxiety seemed to put life back into Oz. Rubbing his hands and chuckling to himself, Oz Osbourne, Gateshead's own anti-hero, pulled open the driver's door with a flourish and began to sing:

'*If I were a carpenter,*
And you were a lady ...'

They had passed through the German border a while ago. More banter between Dennis and Oz about fake passports, spy novels. Neville didn't know what to think at the moment. In some ways he felt older than his two mates, while in others he knew he was painfully young and inexperienced. Oz he found particularly confusing. The bloke was married, thirty, but seemed to have no feelings for his home and family at all; he apparently didn't care about anything except booze and birds, and life was just one big joke. Neville, for his part, had dreamed of his own Brenda all the way from when he had fallen asleep just east of Aachen – that last night at home in their little flat; her all tearful and achingly pretty in her housecoat, him clumsy but determined. If he had to go to work in Germany to get him and Brenda and their family-to-be a nice house on a nice estate, then that's what Neville would do. Brenda had said she understood. They'd kissed on that ...

Neville was reliving the last kiss with Brenda – and beginning to get into an action-replay of what had followed – when a jolt and a bang tore him out of his dream world. He groaned, rubbed his eyes. The Zephyr was kangaroo-hopping onto the autobahn hard shoulder. Oz was wrestling with the wheel, silent for once in the face of adversity, his face blanched even beyond its usual bar-room pallor.

Finally the car juddered to a halt and they were stopped safely on the hard shoulder.

'Whoa, girl,' said Oz, trying to be cool but obviously still a bit sick with fear. He was breathing heavily, and it wasn't over a copy of *Penthouse*. He slapped the dashboard. 'Teach me to give you yer head, eh?'

Dennis sat like a rock. Only his eyes were alive. 'Damn,' he said simply. 'You can get the bonnet up on this thing, can't you?'

Oz frowned and peered around for the bonnet catch.

"Spose so. Never 'ad reason before. Bloody thing's always worked up till now, hasn't it?'

Neville heard Dennis use a number of words he'd never heard before – and he hadn't led *that* sheltered a life.

Ten minutes later, Neville was at the wheel, waiting for orders to try the ignition while the other two fiddled with the works, when a big German juggernaut pulled in in front of them, at a slight angle so that the cab had a view of the stricken Zephyr. They saw a German stick his head out, then the lorry driver was joined by the grinning face of the cockney lad they had seen back at the railway station in Holland.

'What's the word, then?' he bellowed.

Dennis looked up reluctantly from his work. Oz, who was made of sterner stuff – or maybe cared more about losing face – carried on pretending to clean the plugs.

'Choked's as good a word as any,' Dennis called back.

The cockney smirked. 'I'd offer you a ride, chaps, but there's not really room. Not for the three of you, and all your gear.'

'On your way. We'll manage,' said Oz, still refusing to face him.

'Hope so. See you.'

The juggernaut pulled away.

'Not if I see you first,' growled Oz.

Meanwhile, Neville had got bored with sitting in the car and had climbed out onto the tarmac. He wandered round to the back of the car, glanced morosely at the speeding traffic, then at the vehicle again. Suddenly he crouched down.

'Hey,' he yelled to the two men working at the front. 'Look at this! Sump's dropped off!'

Oz popped up round the raised bonnet. 'The what?'

'The sump. All the oil's drained out. No wonder the engine seized.'

Dennis moved round quickly to join him. 'Can it be fixed?'

'No,' said Neville, shaking his head. 'New engine, that.'

They were forced to wait as another big juggernaut passed, drowning all hope of conversation. Which was probably lucky, because Dennis had been using those dirty words again. By the time he could make himself heard, though, he had calmed down a bit.

'All right,' he said to Oz. 'Damage's done. I 'spose your insurance'll cover it if it's fixed in a German garage?'

Oz stiffened. As usual when he knew he was about to be put in the wrong, he put on an aggressive stance. 'I doubt it,' he muttered. 'It's not insured.'

The other two stared at him in horrified disbelief.

'It has to be insured,' Dennis said finally. 'It has to be, man! Otherwise you couldn't have got the green card to bring the car out of England.'

Oz looked up heavenward, or at least away from his mates' accusing eyes. 'Ah, well. I cancelled the insurance after I got the green card. To give me some spendin' money for the trip, like.'

'You were intending to drive all round bloody Germany without insurance!' Dennis exploded. 'What if we'd had a crash? What if one of us had ended up in a Kraut hospital? We're not on the German National Health, you know!'

'We didn't, did we?'

'We could've done. What if the engine had packed up in the fast lane? With one of them juggernauts up our arse?'

'We've never been in the fast lane!' Oz protested, as if it let him off.

Dennis shook his head in weary resignation. 'I blame meself. I should never have left owt to you. I won't make that mistake again. You're totally irresponsible, Oz, it has to be said.'

'We got this far! Think of the money we saved on train fares.' Oz suddenly brightened. 'Which reminds me, you two still owe me for the petrol.'

For a moment it seemed that Dennis would be unable to stop himself from clobbering Oz right there and then. Instead, he managed to divert his violence in the direction of the hapless Zephyr. He delivered a hefty kick to the back bumper, before he could help himself. The boot flew open like a jack-in-the-box. The bumper hit the road with a heavy clang. Dennis stared at the scene for a long moment, then stoically began to unload their gear.

'So which way do we go to Düsseldorf from here?' asked Neville plaintively.

'The hard bloody way, that's which!' Dennis snapped, swinging a suitcase in his direction.

Oz stood thoughtfully with his hands in his pockets, watching the autobahn traffic stream by.

'Hard?' he said. 'You don't know the meanin' of the word. When I were a kid, I 'ad to walk five mile to school.'

'Aye. It were only a hundred yards as the crow flies, but you was tryin' to evade your creditors.' Dennis chucked a canvas bag. Oz caught it full in the stomach and grinned.

'I still owe the buggers,' he said.

Oz was what you might call irrepressible. Which is basically the polite way of describing a pain in the backside that won't go away.

The Germans thought big, even in bad times. The building project on the outskirts of Düsseldorf looked chaotic, as they always do, but out of the confusion of excavations, half-finished buildings, huts, cranes, trucks and on-site machinery of about every kind, was starting to emerge an integrated development of low blocks of family flats, offices and old people's chalets that the city on the Rhine would one day be proud of. The Germans are thoughtful when it comes to up-to-date design. Maybe not quite so thoughtful about the workers who have to turn it into reality.

Dennis was in the lead as usual as the trio of Geordies trudged the final muddy stretch across the far corner of the site towards a cluster of portakabins. He stopped, put down his bags for the last time and stared around him.

'It's the green hut in the middle,' he announced to the other two. 'Gaffer should be in.'

Oz, meanwhile, was energetically giving the two fingers to someone up among the scaffolding to their left, a someone who turned out to be the young cockney they had met in the station car park and then on the road. He was in the middle of his first day's work now – as a carpenter, they could see – and he was obviously amused to see the time and manner of the Geordies' arrival.

13

'Not only a Spurs supporter but a ruddy chippie. I shoulda known,' Oz said. 'Beggin' your pardon, young Nev.'

They picked up their stuff again and walked the final twenty yards or so to the entrance of the green hut. They were still a short way off when a large, formidable-looking man with a bald head, gold-rimmed glasses and a spotless suit emerged and stared at them keenly.

Dennis stopped. 'Herr Grunwald?'

'Ja,' the German foreman answered, and then waited.

Dennis stepped forward and wordlessly handed over the three contracts that they had signed with Herr Pfister the previous day.

'Reporting for work, sir,' he said in English. 'Patterson, Osbourne and Hope. Herr Pfister signed us on. Two brickies and a chippie.'

The German took the documents and without more ado began to scrutinise them. After a couple of seconds' silence, Neville nudged Dennis meaningfully, as if to remind him of something they had agreed beforehand. Dennis cleared his throat.

'Unless, that is, you need another brickie,' he said quickly.

'Why?' asked Grunwald, looking up quizzically.

'Well, we know of one.' Dennis shrugged. 'If you do.'

'*Nein*,' murmured Grunwald and went back to checking the contracts. Dennis flashed Neville a look that said: 'I tried.'

So they stood for some minutes – or so it seemed – and waited while Herr Grunwald got his pound of flesh. The wait was just getting a bit silly when the German folded the papers and stuck them in his pocket. He sighed.

'It is not good, I think, to arrive so late.'

'Had a bit of bother on the road, sir,' Dennis explained hastily. 'Should we just check in the hostel and then get back here smartish?'

Grunwald smiled humourlessly. 'The hostel is full. You will have to stay on the compound.'

Dennis's face fell. 'Oh,' he said. 'I'd reckoned we'd be in the hostel.'

'First serve, first come,' Grunwald quipped in his clumsy English. 'Put your things in your hut, then report for work.'

Then he stalked off back into his own lair without another word, leaving the three Brits standing in the mud like lost kids.

'Hut? What hut?' Oz was the first to speak.

'Pro tem, pro tem,' retorted Dennis.

'You said we'd be in a hostel with table tennis and baths,' Neville said as they tramped back towards the compound in the other corner.

Dennis looked daggers at Oz. 'We would've been if we'd arrived on time.'

'Then where are we going to be?'

Oz answered for Dennis. He nodded in the direction of the forlorn, bitumen-roofed huts ahead. The bitterness in his voice matched Dennis's. 'Stalag Thirteen, by the looks of it.'

The comparison was apt, too bloody apt. Reminders of all those POW films – and of course the fact of the country they were in. They pushed on past a half-completed structure, suddenly in no great hurry any more.

'Is there anywhere to go round here?' Neville asked with a hint of desperation.

Dennis shrugged. 'How should I know? You've seen as much of it as me.'

'But you've been here before.'

This time, Dennis had to grin sourly. 'Not this site, I haven't. I can't choose the site. I'm a bricklayer, not a bloody architect.'

'Sorry,' Neville said, realising what a stupid question it had been. From what he'd seen of Düsseldorf, it was probably bigger than Newcastle and Gateshead put together. You'd have to live here half a lifetime before you knew every part of it.

Suddenly a bear-like figure loomed out of the mud. He must have been six-three and built like an all-in wrestler. Despite the chilliness of the morning, he wore no jacket, and his shirtsleeves were rolled up to reveal tattooed biceps like Christmas hams.

Dennis stopped. Not that he had much choice. The bloke

blocked out what there was of a pathway. In fact, he blocked out the daylight.

'Excuse me,' he said very slowly and deliberately to the huge apparition. 'Do-you-speak-English?'

For a moment, the giant seemed puzzled. Then he smiled slowly. "Tis me mother tongue, my dear,' he said in a surprisingly soft Somerset burr. 'Moi name's Bomber. Leastways, that's what I'm known as ...'

Dennis nodded a greeting. 'Which is the best hut, Bomber?'

A massive thumb jerked in the direction of a blue-painted hut twenty yards or so further on. 'Oi'd take that one. The other one's got all the Turks in it. We calls that the Casbah.'

'Ta.'

Bomber went on his way with a smile.

'Turks?' said Neville. 'What's this? Lawrence of Arabia?'

Dennis nodded. 'The Germans ship 'em in to do the labouring work. They're not so bad really; uneducated but amiable enough, though I can't say we have a lot to do with 'em, on site or off. Clash of cultures, you might call it.'

'I must say, I wasn't looking forward to goin' on the ale with a bunch of Levantines.'

'Don't worry, Nev. We'll have some good times. I know Düsseldorf well.' Dennis's bleak expression belied his brave words.

'Oh, I'm not bothered,' said Neville with just as much or as little conviction. 'I want to save me money. That's the whole point, isn't it?'

They reached the hut. One by one they put down their luggage and stood in the doorway at one end looking into the building. If their expressions had been bleak before, now they were arid as the Sahara Desert. Even Oz was struck dumb at the sight that met their eyes. Rows on each side of low, iron bedsteads topped with spartan mattresses and lumpy-looking pillows. Beside each bed a metal locker. In the middle of the floor an old-fashioned iron stove. Some attempts had been made to cheer up the place with pictures – the usual pneumatic, thigh-spreading pinups that you'd find on a million sites all over the Western

16

world. In the far corner stood a hotplate, an old fridge, and an ironing board.

Dennis looked sheepish. Neville leaned down to tug at the laces of his muddy boots, being a well-trained lad. Oz, meanwhile, stomped in, found an empty bed and threw himself onto it. He put his hands behind his head and stared vacantly at the ceiling, obviously setting a pattern for the months to come.

'Get yourself a bed,' Dennis muttered. 'This'll only be temporary.'

Oz snorted. 'Aye. We'll start tunnelling tonight. I'll square it with the escape officer. The problem is the dogs. And then, of course, there's where we put he sand ...'

'Shut up, Oz,' Dennis snapped, lighting a cigarette. His stock of duty-frees had dwindled alarmingly in twenty-four hours.

'We'll need false papers. And civilian clothes.'

'Oz!'

'Well, it's like that,' Oz grated, turning over to rest on his elbow and stare balefully at the other two. 'I mean: "*Raus! Raus! Schnell! Schnell!*"'

Neville ignored him and padded in his socks over to the locker by the side of a bed that looked free. He opened it, saw two bent wire coat hangers, a couple more nudes pasted inside. The previous occupant had left behind a well-squeezed tube of shaving cream, a German soft-porn magazine and, down in the bottom, one very muddy boot. Not a pair, just one. And caked in the stuff. Times must be tough for one-legged krauts, thought Neville gloomily, if they have to come to places like this. He put his case down on the bed, snapped it open and fished out the picture of himself and Brenda on the beach in Minorca, sun-tanned and happy. He needed a reminder of that other world, and he needed it badly. Unfortunately, for the moment there was nowhere to put it. He'd have to do some thinking. Maybe after he'd dropped her a line to say he was safely here ...

While Neville gazed wistfully at his holiday snap, Dennis moved in to the free bed beside him and began unpacking. Oz sang a country-and-western song as he too began to stow his things in his locker. Trust him, though, not to stay out of mischief for long. Neville had hardly started composing his postcard home when Oz appeared with the spirit-level thrust under one arm like an officer's swagger-stick.

'All mail will be censored, so be careful vat you say,' he barked, putting on his *Colditz* act again. He never seemed to tire of the joke.

Neville smiled weakly. 'I just want to tell her we've arrived,' he said.

To his surprise, Oz lowered the spirit-level and dropped the act with it.

'Are you homesick?' he said with every appearance of sympathy.

Neville nodded. 'Aren't you? Oh no, of course you're not.'

With an airy wave, Oz indicated there were no hard feelings at the mild sarcasm in Neville's words.

'I know how you're feeling,' he said. 'You're thinkin' what it would be like if you were 'ome right now. You'd be comin' in from some windswept site. Into the warmth of a coal fire and Brenda's embrace. And the smell of her Bisto gravy waftin' from the kitchen. "Sit down, pet," she'd say. "Catch the end of *Nationwide* while I put the cauli on . . .".'

There was a wistful expression on Neville's young face. Even Dennis was moved by the description of such a golden idyll.

'That'd be magic,' breathed Neville.

A second later, Oz had rammed the spirit-level back under his arm and was screaming at his bemused mate: 'Put zese thoughts from your mind! Escape is impossible! For you ze var is over!'

Neville's face fell with real disappointment. Joking apart – and the joke was cruel – Oz had to be right. It was goodbye to Brenda, to his tea in the oven and to all the home comforts he was used to. And it was welcome to this hellhole of a hut, to a strange, foreign country where he didn't understand a word, and to a bunch of men he wasn't even sure he liked all that much. Oh, not forgetting the fact that he was supposed to be working as a chippie and didn't know how to hold a hammer straight.

'Ha bloody ha,' he muttered, and went back to finding a place for the photo of Minorca. Happy days.

TWO

Oz was definitely out to cut a dash. He was laying his bricks six at a time, laying down the mortar and trimming it with his trowel with a deftness that seemed out of tune with his bulk and usually slovenly manner. Oz might be an irresponsible bastard, but he could lay bricks; it was his saving grace, or could have been. By his side, Dennis was working just as well, pulling the same six-brick trick, but he wasn't bothered about the flamboyance. It was Oz who caught the slightly resentful attention of the nearby German brickies in their hardhats and neat, uniformly-coloured overalls, which contrasted strongly with the scruffy jeans and bare heads of the Brits.

As if his work rate wasn't enough, Oz insisted on having a meaningful conversation with the nearest pair of Germans, or at least pretending to.

'You lads from round here?' he asked one in his thickest Geordie.

'Round here?' the German echoed, clearly puzzled.

Oz grinned condescendingly. 'Round here. Do ... you ... live? In ... Düsseldorf?' he mouthed, painfully slow as if to an idiot.

The German shrugged. 'Düsseldorf, *ja*.'

'I've 'eard it's a canny place,' said Oz much more quickly, as if encouraged. 'But ...'

The pair of German workers exchanged bemused glances. They spoke a little English, but this tongue the big, dark-haired man spoke was something else entirely. '*Bitte?*' one queried plaintively.

'Aye. Not as bitter as where we come from,' said Oz.

'*Nicht verstanden.*'

Then the two of them went back to their painstaking labours, laying one brick at a time, neatly and thoroughly but with nothing of the Brits' flair or speed.

Oz snorted. 'So much for my attempt to cement Anglo-German relations,' he complained to Dennis.

'I'd concentrate on cementin' bricks if I were you, Oz.'

But Oz was still staring critically at the German brickies. 'Look at 'em,' he scoffed. 'One brick at a time. They don't 'ave our panache.'

Dennis nodded agreement. 'That's why they get the needle, man. 'Cause we're quicker than them.'

'Ironic, really,' Oz said with a sigh. 'Us here, helping erect all this. When it was our lot flattened it in the first place.'

'Not here. All new, this is. This is one of your dormitory suburbs.'

'Ah,' said Oz sagely. 'You mean like a computer belt.'

'Well, you might as well make yourself useful somehow,' Dennis said. He pointed to a near-empty wooden case of mortar. 'We're gettin' low on Darbo,' he told Oz, giving the stuff its German name. 'Give that Turk a shout.'

Oz nodded and shambled over to the bare window frame that faced down onto the main site. There was a Turk below loading fresh mortar into another case, ready to be lifted up to Dennis and Oz's level by crane.

'Come on, Ayatollah!' yelled Oz. 'Shift yourself!'

As a diplomat you're a very good brickie, thought Dennis to himself. He just hoped there wouldn't be too much trouble. Blokes like Oz could breeze on for a while treating foreigners like dirt, and then suddenly things blew up. Dennis had seen it happen before.

When the hooter went for dinner break, Oz was down before you could say *Bratwurst*. The Brits gathered together in what had become their own spot. Someone was asleep in the scoop of an excavator. Dennis and Oz perched on a pile of breeze blocks, each with his sandwiches piled on a paper plate.

'When do we get our Red Cross parcels?' said Oz towards the end of his snack. 'Chocolate and condensed milk, eh?'

'You live in a fantasy world, you do, Oz,' Dennis mumbled through a mouthful of food.

'Mebbe. Lot better than the real thing,' Oz shot back, visibly needled.

The remark seemed to shut Dennis up. The older man concentrated on his lunch, and his eyes took on a faraway look. Oz could strike a chord sometimes. Like those monkeys on a typewriter that were supposed to be able to write Shakespeare if you left them at it long enough.

Oz looked around for other meat. Across the way from them sat the young cockney chippie that they had met in Holland and on the autobahn. Neville – God help him – was working with him in his attempt to imitate a carpenter, and they now knew the cockney's name was Wayne. As usual during breaks, Wayne sat tapping one gaudily-booted foot to the rock music he played nonstop in the portable Sony Walkman that he carried everywhere. In that world, eyes shut and his ears plugged with listening 'phones, Wayne was out of it, and that was the way he seemed to like things. Oz watched him for a while in fascinated disgust. Then he thought of Neville. And come to think, where *was* Neville?

'Hey, Wayne. Where's your new mate, Neville?' he bellowed.

No response. A million miles away. Oz picked up a nearby half-brick and lobbed it casually at the cockney chippie. It missed him by a matter of inches. Wayne wrenched off his earphones.

'Did you frow that?' he asked indignantly.

'Aye,' said Oz, all innocence. 'Where's Neville?'

Wayne didn't seem to have heard him. 'You could've split my head open, you lunatic.'

'I wanted to know where Neville was.'

'He's over at first aid, in' 'e?' Wayne answered, still frowning. 'An' I'm bleedin' lucky I'm not there with him.'

In fact, it was evening before they saw Neville again. Dennis and Oz came into the hut to be greeted by the sight of Neville sitting on his bed, looking very sorry for himself.

Dennis got the first word in. He didn't trust Oz to say the right thing. 'Hey, Nev. Y'all right, kid?'

Neville said nothing, merely held up his right hand. It was bandaged.

'What happened?' Dennis asked.

Neville grimaced. 'The saw slipped, didn't it?' he said with bitterness in his usually even voice. 'It's only a question of what I'll lose first – the job or me right hand.'

Bomber, the big man from Somerset, was sprawled on his bed across the way. He couldn't help but overhear. He raised himself on one elbow and made a trembling motion with his right hand.

'Too much o' *that*, if you ask Bomber,' he called over.

Oz put a comforting hand on Neville's shoulder.

'I'm afraid you've written your last postcard, Nev,' he said in a parody of a bedside manner.

'Leave us alone, Oz,' Neville hissed, shaking him off.

But Oz was implacable. 'That's your dart hand, an' all,' he continued. 'Serious injury when you can't chuck an arrow. Can't even hold a hand of doms. What's left, I ask you ...'

'That'll *do*, Oz,' Dennis intervened.

It wasn't enough, though.

'Least he'll be popular wi' the Germans,' Oz said. 'They won't have any trouble keepin' up with *his* work rate.'

The shoebrush thrown with Neville's good hand hit the already ducking Oz square between the shoulderblades.

'Oh, she's throwin' a tantrum, is she?' he whooped, then peered down at the brush. 'Oh no, it's a shoebrush.'

Neville stared morosely at the ceiling. 'Everything's a joke to you, isn't it, Oz? Just a permanent clown, you are.'

'Better a clown than a bloody misery like you. Like death warmed up, you are,' said Oz defensively.

Bomber's gentle West Country voice drifted over: 'Oh dear. Trouble in paradise!'

Neville ploughed on, using the chance to vent his feelings. 'I'm not here 'cause I like it! Some of us, like Dennis and me, are going through with this 'cause we got a purpose.'

Oz leered. 'Oh, I'm sorry. I thought you just had a wife. I didn't know you 'ad a *porpoise*. What d'you feed it on?'

'Oz,' Dennis hissed. 'You never know when to leave it alone.'

Neville nodded, pursing his lips. 'You're the one that's out of step, Oz. What's so comical about me writing to me wife? What's so strange about me caring about her, worrying about her? Dennis is the same with his Vera. You're doing this for her, aren't you, Den? Her and your bairns?'

He was glancing to Dennis for support. The older man at his side paused for just a moment, and a look of sad reflection flickered across his face. Then he said: 'Why, aye, son. 'Course I am.'

Maybe a lad like Neville would understand that he could only give him a half-truth, and maybe he wouldn't. Either way, Dennis thought at that moment of Vera and her supermarket manager, and of the kids just before he had left for Germany, and he knew this wasn't the time or the place to start distinguishing between different levels of truth. If he started on that tack, then he might have to think about why he was really here, and that was something Dennis most assuredly didn't want to do.

It was Friday, and the working day was over. Herr Pfister had been and gone, and the lads had money in their hands, crisp wads of Deutschmarks. Neville sat on his bed, staring at the unfamiliar money, which he had succeeded in translating into pounds. It made an impressive enough sum by the standards he was used to.

'That makes it worthwhile, Nev,' said Dennis, as if reading the lad's mind. 'Your first pay packet.'

Nev nodded. Then Bomber, who had been brushing down a blazer that hung in his locker for special occasions, chipped in: 'And Bomber's last.'

The others turned and stared at him.

'Not soon enough, me ducks,' Bomber proclaimed proudly. 'I've got a nice job lined up, I have. In Bristol. A new by-pass. Good money, home every night, and English Ale.'

Dennis smiled. 'They'll need a brickie. I'll steam in there Monday.'

Bomber's booming laugh almost seemed to shake the wooden frame of the hut. He laid out his blazer on the bed, stripped off his workshirt. Elsewhere, someone was ironing a pair of trousers on the battered board, while Wayne dried his billowing locks with a dinky little Moulinex hairdryer. A bizarre scene but at the same time cosy. It was amazing what men alone could do to make themselves at home; in its small way, the hut was a memorial to the unquenchability of the human spirit.

More memorials were all over Bomber's body. Neville stared at him in fascination as the big man polished his shoes, still stripped to the waist. Hearts, flowers, snakes wrapped around busty girls, Bomber had the lot; his flesh was as crowded as a cartoon by Giles.

'You admirin' the tattoos, lad?' said Bomber kindly.

Neville was fazed for a moment, but then he nodded. He was repelled, too, but, yes, he supposed he was admiring them. 'Oh ... yeah.'

'Souvenir of my travels, these are,' Bomber chuckled. 'You youngsters sew badges on your rucksacks. Bomber bears them on his body.'

'I've never seen so many!'

Bomber slapped his thigh. 'This is nothing. My mate Plugger from Teignmouth, he's got a fox hunt on his back. An entire pack of hounds down the spine. And you can just see the fox's brush peeping out his arse.'

Just then, Oz came thundering in from the showers a hundred yards away across the site, wearing nothing but a towel and a pair of wellies. He was shivering, but irrepressible as usual.

'Ruddy showers are hot enough,' he bellowed to no one in particular. 'But by the time you get back here, you've lost the benefit.'

He strolled through the hut to his bed, grinning at all and sundry, singing *I've Been Looking For Love In All The Wrong Places* and wiggling his capacious belly like a hoola dancer. His eyes lighted on Wayne, who was staring intently at a small mirror, flicking the blue blaze in his hair ready for an evening's hunting.

'By God, look at London!' said Oz. ''Ere, you musta been

lookin' for love in some peculiar places for your hair to turn that colour!'

Wayne ignored him. This was getting to be a pattern. But Oz was too chuffed to be going out on a Friday night to get involved. He made a face and continued on his merry way. Meanwhile, Dennis buttoned his shirt and had another go at cheering up young Neville.

'C'mon, shift yourself, Nev,' he said.

The lad shook his head. 'I'm not going out, thanks.'

'Might do you good. Get yourself out of yourself.'

Oz, who was hovering in the background half-naked, leered and smacked his lips noisily. 'Aye. Bomber's takin' us to a brothel.'

'I'm not going to a brothel, thank you,' said Neville disapprovingly.

Oz smiled encouragement. 'Hey, there's no panic,' he said. 'It's all perfectly above board here, y'know. State owned.'

'State owned?' asked Neville incredulously, curious despite himself.

'Aye. The girls are all civil servants. It's kind of like the National Health, only a bit more fun, like.'

'It's a nationalised knocking shop,' Wayne chipped in.

Neville shook his head.

'Come an' have a few jars anyway, Nev,' Dennis coaxed. 'You don't have to go with that lot.'

Neville said he was tired. He'd rather just read and have a quiet night in. Maybe he was waiting to be persuaded just a bit more, to salve his conscience, but at that moment something like a war-cry echoed from the far end of the hut. Bomber had finished dressing and was standing arms akimbo, resplendent in polo neck, a navy-blue double-breasted blazer teeming with gold buttons, and shoes like two halls of mirrors.

'Bomber's ready! Bomber's away!' he roared.

Dennis turned away from Neville and looked at the astonishing sight of Bomber ready to go on the razzle.

'Oh aye, Bomber,' he said in mingled amusement and awe. 'Unstoppable.'

As the rest of the lads piled into a couple of taxis they had ordered, Neville sat on his bed, where he could just see them through the darkness, and sighed. Then he began the inevitable letter home:

Dearest Brenda, It is Friday night and the lads have just gone out. They asked me to join them, but without you there didn't seem much point ...

The owners, with a bow to the world of *Cabaret*, had called the bar the 'Kit Kat Klub'. It had the slightly flash, slightly naughty, though basically respectable atmosphere of a lot of watering-holes in the old quarter of Düsseldorf. It didn't deliver what it promised, but by the time people realised the fact they were too pissed to care. Either that, or they used the club as a staging-post on the way to the lower depths of the city's nightlife. As the Brits were doing tonight, crowded in a heaving phalanx around the long, narrow bar.

Somewhere over the other side, the trio – bass, guitar, drums – were pounding away, and the pert girl singer (slightly shopsoiled) was doing her version of *Knowing Me, Knowing You* in German.

Oz was talking to Wayne up against the bar. Or at least he thought he was. In fact, Wayne was moving his lips occasionally, but what he was really doing was making eyes at the pretty blonde barmaid behind the Geordie's broad back. As Oz finished recounting a particularly filthy piece of Gateshead folk legend, the barmaid, as if drawn by magnetism, appeared close by, looking at Wayne and then at his empty glass with a broad, come-on smile.

Wayne grabbed his chance.

'Want another?' he asked Oz.

Oz half-turned, saw the girl, realised Wayne's game. 'I think we're off in a minute,' he said, then called out to Bomber. 'Aren't we, Bomber?'

'That's it!' the big man boomed. 'Sup it up. Things have to be done, and that's a fact!'

When Oz turned back, he found Wayne looking at him with a sly smile. 'You ever been to a brothel, Oz?' the cockney asked.

Oz shrugged. 'I haven't, as a matter of fact. But I have a

very vivid picture in me mind of what it's like.' His eyes took on a dreamy look. 'It's all red plush, see. An' there's a bloke in the corner playin' the piano in his shirtsleeves. An' all the girls – right crackers, like – are standin' around in high-heeled shoes and corsets ...'

'I think it might be a bit different here, from what I've been told,' Wayne said.

'Soon see, won't we.' Oz motioned for him to drink up. Bomber was getting restless, and so were the other lads.

Wayne shook his head. 'I'm not going.'

'What?'

'I'm not paying for it.'

Oz looked at Wayne first with disappointment, then with disbelief. 'You're not goin' to pull here!'

The Londoner's clear eyes twinkled. He had been playing games all along. Lord alone knew how he did it.

'Already have, son,' murmured Wayne.

He grinned at the barmaid, who melted. He grinned at Oz, who snarled.

'Some of us 'ave got it, mate,' he said. 'See ya later.'

And, in fact, where Bomber led them to gave Oz a bit of a shock. Instead of the Best Little Whorehouse In Texas, he found himself in a building that was more like the Best Little Block of Council Flats in Dagenham.

The group of half-a-dozen Brits shuffled into an oblong courtyard lit by sodium streed lights and the glow from the main building. A train clattered by a hundred yards or so away. Other men were waiting in line: servicemen, salesman types, a lot of foreign 'guest workers' and a few other Brits. The girls were wandering none too purpose-fully up and down in front of the potential clients, occasionally making an effort to break the ice.

'You said this was the best brothel in Germany,' Oz hissed accusingly at Dennis.

'No I didn't. I said it was the biggest.'

Oz surveyed their fellow-clients and with his gimlet eye spotted the Turkish labourer from their part of the site.

'Hey, there's the Ayatollah, Dennis,' he said, cupped his hands round his mouth and bellowed cheerfully at the embarrassed Turk: 'This is not allowed in your country! If they find out, they'll chop it off.'

He chortled, but it didn't take much to realise that he had merely found a scapegoat to mask his own awkwardness.

Not so in Bomber's case. The big man wasted no time. He walked boldly forward like a farmer at a cattle sale and looked the girls up and down as they passed close to him.

'That's it! That's what Bomber wants,' he declared. 'That's what Bomber came for.'

Bomber's unashamed sexual appetite encouraged some of the others, who had been lurking rather sheepishly in the background.

'How much is it, Bomber?' asked one of the group, a Scots chippie.

'Oh, eighty deutschmarks,' Bomber explained matter-of-factly. 'That's your basic rate. It can go up to two hundred, depending on your proclivities.' He winked and turned back to the business of the evening. His eye rested for a moment on one girl and his mind was made up. 'Come on, my beauty! You belong to Bomber!'

The girl, a delicate-looking waif of a creature, seemed momentarily put out by her prospective client's size, but nevertheless she took his hand and led him off towards the building.

Oz watched him go, then went back to watching the talent parade. Some of the girls weren't half bad, in fact. He nudged his mate.

'I fancy that one, Dennis,' he whispered.

'Which one?'

Oz indicated a Eurasian girl. She was certainly a looker, and dressed up to the nines, like a fetishist's treat.

'That one there with the ear-rings and the ... well, everything. Suzie Wong ...' Oz said. 'What about you?'

Suddenly Dennis felt and looked his age. He was finding the whole thing more than a bit sad. Money ... sex ... paying to relieve your loneliness just for a half-hour ... it was all too close to the bone.

'I've gone off the idea,' he said slowly.

Oz laughed nervously. 'What? You? Never ...'

'I'll wait for you. Don't mind me. I'll have a smoke and then we'll share a taxi back,' Dennis told him gently.

Already straining at the leash, Oz slapped him on the shoulder and headed off. 'I 'ope you've got a full packet. In a manner of speakin',' he called out over his shoulder. Then he and Suzie Wong disappeared into the brightly-lit block.

Naughty nights, German-style, thought Dennis. Brightly-lit, functional and cold. He lit a cigarette and looked around for a bar of some sort in the neighbourhood. A quick beer and Oz was sure to be through. At heart he was the basic whack type, was Oz. Eighty deutschmarks maybe, certainly not a lot over that. In and out.

Neville hadn't slept much, but he was determined to pretend that he had when he heard the cab door slam and a couple of blokes start to squelch through the site mud towards the hut. Before long, he picked up the accents and knew who was coming. The door opened and someone fell in.

'Bloody hell!' hissed Oz in a drunken stage whisper.

Then Dennis: 'Shut up, man. You'll wake the others!'

Neville watched over his bed clothes, careful to keep his eyes half closed, while the two of them struggled to remove their shoes and then began to tiptoe unsteadily down the centre aisle of the hut. Before long there was a loud clattering noise and a yelp. Oz had kicked over the coal scuttle.

'Shut up, for Christ's sake!' growled a sleepy voice.

'Sorry!' Oz's apology must have woken up anyone who wasn't already a hundred percent conscious.

Muffled curses and loud shufflings as he and Dennis made their way to their beds.

Neville heard the springs on Dennis's bed go. 'Is that you, Dennis?' he muttered.

'Aye, Nev. Sorry, did we wake you?'

'I wasn't sleeping,' Neville admitted. There was no sense in pretending just to make the blokes feel guilty.

Oz, though, obviously took this as an invitation to make a night of it. Oz coughed and said gruffly: 'Is that you, Neville?'

'Yes,' said Neville, then paused awkwardly before asking: 'Did you have a good night?'

'Magic, man!' Oz said without a hint of reservation.

31

'Ah. Did you, er, go to the, er ...'

'Oz and Bomber did,' Dennis explained. 'I gave it a miss.'

Neville was a bit relieved. He'd been relying on Dennis to provide a spot of sanity, and he'd been proved right. 'So where's Bomber?' he asked.

Oz laughed throatily. 'Still there. He's bought a season ticket, has Bomber.'

Fascinated despite himself, Neville couldn't stop himself from asking the other, obvious question. 'What was it like?' he said, like a kid who'd been left behind for the treat because he'd had the mumps and was now trying to enjoy the thrills vicariously.

'Great,' said Oz. 'I had this gorgeous girl. Now admit it, Den. She was gorgeous, wasn't she?'

'Not bad.'

The voice from the far end of the hut came again, louder: 'SHUT ... UP!'

'Bollocks!' Oz snarled jauntily, but dropped his voice a bit. 'She was Eurasian, Neville,' he said with slow relish. 'I mean, I've never seen owt like it. You don't get the chance at 'ome, do you? Not with girls like that.'

'Was ... was it different, like?'

Oz sighed heavily at the memory of it all. He took another, suspense-building drag on his smoke.

'I'll tell you one thing, Nev,' he said. 'Sex is in its infancy in Gateshead.'

Bomber was all alone in the hut when Neville burst in, muddy from running around the site's improvised football pitch but more cheerful than he had been for days past. Hard exercise had helped him forget his misery. He seemed as frisky as a young dog.

'Turkey two, England three!' Neville announced delightedly, painting an imaginary headline in the air in front of him.

Bomber forced a smile. 'Oh. That's good, me dear.'

'Right. Five minutes left, I get the ball on the right wing, go past their left back ...' Neville dodged and ducked, mimicking his movements on the pitch. '... Then a cross an' that Scots lad slots it in. He's an animal, but he's a canny player.'

'So where are the victors, then?' asked Bomber, strangely listless.

Neville shrugged. 'They've gone to that bar down the road. I wanted to catch the showers while they're hot.'

The Geordie lad fetched the soap from his locker, grabbed a towel, was about to leave and then suddenly had a thought.

'Hey, Bomber,' he said. 'I thought you were goin' home. Shouldn't you be at the station by now?'

'Should be, yes.'

'Better get your skates on, hadn't you?'

A gentle heave of Bomber's massive shoulders. 'Not going now. No point.'

'Why?' Neville's face showed genuine concern.

'No money.'

'You're jokin', man,' said Neville, sitting down on the bed opposite Bomber. 'You told us you were takin' home almost nine hundred pounds!'

Bomber got up, as if to escape his sympathy. 'I had it,' he said quietly. 'But now I haven't.'

'How many girls did you have?' Neville's face was a picture of amazement. In another mood, Bomber would have found it hilarious. Not so now.

'It weren't that,' he said. Then he took a deep breath, as if he wanted to get it off his chest, and launched into the sorry story. 'Went out after ... Back to the hostel with some of the other Brits ... Poker was my downfall. I was feelin' lucky ... But I reckon the William schnaps affected Bomber's judgement ...'

Neville's attitude changed from one of sympathy to intense disquiet. It was obvious that he found Bomber's story an affront to his entire way of life.

'That ... that's tragic,' he said. 'What will your wife say?'

'I know exactly what she'll say,' the big man sighed. 'That's why Bomber isn't giving her the chance to say it ...' He saw Neville shaking his head in disapproval. 'Aye, well it's not the first time, boy. Daft as a brush, that's always been Bomber's trouble ... I dunno – you work every week

33

an' you hand it over to the wife. Pay for the house, new clothes for the kids . . . it don't leave you much for yourself, like. Then suddenly you got a big wad o' spendin' money in your fist. It throws you off kilter. Great feelin', you know, bein' able to buy drinks for your friends. Even for strangers.'

The big man's voice died away. His brows furrowed in recollection of the night before.

'All the same –' said Neville.

Bomber laughed, but his eyes were still a bit sad. 'Oh, I ain't sayin' be like me. Don't suppose you will be; you seem like a sensible lad. I'm just sayin' you should try and understand.'

Neville nodded. 'So what'll you do?'

'Oh, as much overtime as I can crack,' said Bomber. 'Work me nuts off. It's the straight an' narrow from now on . . .'

Suddenly he was looking at Neville with a real, open grin on his battered face. Bomber was well on his way to bouncing back.

'Now,' he said. 'Which bar did you say the lads had gone to?'

Sure enough, though, come Monday Bomber was laying bricks like all the hounds of hell were after him – which if his missus found out what he'd done with the nine hundred quid, they would be. Even the Germans were forced to try to slow him down; the crazy Englishman was working so fast he was making them look pathetic.

In his way, Bomber had accommodated himself to the situation. He knew what he had to do, and he set to doing it. Not so Neville. The football match on the afternoon of his chat with Bomber had been a high spot, but it had been all down hill from there on. He was unhappy, and he wasn't one to let it out in the open like some people. Neville's ways were dark and mysterious; when he came under pressure, he withdrew.

So it was that Dennis burst into the hut one day the next week to find Neville sitting on his bed, pulling off his wellies. The older man was concerned, but also a bit hurt.

'Neville?' he said sharply. 'The Capo tells me you've jacked it in.'

The lad knew right enough that Dennis shouldn't have had to hear it second hand. 'Oh, did he . . .?' he mumbled.

'Is it true, man?'

Neville cleared his throat. 'Well, yeah. No choice, have I?'

'Why?'

'If Bomber had gone, I'd have stayed,' Neville said with a shrug. 'But I'm not a chippie. I can't keep fakin' it.'

Dennis sucked in his cheeks, looked thoughtful. He could see the lad was in a genuine dilemma. Neville was having to live a lie, and when you were as honest and straightforward as he was, that came hard. Pity in a way that he hadn't picked Oz to play the chippie. Oz would've collected a couple of Oscars by now. Or killed himself. That was the trouble with Oz, he didn't know the meaning of the word moderation. He didn't even know how to spell it.

'Look,' he said slowly. 'I'll have a word with the Capo. Explain the circumstances. I'll tell him you're dead keen to stay on. He'll switch you back to bricklayin'.'

Neville reddened. It was as if Dennis had stripped away his flimsy alibi. 'It's too late for that,' he stuttered. 'I've already rung the wife, haven't I?'

'Was it her letter, like?' Dennis asked as gently as he could, though it was impossible to keep a knowing smile from his face.

'No,' Neville insisted. 'It wasn't her. She's put no pressure on. It's me, Dennis. I hate it here. I admit it.' He looked imploringly at Dennis. 'So maybe I could save a thousand quid, but it'd take me six months and I can't stand the prospect.'

Dennis sighed. 'Maybe it's partly my fault,' he said. 'I painted too rosy a picture.'

'No, it's not that, Dennis. I know me, and I know I'd never last the distance.'

'When do you leave?' Dennis said abruptly. Suddenly he was a bit tired of sorting Neville out. He was very fond of the lad, but you couldn't go on nursemaiding him. After all, he was a married man with his own life to lead.

'I'm workin' out the week,' said Neville.

Dennis lit a cigarette and smiled. The lad looked right hangdog. Soddit, he deserved a bit of fun.

'Tell you what, Neville,' he said firmly. 'Friday night you're goin' out with us. You've not come all this way to spend two weeks in a hut readin' Oz's overdue library books.'

Neville swallowed hard. 'Oh, I'd just as soon –'

But Dennis was not to be denied.

'No arguments,' he rasped. 'That's settled, Neville.'

The restaurant was not too flashily furnished, but the decor had a kind of quiet dignity that made you mind yourself just a bit. Dennis had been here before and he liked it. Not that the three of them were likely to disgrace the place. They were all well suited and tied. Neville, in particular, was freshly showered, hair washed, looking like he'd decided to join the human race. When he took that pining look off his face and had a drink or two, he was a pleasant, presentable sort of bloke.

Oz was giving the *coup de grâce* to a bottle of the local Rhine wine, shaking the last drops into Neville's glass. They had managed to get through the lot while still studying the menu. A waitress came over. Easy on the eye and discreet she was, and asking if they were ready to order.

'Ja,' said Dennis, the lads' spokesman. 'Almost. What you can get, pet, is another one of those ...'

He pointed to the empty wine bottle. The waitress smiled, took it and bustled off. She was in no hurry to rush them through their meal. This wasn't that kind of place.

'All right with you, Nev – you like the wine?' Dennis asked, pleased with his choice of venue for their night out.

Neville nodded. 'Very nice. It's the same shape bottle as Blue Nun. Brenda and me sometimes have that with our Sunday dinner.'

It might have been Neville's mention of Brenda, but Oz chose that moment to fart loudly. 'I could murder a pint,' he commented, as if the two things were connected.

'Well, you're not having one,' Dennis growled. 'Sit up straight. And when the food comes, I don't want you to talk with your mouth full or shovel your peas.'

Oz looked offended. 'Hey! Hey! I've been out before, you know.'

'To chip shops, yes. Not to a proper restaurant like this.'

Neville, meanwhile, was still scanning the bewildering array of dishes on the menu. He obviously had no idea what to choose.

'Can you translate these, Dennis?' he asked shyly.

'Some of them, some of them,' Dennis said. 'For a start, *mit* means "with".'

Oz snorted. 'Oh, that's a big help.'

Dennis pressed on. '*Wiener* is veal. All the lot down that side's veal,' he said, leaning over and pointing at a section of the menu.

Brenda, apparently, didn't like them to eat veal because of what they did to the calves, keeping them in the dark and all. To keep the peace, they decided to move on to other things.

Suddenly Oz turned and stared at the next-door table. A waiter was arriving to dish out a main course to a German couple. The food looked a bit like a hock of ham covered in sauce, with some kind of stringy vegetable.

'That looks all right,' said Oz. Before the others could stop him, he had leaned across until his elbow threatened to do the waiter an injury.

'Er ... 'scuse me ...' he said slowly and very loudly. 'D'you mind tellin' me what that one's called?'

Dennis was cursing under his breath. The German diner, meanwhile, was affable but puzzled. Then his wife, who seemed to have understood Oz, spoke to him in rapid-fire German. The diner nodded and turned back to Oz.

'*Eisbein mit Sauerkraut*,' he said simply.

Oz beamed. 'Oh, thanks very much. Looks great,' he said, and then turned back to his own table, looking inordinately chuffed with himself.

'What is it?' said Neville.

'Dead simple,' Oz declared. 'It's ... Eisbein ... with ... sauerkraut.'

Luckily the waitress returned just at that moment with the second bottle of wine.

'You have decided?' she asked, in English this time. 'Or you need something explained on the menu? We have many delicious specialities ...'

But Neville had obviously had enough. He looked at the others, then at the waitress, and closed his menu. 'I'd like a steak, please,' he announced firmly. 'Well done.'

'Aye. Me too,' agreed Oz.

Dennis sighed, though if he had been honest he would have admitted to being relieved. 'Make that three, pet,' he said, handing his own menu back to the waitress.

'Yeah,' drawled Oz. 'Mit chips an' peas.'

A couple of hours later, well wined and dined, the trio were to be found strolling through the traffic-free precincts of the old city. As ever on a Friday night, Düsseldorf's shopping and entertainment centre was crowded with sightseers and pleasure-seekers. For the three Geordies, and especially Neville, it was wonderland.

Neville peered with undisguised envy into the elegant window of a high-class furniture shop. 'There's some fantastic things in the shops here,' he said.

'Lot of money in Germany,' Dennis told him.

Neville nodded and moved on reluctantly, obviously impressed with what he saw. 'It's not what I expected,' he said after a while. 'Much nicer place than I thought.'

Oz, meanwhile, was getting bored with window-shopping and was eyeing the passing talent.

'An' there's some beautiful lookin' women, I tell you that,' he boomed.

Right on cue, a passing blonde flashed a smile – though her target wasn't Oz but Neville. The youngster's eyes lit up, despite himself, and he smiled shyly back at her before he remembered Brenda and forced himself to go back to the shop windows.

Dennis chuckled. 'Hey, I saw that. Don't forget you'll be back with your Brenda this time tomorrow.'

'That's true,' Oz agreed. 'Better get in there quick.'

'Good job we're with him, Oz, or he'd get into all sorts of mischief,' said Dennis with a wink.

He was joking. Little did he know.

The rot – if that's what it was – set in when they arrived at the Kit Kat Klub for a nightcap, knowing that the Brits from the site would be in there of a Friday. The place was packed, but they soon spotted the towering figure of Bomber at the bar, well into his cups and beaming a delighted welcome at them.

'Over here, my beauties!' he bellowed. They pushed through the crowd, past Wayne, who was busy with his barmaid, towards the big man from Somerset.

'What's your pleasure, lads? 'Tis Bomber's shout,' he declared.

'Three Pils,' Dennis answered automatically.

Oz grinned. 'Your spirits have risen, Bomber.'

'In proportion to the amount I've sunk tonight, me dear,' Bomber chortled.

'What's that you're drinking?' asked Neville before he could turn away to order the drinks.

'Bomber's ruin, lad. William schnaps is what this is.'

There was an unaccustomed twinkle in Neville's eye as he said: 'Can I have a sip?'

Bomber guffawed. 'Be my guest.' Then he caught the barmaid's eye at last. 'Three Pils here, Fräulein! And three Williams!'

Dennis moved in. 'Oh,' he began, 'not for the lad ...'

But Neville was already trying the spirit. 'No, it's quite nice,' he said. 'I like it. Tastes of something. Is it pears?'

It was a couple of Williams later when Dennis found Neville standing away from the bar, watching a group of customers at a table playing dice. Neville was slightly flushed and had loosened his tie.

'What's this game, Den?' he asked.

'Oh, all the locals play it. Don't you get any ideas.'

Neville nodded cheerfully. 'I've been watching. It's quite simple, really.'

'Look, I did in fifty quid last week. No bother,' Dennis told him. 'And I want you goin' home with your wages intact.'

Neville tore his eyes away reluctantly. Trouble was, when he stopped watching the dice game and enjoying himself, he immediately started to think about Brenda and got the old guilt coursing through his system again.

'I should've bought her something,' he said.

Dennis motioned for him to get his beer down him. 'She'll be happy enough just with you.'

'Yeah, suppose so.'

The mention of home attachments made the lad thoughtful. He stood sipping his drink a little morosely. Then he turned to Dennis with an embarrassed smile.

'Brenda said on the phone that she'd seen your Vera ...' he began.

Dennis's 'Oh, aye' was brisk and immediate, but Neville continued regardless.

'Vera told her, like,' he said. 'About you and her having problems. I'm sorry, Den. You never said.'

'These things happen.'

Dennis's tone was not encouraging, but it seemed as if Neville needed to talk about things as well, to see life for a while through the eyes of the older man whom he admired so much.

'You been married ... how long is it?' he asked.

'Sixteen years,' said Dennis, unbending a bit. 'We were both nineteen.' He shook his head in disbelief that anyone could have been so stupid – particularly his own younger self.

But Neville nodded. 'Us too. Well, Brenda was eighteen.'

'Nearly everybody out here's married with kids,' Dennis mused. The words came out. 'Shall I tell you why they come?' he asked with a harsh laugh. 'It's not just for the wages they send back. It's to try to relive their adolescence. Which most of 'em missed by gettin' married at nineteen like you and me.'

'I don't want to do that,' countered Neville firmly, even though his voice was slightly slurred. 'Maybe that's why I've found it so tough out here.'

'Aye. Well, you're the exception. Most of 'em lap it up. Go right over the top. Speakin' of which –'

Oz appeared, three glasses of Williams in his paws. He thrust them at his two mates, peered at them searchingly.

'Who died?' he said.

'Why?'

'You look so serious, Dennis.'

40

'Just talkin' about the meanin' of life.'

Oz scoffed. 'Oh, that.' He gulped at his schnaps. 'I give that a lot of thought. Bein' a brickie makes you a bit of a philosopher.'

Neville looked at him in exasperation. 'Have you ever had any ambition, Oz?'

'Ambition?' echoed Oz. He looked thoughtful, seemingly hunting through the murky files of his memory for an instance when he had been tempted to think beyond the basics of the here and now. No luck.

'His only ambition's to see Friday come round again,' said Dennis.

It was gone midnight. Dennis emerged from the door marked *HERREN*, still adjusting his zip and a shade unsteady on his feet but well in control of his reactions. Wayne was just leaving with his pretty barmaid. He'd done himself all right there, had the cockney, thought Dennis. What these birds saw in the likes of him was a mystery, but then wasn't it always?

'G'night, London,' he said with only a hint of envy.

'G'night, squire.'

Wayne winked as he ushered the well-stacked blonde out into the night. It occurred to Dennis that one of these days he was going to need a woman himself. After sixteen years of being a one-woman man, the thought of going hunting again was strange, but maybe not so unattractive. He worried about kids like Neville, tying themselves down, grafting away, always putting their duty first – and for what? For your missus to decide she needed a spot of strange, a bit of excitement. You couldn't win. Or at least, he hadn't with Vera.

It was a while before Dennis caught sight of Neville, who had disappeared from their regular place at the bar. He groaned. The lad was sat down at the dice table.

'Aw Nev, what did I tell you!' he said when he got over there.

Neville looked up happily, pointing to a pile of plastic chips in front of him.

Oz was standing at Neville's other elbow. He grinned cynically at Dennis. 'He's winnin'. And he likes it.'

Dennis suddenly felt his age. 'I fancy getting back,' he said, touching Neville gently on the shoulder.

The lad didn't look up again. 'Oh, there's no mad rush.'

And, in fact, that moment brought him another win. Dennis made a decision that his nursemaiding days were over. By mutual consent, as the saying went.

Dennis's consciousness drifted slowly and unwillingly back to the surface of his mind. He half-opened his eyes. His forehead was a bit tight, but he'd escaped the worst of the hangover risk by controlling his drinking the night before. For Neville's sake. The lad would need someone who was all there to get him off this morning.

Dennis opened his eyes, gazed blearily at his watch. All right for time ... Then he glanced to his right and saw the empty bed.

Within seconds, Dennis was out of bed in his underpants. The rest of the hut were still asleep. Including Oz across the way. Dennis shot over to him and shook him savagely.

'Oz, wake up, man! Come on, Oz!'

His mate's dark thatch was all that was visible. Dennis shook him again, and a pasty, puffed face appeared, staring evilly at him through early-morning slits. Oz was no oil painting at the best of times; at this hour of the morning after a Friday night on the beer, he wasn't even a coat of metal primer.

'W-what?'

'Where's Neville?' Dennis snapped urgently.

Oz looked at him listlessly. 'Well, he's not bloody well in here with me, man!'

'Didn't he come back with you last night?'

Oz made an attempt to raise himself on one elbow, then collapsed feebly back onto his pillow. 'No. He went off with Bomber and some of the lads. I forget where.'

'Aw. I shoulda known not to leave him with you.'

'Divn't fret man,' Oz said loudly, suddenly awake and a bit angry. 'You've bin wetnursing him ever since we left. He's old enough!'

A muffled voice from the end of the hut told Oz to shut

up, but he wasn't about to be stopped in mid-flow.

'Bollocks!' he snarled.

'Some of us are tryin' to sleep.'

'Double bollocks!'

Dennis, meanwhile, shook his head, concerned. He looked at Neville's bed. The picture of him and Brenda on that Mediterranean beach was still holding pride of place. He hoped the young bugger hadn't done anything fatal. Such extremes had been known.

Dennis was in the shower hut having a shave when Oz stuck his head round the end partition.

'He's back!' he bawled.

The two older men made their entrance into the dormitory hut together. Neville was sitting on his bed in his shirt and trousers. His suit jacket was lying crumpled by his side. He looked up, smiled sheepishly, obviously hungover and ashamed of himself.

'Look at the state of you,' Dennis chided him. 'Where did you go?'

Neville shrugged. 'Lots of places. Can't remember in what order.'

'Where did you wake up?'

'At the railway station. On a bench.'

'Pity you didn't have your bags with you. You could have hopped straight on the train.'

Neville didn't answer that.

Oz asked: 'Where's Bomber?'

'I think he went to the brothel.'

'You mean you didn't?' said Dennis.

For a moment the colour came back into the lad's face. 'Certainly not!'

Dennis seemed relieved. He double-checked the time, smiled encouragingly.

'Howay, kid,' he said. 'Get your gear together. You can still make the train if you shift yourself.'

There was a long silence. Neville stared at the floor.

'I'm not going,' he said finally.

'What?'

Neville swallowed hard. 'I'm not going back.'

Dennis and Oz exchanged bemused, worried looks.

'Let me guess why,' said Dennis with heavy irony. 'You've lost all your money, haven't you? You've blown it all on booze and gambling just like Bomber.'

Neville made no move to confirm or deny it. He just said tonelessly: 'I don't know how I ended up. I still don't understand German money.'

He reached into his jacket pocket and fished out a creased wad of Deutschmarks. One or two fives fluttered to the ground. The rest were mostly higher denominations, tens and twenties. Both his mates' eyes went wide with astonishment.

'Look at that!' gasped Oz.

Neville smiled nervously. 'Did I win?'

'You're rich, bonny lad.'

'Am I?'

'Comfortably well off, anyway,' Oz said. 'We'll charter a Lear Jet,' he suggested to Dennis. 'Have him home by tea time.'

Somehow the news of his win failed to cheer Neville up. He put his head in his hands.

'I can't go home,' he moaned. 'Not ever.'

Dennis looked at him with a mixture of puzzlement and concern. 'Why not? So you didn't stick it out, but you're goin' back with some cash in your pocket. Got nowt to be ashamed about.'

Neville's face was a picture of agony. 'Oh no?' he said heavily. 'Haven't I? How can I go home to Brenda with this?'

Slowly he unbuttoned his shirtsleeve, then rolled it up to reveal a gleaming new tattoo. It featured a heart with an arrow through it. In the top left hand corner of the design was the name of Neville. At the other extreme, by the tip of the arrow, by the tip of the arrow, sat the name of one Lotte.

'Lotte? Who's she?' said Oz, struck with wonder.

'That's the thing,' Neville answered between clenched teeth. 'I can't remember ...'

THREE

They were having an intense discussion about the origins of various pop songs. Bomber was giving Oz and co. a spirited rendering of *The Happy Wanderer* as an example of how we had pinched songs from the krauts, to answer Oz's complaint about the way the German fellahs murdered Brit tunes.

'Watch it,' said Dennis. 'Here's mein Führer.'

They were all grafting away at their usual pace, which was pretty respectable, but it always did to know where the management was. Gave a bloke a sense of his back being covered. In this case, the management was represented by Herr Ulrich, Grunwald's number one assistant.

Oz spat deliberately on the ground. 'Is he heading here?' he said.

'Looks like it,' answered Dennis.

'Right.'

Oz put down his trowel, rubbed his hands together and picked up the battered Newcastle United Supporters Club bag that held his sandwiches and tea. Within seconds, he was perched on the half-completed wall, pouring himself a cuppa from his thermos.

'Is he barmy, Dennis?' queried Bomber. 'Takin' a tea break when the charge hand comes round?'

Dennis smiled wryly. 'He does it on purpose, Bomber.'

'Principle,' Oz agreed.

Bomber, who had continued to work at his smooth, efficient best, paused to tap his forehead pointedly. 'I sometimes think that Oz ain't playin' with a full pack, y'know.'

One or two of the Germans nearby also registered Oz's act of defiance. They nudged their mates, grinned or shook their heads. But they stepped up their work rate. The point was not lost on Oz.

'I don't kow-tow to authority like what they do,' he said loudly, jabbing an accusing finger at the German workers. 'If you put a chimpanzee in a uniform they'd salute it. 'I voz only obeying orders.' That's like their national motto ...'

Ulrich had entered the work area. With a quick glance at Oz he continued past them to where several Germans were working. He spoke harshly to one in particular, shoving what looked like a time sheet in his face and smacking his fist to emphasise his points. The argument between the two Germans continued for a couple of minutes, until Ulrich happened to glance around again in the direction of the Brits.

'If you've got a complaint, say it to me face!' growled Oz.

Dennis put a hand on his shoulder. 'He's talking to the Erics,' he said. 'He's not talking about you, Oz!'

'Erics' was their slang for Germans. It meant you could talk about them on site, saying 'Eric did this or that', without their realising you were doing it. Luckily they hadn't had anyone who was really called Eric work here yet.

'He is talkin' about me,' Oz insisted.

'How can you know when you don't speak a word of German?'

Oz wouldn't listen to reason from Dennis. 'I know more German than you think,' he said.

Ulrich suddenly turned round and began to walk towards them. Then he stopped a few feet from Oz. He was in his early thirties, quite handsome in a boney, Prussian sort of way. Fancied himself. And, in fact, was pretty good at his job.

'And I know more English than you think,' he said, smiling wolfishly. 'For instance ... I am familiar with the English word "tea break".'

Oz was fazed. Ulrich's English was a bit heavily accented, but he was fluent and obviously couldn't be fooled. Oz wasn't going to give up easily, though.

'Listen here, Mr Ulrich,' he countered. 'I do my whack as well as the next man. And if I do it faster, it entitles me to take my tea break when I choose. At the end of the day, you'll find no fewer bricks laid here than any other place.'

Ulrich looked Oz up and down, still smiling coldly. 'If this is true, everything okay,' he said, obviously deciding to avoid a fight. He nodded to the other Brits. '*Danke schön*,' he said and turned away.

'An' donkey shite to you, too!' hissed Oz at the back of the retreating charge hand. Ulrich stiffened momentarily, but he didn't break his stride. He'd remember Oz, though, if their paths crossed again.

Dennis looked accusingly at Oz. 'Oz,' he said, 'why do you antagonise people for no good reason?'

'I just don't like them Germans gangin' up on us lot.'

'They're not,' Dennis protested. 'Those lads are just doin' a job of work, same as us. We're workin' on their turf, man. And we're happy enough to take their Deutschmarks come the end of the week.'

Oz grunted sceptically. 'What's that got to do with anything? We earn it, man, 'cos we're the best.'

Oz's combination of bolshiness and primitive national-ism was getting too much for Dennis. He turned to Bomber for support.

'Christ, he's always got to have the last word. I tell you, Bomber, it's like beatin' your head against a brick wall.'

'Aye well,' said Oz. 'If you do, don't beat it against a German bit, 'cause it'll fall doon.'

'He's talkin' about me,' Neville muttered.

Wayne looked up from the piece of shuttering that he was easing into place. 'What?'

'The Capo. He's lookin' this way. They know my work's not up to snuff.'

The cockney chippie shook his head. 'He could be talkin' about anything. The weather,' he suggested. 'Or dandruff.'

Neville refused to be amused. 'Sooner or later I'm going to be collared,' he told Wayne solemnly.

Wayne carried on working, and made a motion with his hammer that implied Neville should be doing the same.

'I've told you what to do,' he said. 'Every time a gaffer comes around, whip out your extendable steel tape and measure something.'

His instructions were followed, though Neville continued to cast anxious looks in Ulrich's direction.

'You're gettin' better,' Wayne said, making an effort to be positive. 'It's not the first time you've 'eld an 'ammer in your 'and. You told me yourself you put up your Brenda's pelmets.'

'I didn't tell you they fell down, though, did I?'

'Come on, you're gettin' by.'

Wayne's attempts to comfort him only seemed to irritate Neville. He was not to be assuaged. 'I don't want to "get by",' he snapped. 'It's not fair. To you and the other lads.'

'I think you're just embarrassed,' said the imperturbable Wayne. 'Bein' a chippie's put you a step up on the social scale. Cut above, innit?'

'It is not! Nothing wrong wi' bein' a brickie!'

Neville bit his tongue, then smiled wanly, realising that Wayne had been taking the mickey. The hooter went for mid-day.

'Oh good,' he said then. 'I can do with me dinner.'

Wayne looked down his nose. 'Hus carpenters calls it "luncheon", my good man.'

'Silly sod.'

They began to put their tools away. Wayne looked up and saw a young German carpenter, in his late twenties with an open, friendly face, standing not too far away. He was smiling shyly, holding a football in one hand.

'Hellow. I am Helmut,' the German introduced himself.

Wayne looked him up and down. 'Oh yeah,' he said non-committally.

'Neville,' said his Geordie companion with a much more open grin.

Helmut smiled back, nodded. He indicated the ball in his own hand. 'You play, I see. *Sehr gut.*'

'Sure. He's a bit tasty, our Nev,' agreed Wayne.

'You play now?'

Neville blushed, then shook his head. 'Oh, I see,' he told the young German. 'No, I can't now. I've got to go and see someone about something.'

'Okay,' Helmut said with a shrug.

Maybe he was a little put out, but not too much. A happy-go-lucky type. Not your usual stereotype of an Eric, the stiff Prussians Oz was always fond of imitating.

'Donkey shite, all the same,' Wayne called out after him. It was the Brits' standard corruption of the German *danke schön*, and the Germans were used to it by now. 'Who have you got to see then?' he asked Neville.

The young Geordie looked grimly determined. 'I want to 'ave a word with Dennis,' he said.

Dennis and Oz had sidled into the little bar across the road from the site as soon as the hooter had gone. The past week or two, the place had become their 'local', comfortable and friendly and about as close to an English pub as you were likely to get over here.

Dennis had been trying to read a letter from his solicitor that had arrived that morning. About the divorce. The gory details. Fat chance, though, with Oz around.

'... Already they're on about child maintenance,' Dennis was saying gloomily.

Oz scoffed. 'You're all right there, Den,' he breezed. 'Workin' over here, no one knows what crack we make officially. Keep a bit back for yourself.'

'Oh, I don't want to do that. They're my kids, man. They're the reason I'm over here. Whether I'm livin' with them or not, I want them well clothed and well fed.'

Oz gulped down a good portion of his beer, smacked his lips in satisfaction and glanced knowingly at Dennis.

'Course you do,' he said. 'But you want to keep a few readies for yourself.'

'Not especially,' Dennis muttered. And he meant it. With a shrug of resignation, he folded up the letter from the solicitor and put it back in his pocket. Right on cue, Neville appeared with three beers.

'Three Pils, right?'

Oz nodded graciously. 'Good lad.'

'Cheers, Nev,' said Dennis. He made an effort, got himself out of his preoccupied state sufficiently to take proper notice of the new arrival. 'You don't normally get yourself over to this place in the middle of the day,' he said.

'I'll tell your Brenda,' mocked Oz.

Neville took a sip of beer, began to play with his beer mat, obviously embarrassed.

'It's the situation, Dennis,' he said after a while. 'I need a word with you. I can't keep pretendin' I'm a chippie when I'm not.'

'What am I supposed to do?' answered Dennis, a hint of irritation in his manner.

'You got me into this,' the lad said.

That was too much. Below the belt.

'I *what*?' Dennis growled. 'Let me tell you sommat – it was either that or splitting up. You'd 'ave been on your tod now. In Munster or Koblenz.'

'Yes, but you said once we got here you'd straighten it out.'

There was a heavy silence. Dennis knew that wasn't exactly what he'd said back in that railway restaurant in Holland, but the important thing was that Neville *thought* he'd said something like that. People were always *thinking* that Dennis was going to sort their lives out for them. It was a well-established pattern in Dennis's life, and it was starting to really piss him off.

'Look, Neville,' he said with a sigh. 'I do have a few problems of me own.'

'Like what?' said the lad in astonishment. Blokes like Dennis didn't have problems so far as he was concerned.

'My business,' said Dennis evasively.

Oz snorted. 'His divorce,' he said.

'Oz,' Dennis snapped angrily, 'one of these days someone is going to put their fist right down that big mouth of yours. And it may well be me.'

'What 'ave I said now?' Oz was trying to look as though butter wouldn't even get a little soft in his mouth.

Neville, meanwhile, had begun to absorb the information. 'Hey, Den. I'm sorry. I didn't realise. Must be very difficult for you.'

'Aye, well.'

They busied themselves with their beer, each for his own different reason. Oz and Neville observed a few minutes' silence in acknowledgment of Dennis's delicate problem. Then Neville cleared his throat and encouraged himself with a hefty swig of Pils.

'Still . . .' he murmured. 'What's going to happen to me?'

Five minutes later, Dennis and Neville marched into the site office. The blue-painted portakabin contained Herr Grunwald's office, which was tidy, partitioned-off in accordance with its inmate's prestige, and a larger, open work area festooned with architectural blueprints and flow charts illustrating the distribution of the work force and the work in progress. The place had an atmosphere of crowded, but almost clinically tidy activity, and was surprisingly clean. Ulrich's desk was at right angles to the door; across in the far corner of the open area sat Dagmar, the secretary, filing work sheets. Dagmar's desk was connected to Grunwald's office by a hatchway, through which as he entered the hut Dennis glimpsed the Great Man, puffing away on his pipe in his lair and apparently uninterested in the advent of the two Brits.

Not so Ulrich. The young German chargehand's keen eyes narrowed and his thin mouth turned up in an ironical smile as he motioned Dennis and Neville over towards his desk. He did not ask them to sit down. Not even – or perhaps especially – when Dennis told him the problem.

'You are telling me,' said Ulrich in his clipped English, 'that this man has worked here for almost two weeks without credentials?'

Dennis met the German's hard stare. 'Oh, he's got credentials, Mr Ulrich,' he said. 'But as a bricklayer. One of the best, mind. I can vouch for that meself –'

Good try, said Ulrich's ever-tightening smile, *but not good enough.*

'Come,' he interrupted Dennis. 'He is working here as a carpenter. How can this be?'

A pause. 'I can only assume it was some administrative cockup,' Dennis said innocently. Neville cleared his throat, shifted his feet.

'Cockup? *Was ist das?*'

'Oh, a mistake. A blunder, like. With the agent.'

Ulrich frowned. 'I think not . . .' he turned to Dagmar

51

and spoke quickly in German, clearly an order for her to check. '... You see,' he said, turning back to Dennis, 'my requirement is always exact. I cannot believe that the agent would make a mistake.'

'He's handling people for all over Germany,' Dennis said, making a last, desperate throw. 'There's thirty thousand of us workin' over here, so there's bound to be the odd error, like.'

Ulrich shrugged. 'Herr Pfister is most dependable.'

Just then, Dagmar glided over with a file for him. A good-looking girl. Or rather, woman. She was slim-hipped, firm-breasted, but there was a mature quality about her that was reflected in her humorous, intelligent eyes. Dagmar had been around a bit. Dennis, for one, was surprised to find her working in a place like this. She had that indefinable element of class.

Ulrich took the file. He didn't even look up. Obviously Dagmar wasn't his type.

Dennis managed to tear his eyes away from Dagmar. Neville was glancing at him uneasily as Ulrich leafed through the file. The lad could see the conversation wasn't going quite as hoped. His fears were confirmed a moment later. Ulrich nodded and pursed his lips in satisfaction.

'*Ja*,' he said, reading from the file as if to himself. 'Here is my letter to Pfister dated August 4th. My requirement is exact. Carpenters three, plasterers five – he sent four only, one comes today – and bricklayers ...' Ulrich looked up sharply. '... two only. There is no "cockup".'

An uneasy silence. Then Neville nudged Dennis, whispered to him: 'Ask him if there's any chance of a vacancy.'

'He does speak English, Neville,' Dennis hissed back, making a gesture towards the stony-faced Ulrich.

'Yeah, but you put things better than I do, Den.'

Dennis cursed quietly under his breath, took a step forward.

'Look, Mr Ulrich,' he said. 'I've worked in your country three times before. You can ring around any of the Stompenführers I've worked for, and they'll confirm I'm solid, right?' Still no reaction. Dennis pressed on. 'Now, as he was under me wing, like, we didn't want to split up. I'm pretty sure the occasion's going to arrive soon when you need another brickie, right? In the meantime, he'll do anything you want. He can shovel . . .' the desperation was starting to show in his voice and face now. '. . . Fair enough?'

There was no time for Ulrich to answer, as it happened. Grunwald, as if drawn by some special antennae that he carried around on his glistening pate, loomed silently out of his office, pipe clenched between his teeth. The briar seemed to twitch like an exploratory probe. He rocked on his heels for a moment, then took his pipe out of his mouth and fired a question at Ulrich. The chargehand explained deferentially but clearly, obviously referring to the document from Pfister that was still open in front of him. Grunwald nodded heavily and turned to the two Englishmen.

'This is true? You are a bricklayer?' he said in English to Neville.

Neville looked guilty. 'Yes,' he answered, nodding gloomily.

'So what if there had been an accident?' snapped Grunwald. 'You would want compensation, okay? But the fault would be yours.'

'I never thought about that . . .'

But Grunwald had already turned back to address Ulrich. It was clear he was putting responsibility squarely on the younger man and that he was in a hurry to go somewhere. He swept out without another glance at the two Brits.

Ulrich watched him go, smarting slightly from the damage inflicted by his superior's tongue. Then he looked first at the file, afterwards at Neville. The expression on his angular face changed to one of ill-concealed relish. Ulrich bounced back quickly, it seemed.

'You do not work today,' he said softly, easing himself back in his office chair. 'I must think. We talk of this again tomorrow.'

And that was that. Out they shambled, tails between their legs, to wait on the chargehand's pleasure. Neville said a brief farewell to Dennis and went off to pack up his tools.

'Blimey, you look sick, my son,' said Wayne.

Neville just nodded. The lad's face was a picture of dejection. The fragile bubble of his self-confidence had been pricked.

'You'll be all right, no bother,' Wayne continued in a vain attempt to cheer him up. 'That Ulrich just wants to make you sweat. They're all the same, gaffers. Power trip, innit?'

Still Neville could only shrug. He obviously expected the worst, and nothing Wayne said would convince him otherwise. After all, if the management here let him get away with this, they could get all sorts turning up claiming to be craftsmen and then changing their tune when they'd been hired ...

'I hear ze news. I am sorry.'

Both the Brits turned and saw Helmut, the young German who had offered Neville the chance of a lunchtime game of soccer. He was smiling shyly, apologetic.

'My own fault,' Neville admitted heavily.

Helmut shrugged. 'But I zink you are happy to go home, no? You not like Germany, I zink?'

If the comment was intended to comfort Neville, it failed. The lad looked even gloomier.

'I've got nothin' against Germany,' he said. 'I don't even know the place. Except for a night out with the lads.'

'You are married?' Helmut asked.

'Oh yeah. Five years.'

'Me also,' said Helmut, tapping his own chest, half proud, half rueful.

Smiling wanly, Neville, fished into his overall pocket and produced a well-thumbed snap of himself and Brenda.

'That's the wife. It's not a very good picture.'

Helmut looked genuinely appreciative. 'She is very pretty.'

'Aye, well.' Neville flushed slightly, but he was chuffed all the same.

No sooner had the photo of Brenda disappeared than Helmut produced one of a young blonde woman.

'This is my wife, Eva.'

54

Neville nodded, expressed approval. 'Oh yes. She's pretty an' all.'

This was a chance for Helmut to congratulate him on his choice of mate. And take a small step further towards the Englishman.

'I like very much if you meet her. Tomorrow you come to my house.'

Neville eyed him for a moment, genuinely surprised. 'Me?' he murmured.

'*Ja*,' Helmut chuckled. It was obvious there was no side to him, no ulterior motives. 'We eat,' he said. 'And also we drink?' He grinned. 'And zis way you meet German ... er ... home.'

'Family,' Neville said helpfully.

'*Ja*. Family. Okay?'

Neville began to relax for the first time in days. He grinned back at Helmut and nodded. 'Okay,' he said simply.

'Good,' said Helmut.

Barry was ironing a shirt, when Bomber sauntered over.

'Goin' out then, Barry?'

'No, none of us is,' said Barry. A keen student of the world of politics and science was Barry. He'd read a ton of paperbacks. some of them he'd even got close to finishing. 'So we'd better vote on what we're going to eat,' he announced.

Neville, who had just finished writing a postcard to Brenda and had sunk back into his now-habitual gloom, lay back on his bed. 'Not much choice, is there?'

'Yes, there is,' Barry said. He put down his iron and checked off on the fingers of one hand. 'We can have sausage, egg and beans. Or we can have sausage and eggs. Or alternatively we can have egg and tinned tomatoes on fried bread ...'

'Why can't we each have what we want?' boomed Oz from the far side of the hut.

Barry looked pained. Some people had no concept of how human societies worked. Particularly those, like Oz, who had had most of their brains scrambled at birth.

'It don't work like that,' he said, looking at Oz as if he was a madman to be humoured. 'We've got to abide by the majority's consensus. Otherwise, what have we got? Anarchy!' Inspired by his own words, he stepped out from behind the ironing board and raised his arms. 'If I could have everyone's attention for a moment!'

Most of the lads cast a glance in his direction, except for Wayne, who was lost in a world of his own, headphones over his ears, twirling imaginary drumsticks in time with whatever was playing on his Sony Walkman. Barry moved over and took off Wayne's 'phones.

'Do me a favour!' snapped Wayne, torn out of his reverie.

'This includes you, Wayne,' Barry said.

'What does?'

Wayne's question was left unanswered. Barry's great moment had come, and he had already turned to the others.

'From my experience,' he announced, 'what each hut needs is a leader. When I was working in München-gladbach, we had a bloke in our hut called Sid Henderson. "Hacksaw", we called him. And he was our democratically elected leader, like. That way we saved a lot of time in fruitless debate about who was goin' to have tinned tomatoes.'

Oz yawned. 'I don't follow . . .'

'You will in a moment,' Barry insisted. 'For example, one night we all wanted to go to the pictures. Some of us wanted to see *The Empire Strikes Back*, albeit in German. And some of the lads wanted to see a Swedish sex film. So it was up to Hacksaw, wasn't it?'

'Just a minute,' interrupted Neville. 'Why does it have to be up to anyone?'

'It makes life much simpler in the long run,' Barry said, frowning with the frustration of trying to get such sophisticated ideas over to a bunch of *Sun*-reading, witless sheep like these blokes. 'I mean, we were unanimous about that in Münchengladbach . . .'

Wayne grinned knowingly. 'You're puttin' yourself forward, is that it?' he asked.

'No, not at all. That should be a democratic decision. By consensus.'

As if he had done his duty by chipping in just the once, Wayne slipped his headphones back on. His eyes glazed over within moments, and he was back in his foot-tapping dream.

Dennis, meanwhile, had come in from having a shower.

'Hey, Dennis! D'you want to be our leader?' growled Bomber cheerfully.

'What?'

Bomber laughed. 'Barry here reckons we need a leader,' he explained. 'Someone to make all the crucial decisions – like whether to have beans or fried bread for our tea.'

'Well don't look at me,' said Dennis, heading for his bed.

Then another voice cut through the conversation: 'Aye. You didn't do a very good job for Neville, did you?'

It was Oz. Who else? And something about the way he said it got to Dennis. Dennis turned quickly, and there was anger in his eyes.

'What's that?' he barked.

'I'm just sayin' . . .'

'Just sayin' what?' Dennis's voice was going ominously quiet.

'Come on, it's not Dennis's fault,' said Neville.

But Dennis was standing with his hands on his hips and a scowl on his face. 'I'm talkin' to Oz, Neville.'

Oz shrugged. 'Whose fault is it then?' he said, jabbing a finger at Neville. 'Den's the one who brought you here. Brought me an' all. Told me I'd be livin' in a hostel. Didn't say owt about a wooden hut. With a bog two hundred bloody light years away.'

'You're like bloody kids, you are. Need wet-nursin'.'

'This is why we need a leader,' said the ever-eager Barry. 'To eliminate all this dissension.'

Oz snorted. 'I don't reckon we need a leader who backs down in front of Krauts.'

'Backs down?' Dennis had half-turned away, but Oz's latest gem brought him back into the argument.

'Why yes, man. You don't go askin' *them* favours. *You*

57

lay down the terms. Just remember they need us more than we need them.'

Dennis cast his eyes to the heaven that must lie somewhere above the bitumen roof of the hut. 'Oh, we don't need them do we not?' he said, his voice heavy with sarcasm. 'Why are we here then? You're complainin' about the conditions and you can't stand the Germans. So why are you here, Oz?'

For a moment there was silence. Oz squirmed a bit on his bed, hesitated.

'Makes a change,' he said finally.

'Aye, it makes a change from the dole queue, doesn't it?' Dennis snapped. He moved a couple of paces into the centre of the hut, staring hard at Oz. 'We're here because we can't get work in England, man. We should be grateful to the Germans; thanks to them we've got some money in our pockets and the dignity of knowing we've worked for it. And I can tell you,' he said passionately, 'that I 'ad precious little of that for the last four months in Sunderland. Kickin' me heels waitin' for the pubs to open. Pickin' the bairns up from school 'cos it was the wife who was earnin'. Then seeing her trying to make a decent meal out of tins ...'

Oz seemed to be taking the message to heart at last. He looked solemn, attentive. When Dennis reached the end of his piece, he nodded sagely.

'I must admit,' he said. 'I must admit that's the other reason I left. To get away from the wife's cookin'.' Suddenly he was smirking maliciously. 'Least *you* don't have to worry about that any more.'

Dennis moved quickly, and his intention was violent. Oz slid off his bed, grabbed a boot from the floor to defend himself. Wayne was still lost in the world of his Sony Walkman, but Bomber knew what to do. He moved even quicker than Dennis and grabbed him before he got to Oz.

'Take it easy, boy,' he said gently but in a way that brooked no messing.

Dennis shook his head. 'None of your business, Bomber,' he growled. But he didn't actually move to break away.

'The harmony of this hut's everyone's business,' said Bomber.

Oz stared around him, looking for support. 'What's he havin' a go at me for?' he said. 'Harmless enough remark . . .'

'It was bloody tactless,' Neville said, the disgust showing clearly on his young face. 'You owe Dennis an apology, I reckon.'

'Oh, if I've given offence I'd be the first to admit. Very sorry, I'm sure.'

Oz's 'apology' fooled no one, but for the moment it was enough. Dennis's eyes were still murderous, but his body was relaxing. Sensing that the danger-point had passed, big Bomber let go.

'There y'are, Den,' he said. 'That's the nearest you'll get to an apology from a pranett like him.'

That got a shamefaced scowl from Oz. Bomber might have pursued the question, but at that moment the door of the hut swung open and a bizarre figure stumbled in. The stranger wore a huge overcoat and a scarf that wound round his neck like a woolly anaconda. He carried a battered suitcase and a big, flat, circular package wrapped in tatty brown paper.

'Good evening, lads,' he said. He had a scouse accent, and it complemented his catarrh beautifully. 'The name's Moxey. The fella told me to come to Hut B.'

One or two of the blokes in the hut exchanged wary glances. Whoever he might be, Moxey was collecting negative points fast. And as if that wasn't enough, as he stood there he coughed convulsively, finishing the performance off by wiping his nose energetically on the sleeve of his overcoat. Bomber summed up the mood of the hut.

'Are you sure he said Hut B?' he asked.

'Oh, y-yes.' The bugger had a stutter too, for goodness' sake.

'Well, I don't think so,' said Bomber brazenly. 'Must be some mistake. Try the next hut along.'

Moxey stared around, found no one who was going to

gainsay the big man. 'Oh,' he mumbled. 'Maybe I'd better check with the gaffer. If I can just leave me gear here for the minute . . .'

He put his stuff down, backed out nervously. When he had gone, Dennis was the first to speak.

'Why d'you tell him that?' he asked.

Bomber looked him straight in the eye. 'I reckon this hut's got enough problems as it is, without adding to 'em.'

Dennis met his gaze for a moment, looked away and shrugged. Bomber could well be right. And he hadn't said anything while Moxey had been there, had he?

Meanwhile, Neville had wandered over towards the door. He was looking curiously at Moxey's belongings. 'He must be the missing plasterer,' the lad mused, bending to check the disc-like brown paper package. 'What's this, I wonder?'

'Go on, have a look,' said Oz.

Neville glanced briefly at the others, then put his attention back on the package. He gingerly tugged at a loose bit of paper, pulled it aside.

'Hey,' he said after a moment or two, his voice tinged with wonder and delight. 'It's a dartboard!'

With that, Oz was on his feet, racing for the door. He flung it open and his voice boomed through the night:

'Hey, Moxey! You were right the first time! This *is* your hut!'

'That's what I like about Oz,' Dennis told Bomber with a wry grin. 'He's so bloody *obvious*.'

They decided to crack a Pils on the strength of that.

FOUR

Neville worked skilfully with the football, bouncing it from foot, to knee, sometimes to his head, then slamming it against the side of the portakabin. Again ... again ... anything to take his mind off things.

He had sat around in the hut this morning in his pyjamas, drinking tea, until all the others had gone. Then he'd studied his fatal tattoo, his one, all-too-visible reminder of the mysterious Lotte. Then he'd thought about what Brenda would say to him about that, which had made him feel angrier with himself, more depressed than he could remember being for a long while, maybe ever. So he'd fetched the ball and come out here, to where the big excavators were working on the foundations and there was room to kick a ball, and he'd let some of it out. At least he was good at something. There was something he could enjoy. Up in the North-East, they appreciated what the Brazilian player Pele had been talking about: Life and the Beautiful Game. Life was hard, but the game was easy, you knew where you were with it.

Sod Ulrich ... slam ... *sod Oz* ... *sod the hut* ... *sod bloody Germany* ... slam ... *and sod himself* ... slam, harder than the others, because Neville was basically an honest lad and he knew he couldn't blame anyone else ... slam ...

That last time he really put some feeling into it; the kick contained something of the wild, uncontrolled fury that was inside him. The ball sailed right over the top of the portakabin, travelling hard and fast and high in the direction of the excavations.

Neville bit his lip, cursed, watched the ball disappear. Then his features relaxed. That was what happened when you let rip. So be it. Within seconds he was trotting round the side of the temporary hut to retrieve the ball.

A big digger was working some fifty or so yards from where Neville spotted the ball showing amongst the loosened earth of the vast crater that had already been hollowed out ready to take the foundations. Neville waved and shouted to make sure the driver saw him, then dived down into the hole and made for his spot. The ball had penetrated the earth, and Neville had to get down on his knees and scrabble gently to release it. No problem. Except that there was something else there, an object he couldn't immediately fathom. It was big, rounded, well-rusted and metallic, with protruding ... fins ...

'Jesus,' muttered Neville to himself. 'A ruddy bomb.'

Just at that moment, he heard the digger behind change gear. The engine noise got louder. He half-turned, glimpsed the huge machine lurching in his direction, its massive scoop swinging menacingly as if preparing to slice down to where Neville was crouched. He could see the driver perched in his high cabin, waving and shaking his fist, shouting none-too-polite-sounding advice in German above the sound of the engine.

Neville waved back frantically. 'No! No!' he bellowed, finding his voice. 'Stop!'

The German leaned out of his cab window, still working his controls with one hand, with the other making a motion that clearly said: 'Get out of it!'

'There's a bomb, man!' Neville screamed. He cupped his hands: 'BOMB!' His voice rose to a strangled crescendo. 'HOLD IT. PLEASE! NEIN! NEIN!'

But the German, gesticulating furiously, continued to lower his greedy scoop towards the spot where Neville was standing. Neville continued to shriek, but there was nothing else he could do: as the scoop descended, he moved to position himself beneath it. Passive resistance. Like a peace protester. The sweat was pouring down his face, and he wasn't sure where else he might be wet, either, but Neville stayed put, shouting all the while: 'You'll blow us up! STOP, PLEEESE!' He reached out, grabbed the scoop.

For a moment it looked as though the enraged German was going to shovel up Neville and damn the consequences. The slicing teeth of the scoop can't have been more than a foot, maybe eighteen inches, from the ground and the bomb when the driver, with one last explosion of venom, cut the motor and halted its progress.

Neville sighed with relief, watched the German clamber down from his cab with a light heart, though he could see his fury.

'Bomb,' he said simply to no one in particular. 'Bomb . . .'

He was still saying it when the driver arrived and saw what he was talking about.

Four hundred yards away, Dennis was sitting opposite Ulrich in the site office. He had looked for Neville at the beginning of his tea break, been unable to find him, but come here anyway. Naturally he was already way over time, and Ulrich was making it crystal clear that this fact did not meet with the management's approval.

'I think,' said the chargehand, 'that you would be better doing your work than arguing for your friend, who has disappeared, no?'

'He's a good worker,' Dennis retorted stubbornly. 'And he wants to stay. Let's face it, you're always goin' to need one more brickie . . .'

Ulrich shook his head. 'There is a principle here.'

'Herr Ulrich, you want us to say sorry, all right we're sorry –'

The usual peace of the hut was shattered with an abruptness that was almost like a desecration. A German whom Dennis recognised as one of the excavator drivers crashed into the office, breathless from running, and started to pant out some urgent message to Ulrich. The exchange between the two men was brief, but whatever it was that the driver said, it galvanised Ulrich into instant action. With no more than the curtest of nods to Dennis, he was on his feet, reaching for his hard hat. Then he left with the driver.

Dennis watched him go, then turned to Dagmar the

secretary, who was sitting at her desk next to Grunwald's office. She looked surprised and impressed by whatever had gone on, and that was really something, because Dagmar let very few things put her out.

'All right. So what was all that about?' asked Dennis.

She answered in English: 'They find bomb, Dennis.'

He was halfway across the site before he realised that she had used his name. How the hell did she know that?

The four of them stood a foot or two from the find: Ulrich, Herr Grunwald, the driver and Neville. Grunwald was bending over to examine the bomb, impassive and clinically precise, apparently oblivious of the fact that he and his companions were being watched by a steadily-increasing audience of site workers. Grunwald's audience was standing around the perimeter of the crater, following the proceedings with fascination. The boss straightened up and turned to Ulrich. He rasped an order. Ulrich hurried off to get help. Then it was the driver's turn. The man indicated Neville as he explained the sequence of events that had led up to the drama. Grunwald nodded vigorously.

'That was very brave of you,' he said to Neville in English. His usually flat voice had an unexpected hint of warmth. 'How did you discover this?'

Neville grinned, feeling foolish. 'I was just fetching me ball.'

'So,' said Grunwald. There may – just may – have been the ghost of a smile.

Leaving the driver to stand guard over the bomb, Grunwald and Neville made their way up the slope to the edge of the crater, where the rest of the site workforce were gathered. Everyone had stopped working; the news had travelled fast.

'Hey, is it really a bomb?' asked Dennis, who was standing close by with the rest of the lads from Hut B.

Neville smiled shyly. 'Certainly is.'

'There is nothing we can do,' Grunwald announced. 'The army will see to it. Until then, will you please go back to your huts.'

64

But no one had any intention of doing that for the moment.

'What kind of a bomb is it?' Bomber said.

Grunwald looked at him levelly. 'I would think it was left from the war.'

There was a moment's silence while they absorbed that. Oz was the first to get the point. He burst out laughing.

'Then it's a British bomb!' he guffawed. 'Hey, it's one of ours!'

Suddenly the British contingent exploded into a torrent of cheers, backslapping. It was magnificent and it was ridiculous. Dennis was the only one who stayed out of it.

'By jove,' chuckled Bomber. 'It's the jolly old R.A.F.!'

'Could've been one of our dads dropped that,' Barry said.

'Aye, it was us that flattened you lot in the first place,' said Oz triumphantly, turning to Grunwald.

Dennis sighed. 'Oh, knock it off, Oz.'

'Why?' Oz gloated. 'It should make you proud. That is a British bomb, isn't it?'

'Yes ...' agreed Grunwald slowly. 'It did not go off,' he added, then stalked off, exuding quiet satisfaction.

Oz scowled, said nothing. Even he couldn't answer that one. Instead he sulked all the way back to the hut.

A brew-up brought Oz back to spirits. 'My uncle was a bomb-aimer,' he started telling the lads. 'Lancasters.' Then he mimed pressing a button – more space-invaders than World War Two, but Oz was never one to quibble about authenticity – and gabbled excitedly: 'Aim, press, schplatt, schplatt. There goes your munitions dump ...' A whining noise, then a mock explosion. '... There goes the rates office, the knocking shop ...'

'Yeah, well,' said Wayne, ignoring the pantomime. 'One didn't go off, did it? And thanks to Nev.'

Bomber nodded. 'Right. Nerves of steel, our Nev.'

'I think Neville's displayed the qualities of leadership this hut so desperately requires,' Barry announced to a chorus of groans.

Neville, who was sitting quietly on his bed, shook his head. 'I'll probably be going home tomorrow,' he said.

'They wouldn't dare. Not after what you've done.'

The speaker was Oz, and contrary to his usual practice, Neville paid some attention to him. 'You reckon it'll help?'

Even Dennis found himself brightening. 'Can't hurt. You saved the day, bonny lad.'

'Oh, I didn't do all that much. Just an accident, mostly.'

'Listen, you play all the strokes you can chisel, son,' said Wayne, tapping his nose sagely.

'Roit,' added Bomber. 'They owes you, don't they? If that bomb'd gone off, it wouldn't just 'ave done for our Nev. It'd 'ave killed the driver, too, at least. An' he's an Eric.'

Oz chuckled evilly. 'Which was the bomb's original intention,' he said. 'Thirty-five years late, mind.'

'What about it, Dennis?' Bomber asked. 'Good time to push the laddie's case with Ulrich.'

'Aye.' Dennis nodded. 'I'll have a word. When the time's appropriate.'

A few minutes later, Ulrich turned up. To tell Neville he was wanted on the Kraut TV news. Nationwide in Deutschland.

Come evening, they were all in the bar on the corner – so heavily patronised by Brits now that they called it 'The Club' – quaffing away and grouped around the TV above the bar, waiting.

Bomber careened over to where they stood, in a hurry to get the round to them before the bit they'd been waiting for came on.

'Here we go,' he murmured. 'Three Pils, two Williams, one vodka and seven-up –'

'That's mine,' said Wayne without a trace of shame.

'– I reckoned it would be. Two scotches and a Dort. Roit . . .'

Moxey drank thirstily. After a while, a thought occurred to him.

'Well,' he sniffled, 'where's the lad hisself, then? Where's young Neville?'

Dennis frowned. 'I'm not too sure. He went off earlier, wearing a suit and tie.'

'Civic reception, is it?' suggested Moxey.

Oz laughed hoarsely, then took his own look round the bar. 'Aye,' he said. 'Where is he?'

'He's off to Helmut's place,' Wayne told him.

'Who?'

'Helmut. One of the German chippies. Asked Nev to his house, didn't he?'

'What! A German's house?' echoed Oz, sounding as though he suspected Neville had been kidnapped by White Slavers.

'What's wrong with that?'

Oz shook his head incredulously. 'You mean , he's gone to his *house*, like.'

'I just told you, didn't I?'

The other lads had been listening in. Bomber winked broadly. 'By jove, Neville's been fraternising with the enemy. Is that it, Oz?'

Oz didn't see the joke. Oz was serious.

'Just thought he'd have been with us, that's all,' he said airily.

A moment later, Barry snapped: 'Here, shut up. This is it!'

The barman turned up the volume on the TV set and a reverent hush settled over the ranks of the Brits.

Five minutes later and half way across the city, Neville sat in the neat living room of Helmut's modest apartment and watched his own face and voice disappear from the screen as the news item about his discovery of the bomb was concluded. Eva, Helmut's wife, leaned over and switched off the television set. She said something to her husband and his parents, who had also been invited to dinner, and they all beamed proudly. Helmut made a gesture for Neville to drink up the schnaps he was clutching in one hand.

'Oh, aye ...'

Eva said something else. Everyone laughed, nodded.

'Er ... what did she say?' asked Neville, frowning slightly – not that he wasn't happy to be here, because despite the unfamiliarity of it all he was, but because his frustration at the rapid-fire German of the interviews and the reporter's voice-over was starting to get to him.

Helmut grinned. 'She say, er, we not know that . . . that we are when you come to my house . . . meeting a famous man who is on, er, television . . .'

Now Eva and Helmut's parents were smiling at Neville. He nodded shyly, embarrassed and yet flattered to be the object of such attention. When the ever-solicitous Helmut had refilled his glass, he smiled nervously and said: 'Aye, well, tell them . . . I was only fetching me ball . . .'

By golly, it wasn't so bad being the hero of the hour.

Meanwhile, back at the Club, the excitement was over a lot more quickly. Within seconds of the end of the interview with Neville, the lads had turned their back on the idiot box and were clustered round a table. Some Germans from the site had taken over their TV-watching spot at the bar and seemed to be watching some incredibly complicated quiz game. Oz claimed the winner got a Ford Escort, in which he was expected to invade Poland.

'Well, she was a bit tasty, that interviewer,' mused Wayne. 'Nev should've steamed in there.'

Oz nodded reluctant agreement. 'Aye, they've got some canny women, the Germans. I'll say that.'

'Nothing else?' said Dennis.

Oz thought for a moment, took a sip of Pils. 'The beer's passable.'

'You pass enough of it,' Bomber said.

'To be fair, I haven't been here all that long,' Oz said.

Dennis grinned. 'It wouldn't make any difference. You could be here ten years and see nothing more than beer halls and massage parlours.'

'Is he gettin' at me again?'

'C'mon, you could use working abroad as an education, Oz. You could learn from it.'

'I lay bricks,' Oz said forcefully, as if he was proclaiming a principle by which he intended to live or die. 'That's what I do. I go to work at eight o'clock in the morning and for nine hours, five days a week, I lay bricks. Makes no difference to me if it's Düsseldorf or Darlington.'

He sat back with his arms folded, challenging the others to tell him there was anything more than that to it –

particularly anything foreign. Barry, naturally, had some serious observations.

'It's all down to how you use your time off,' Barry droned on earnestly. 'Nev's got the right idea. He's integrating himself. When Kevin Keegan went to Hamburg, that's what he did. And Mrs Keegan. They both learned the language and made a wide variety of friends within the German community.'

Oz looked at him in mock disbelief, then smiled cynically. 'Oh yeah? So how come he transferred to Southampton? I mean, Germany must be pretty bloody desperate if he preferred Southampton!'

The last word was chewed off with such emphatic venom that the other lads were a bit taken aback.

'Have you ever been there, Oz?' asked Dennis quietly.

'Me cousin has.'

Suddenly Oz started. A German from the site who had been standing just behind him had moved over and tapped him on the shoulder.

'I have question for you,' he said in heavily-accented but clear English before Oz had time to react.

Oz looked him up and down. 'Oh aye? Want to see me papers, do you?'

The German nodded, as if it was all he had expected. He looked as though he could handle himself.

'I hear what you say,' he told Oz with ominous calm. 'Okay: if Germany such a no-good place, why do you not piss off back to England?'

There wasn't really an answer to that. Not in words, any way.

And from a different perspective, Neville was also having trouble with words where he was. They had finished dinner, drunk their coffee. Helmut's wife and his mother were at work clearing the table while the men sat over half-empty schnaps glasses. Helmut's dad, a solid, grey-haired gent in his sixties, leaned back in his chair and sighed, then reached for the schnaps.

'Thanks. Er, *danke*,' said Neville as the old boy filled his glass back up to the brim.

Helmut senior smiled appreciatively at Neville's courtesy

in using German. His generation hadn't learned English in school, Helmut had explained on his father's behalf. Those had been different times, of deprivation and many bad things besides . . . That was the closest they'd got to politics all evening. And looking at Helmut senior, Neville had to admit he saw nothing more than a good-natured grandpa who'd worked hard all his life and knew how to enjoy himself these days without harming another soul. Not so bad. Plenty of OAPs at home, identical – though not so well provided for.

Meanwhile, the old man was saying something to Helmut, tapping the near-empty spirit bottle and pressing some notes into his son's hand. Neville got it. He was sending Helmut down the offie for a refill. There was obviously some serious drinking in prospect. The girls had disappeared into the kitchen to do the washing-up. None of your newfangled libby stuff in this particular household, that was for sure.

'I will be . . . soon. Okay?' Helmut said with that gauche, amiable grin of his. He indicated the bottle to make dead sure that Neville got the point.

'Oh, right.' Neville smiled warmly back at his new mate. He was pissed enough to be nice and relaxed, not yet at the silly stage. Just right.

Seconds later, Helmut was slamming the door behind him. Which left Neville and the old man together at the table, alone. Moments passed. Then Helmut senior twinkled, reached over and retrieved a packet of cheap cigars from the centre of the table. He offered one to Neville.

'Er, not smoke.'

When that failed, Neville mimed it out, touching the packet, shaking his head, pretending to push the cigars away – though not too energetically, in case his host felt rejected along with the smokes. But the old man got the point. He chuckled, enjoying the moment of communication, and lit his own cigar. After a couple of seconds' silence, he took an exaggerated drag on it, pretended a grotesque coughing fit. Finally he wagged a school-marmish finger playfully at Neville.

'*Nicht gut*,' he said. No good.

Neville nodded. '*Nein*.'

'*Rauchen ist nicht gut für Sie*,' the old man continued, encouraged by his guest's use of German. When Neville looked a little puzzled, he resumed his pantomime, dragging on the cigar and pretending to cough his lungs up.

'No,' Neville agreed, understanding. 'Bad for you. Right.'

Then Helmut senior chuckled again, said something that referred to himself. He touched his bald head, stroked his lined face. Neville got it. The old man was saying it didn't matter at his age, it was too late to bother about things like that.

They sat in companionable silence for a while longer, until the old man lifted his schnaps glass and waited for Neville. They drank together.

'*Gut?*'

'*Gut*,' Neville agreed. 'very *gut*.'

A reminder from the old man that Helmut had gone to get another bottle. Sign language to show that Neville understood. Helmut senior seemed to be examining Neville closely, and it was a bit disconcerting. The lad smiled, looked away, pretending to study the furnishings in the ordinary little room. When he looked back, the old man was still staring fixedly at him. Neville was just starting to feel seriously uncomfortable when Helmut senior nodded and eased himself up from the table. Neville watched him as he made his stately – maybe slightly tipsy – progress across to an ornate dresser positioned up against one wall. It was from earlier in the century and was obviously a family treasure. The old man opened a drawer and took out a leather bound volume.

It was a photo album, well-filled, though faded with age. Helmut senior brought it back to the table, sat himself down in the formerly empty chair next to Neville and opened it. After leafing through a few of the first pages, the old man smiled in triumph, beckoned to Neville to make sure he was looking. Then he jabbed a finger at a black-and-white snap carefully positioned in the centre of the page.

'*Mich*!' said the old man. Me. And there was unmistakable pride in his voice.

Neville leaned over, peered at the photo. He saw a younger version of the man sitting next to him – not unlike Helmut, in fact. The difference was that the lad in the picture was wearing a uniform Neville had seen a hundred times in war films, always standard-issue clothing for the baddies. Of course, Helmut senior was just the right age...

'*Obergefreiter*,' the old man said, pointing to his younger self.

Neville nodded. He could see the stripes on the soldier's sleeve. If it was the same as the British army, he would have been a corporal. And there were other pictures, all from the same period, when Helmut senior had been young and cocky and ... probably scared most of the time. Neville looked at the photos and he also looked at the old man. It didn't take him long to realise why the photo album had been brought out: these pictures were the only real point of contact that Helmut senior could think of, something that joined him to an Englishman, even one of Neville's generation. It was touching and sad. Neville found himself wanting to give something in return.

They had been leafing through for a few minutes when Neville suddenly touched the old man's arm. 'The Scharnhorst!' he said loudly.

'*Bitte*?' Helmut senior asked with a polite smile.

'The Scharnhorst. German battleship.'

For a moment longer, the old man seemed confused. Then he nodded enthusiastically. '*Ja, ja. Scharnhorst.*'

'My grandad. Er ... ' A mist had descended over the German's eyes again. Neville groped for a way of explaining. 'You Helmut's father ...'

'*Vater.*'

'. . . Yeah, right. *Vater*. And your, er, *Vater* ist Helmut's . . .'

'*Ach! Ist Grossvater!*'

'Right! So, my *Grossvater* ...'

'*Ja*?'

'He was ...'

Neville frowned desperately, mimed the action of a ship slipping down beneath the waves.

'Sunk by the Scharnhorst,' he added, adding some indications of shelling to make it absolutely clear.

Helmut senior ran through Neville's movements, and then his eyes lit up. He said something in German, nodded vigorously, that sounded as though it was about sinking. The words were a bit like the English, enough for Neville to know he'd got through.

'Yes, right! *Ja! Ja!*' Neville exclaimed, delighted to have made real contact.

Helmut senior looked at him with pleasure and a new respect. 'Scharnhorst,' he murmured. '*Grossvater, et ...*'

'Sunk! Glug, glug, glug ...'

'*Ach. Gut!*'

They both roared with laughter and relief. After a few seconds, though, Neville's face clouded over a touch. He sipped some schnaps.

'He were killed,' he said.

But the old boy was still too excited to bother about that. He was calling out to the kitchen, telling the women about this remarkable coincidence – he and Neville's grandad fought in the same war. When he turned back to Neville, he mistook the slightly down-in-the-mouth expression on the lad's face for thirst. Helmut senior clucked, checked the bottle. It still had a drop left in, which he instantly poured into Neville's glass.

'*Wir trinken,*' he said gravely. Drink a toast.

Neville was beginning to feel a bit guilty at having laughed about his grandpa. And he wasn't so sure he should drink to whatever the old boy had in mind to drink to. For a moment, he wondered how he could get out of it. Then he relaxed. The schnaps was there, and nothing was going to bring his grandpa back.

'Might as well,' he said out loud, touching glasses with Helmut senior. 'It was a long time ago.'

Just like that bomb today had been dropped a long time ago. The difference was, the bomb might do someone a bit of good. In the meantime, Neville was enjoying himself and sod tomorrow. After all, in a moment Helmut would be back with a fresh bottle of schnaps, and the night was young.

Helmut's light motorbike bumped over the rough road leading into the site. It was half-seven on a grey morning, and he was having to weave to avoid blokes trudging into work. Neville hung on grimly, as he had been hanging on since they had left the apartment for the trip across town. Helmut stopped not too far from the Brits' hut, held the machine steady while Neville dismounted. The British lad winced visibly as he touched hard ground. He was pale and bleary-eyed. Helmut grinned his grin.

'You are okay?'

'No, I feel terrible,' muttered Neville. 'Just as well I'm not working, with the hangover I've got.'

Helmut chortled appreciatively. 'Schnaps is good.'

'It's bloody lethal.'

'Well . . . I hope everything is good for you. With the job and so.'

They shook hands. Neville managed a genuinely grateful smile. 'Thanks,' he said. 'And thanks for last night, Helmut. For the evening, the kip-down and everything.'

Helmut raised one gauntleted hand in salute and buzzed off towards the place where he parked his bike. Neville was starting to shamble towards Hut B when he heard another German voice calling his name. He turned, puzzled.

It was Ulrich. The chargehand was beckoning him over. Neville obeyed.

'Yes, Mr Ulrich.' Nothing servile, but polite.

'Come with me,' said the chargehand simply.

Neville followed. They picked their way through the site towards the part where the low apartment blocks were being constructed. Puzzled at first that they weren't going to the admin hut, Neville brightened when he saw a group of brickies already at work there, including the group of Brits. Oz, he noted with interest, wore a plaster across his nose. Must've had an accident.

Ulrich stopped, waited for the brickies to look up from the labours.

'Good morning,' he said when he had their attention. He

jerked a thumb in Neville's direction. 'This young man starts work today as a bricklayer.'

'Hey, thanks very much,' beamed Neville.

Dennis nodded, well pleased. 'Yes, thank you, Herr Ulrich. Much appreciated.'

'Aye, well, it's only fair in the light of what happened. As I pointed out yesterday –' Oz growled.

'Ja, I know. I agree, it is fair,' retorted Ulrich. He smiled savagely. 'But also, I now have a vacancy for a bricklayer.'

Oz frowned. 'How come?'

'You, Osbourne,' Ulrich said with relish. 'You are fired!'

FIVE

Oz had disappeared in the direction of the admin hut, still furiously arguing the toss with Ulrich. The other brickies looked embarrassed, ill at ease.

'I feel terrible,' said Neville.

'Too much schnaps, was it?' Bomber asked.

'No, about Oz. I mean, it's taken the shine off me reinstatement.'

Dennis shook his head firmly. 'It's not your fault, Nev,' he said. 'Oz asked for it. He's always gettin' up their noses. And I suppose Ulrich found out about last night.'

'What happened last night?'

'Bit of a dispute with the locals,' Dennis told him. Bomber nodded in support. 'Some of the German scaffolders.'

Bomber smiled grimly. 'What you might call a failure to communicate.'

'Is that the reason for the elastoplast, then? Did one of them hit him?' Neville asked.

'No,' said Bomber solemnly. 'That was his head going through the space invaders machine.'

Neville took a moment to let it all sink in. He sat down slowly on a half-finished wall. Then he said: 'Were you all involved?'

'Only tryin' to break it up,' said Dennis.

Bomber shrugged. 'Den's roit, you know. Oz had it coming, though I don't like to say such a thing about a mate. It had to 'appen sooner or later. Daft as a brush, he is.'

'I know,' Neville muttered. 'But he's okay is Oz. Underneath.'

'Yeah,' said Bomber. ''Tis what's on top makes him such a noitmare.'

They thought about it for a while.

'What'll he do?' said Neville.

Dennis grinned. 'Go back home. Sign on. Make it up wi' the wife. Go down the Fat Ox an' get paralytic . . .'

'Lucky bugger,' murmured Bomber wistfully.

And in fact, for the rest of the morning, it was already as if Oz had decided to disappear off the face of the earth. It was lunchtime, and Bomber was up at the bar in the Club ordering Pils and sandwiches, when a sudden silence fell over the place. Oz had walked in.

Neville coughed into his beer in embarrassment. Bomber, though, just looked coolly at the new arrival. 'What'll it be, Oz?' he said gently.

'The usual.'

'Make that another Pils,' said Bomber to the barman.

The German braced himself on the counter, shook his head. To make his meaning absolutely clear, he jabbed one finger in Oz's direction: He – OUT!' he hissed in English.

Bomber remained level. 'Don't be daft. He only wants a swift half.'

'He . . . is . . . not to . . . come here.'

Oz, of course, was all big, innocent eyes and 'What have I done now?'

Even Dennis moved in to intervene on his fellow-Geordie's behalf. 'It's all right,' he said. 'Get him one in.'

The barman was weakening. He wasn't a bad sort, and he liked and respected Dennis. 'Last night –' he began to protest.

'Last night don't count. Special circumstances. Howway, give him a beer.'

The barman looked at Dennis, at the others, then narrowed his eyes for a final, barbed look at Oz, but he filled up an extra glass of beer, which he slammed down on the bar to make it quite clear he was serving Oz against his better judgment.

Dennis swiftly led Oz away from the counter and

potential trouble towards where Barry, Moxey and co. were standing.

'Hey, did you get the boot then?' asked Barry.

'Aye,' growled Oz.

Neville had followed up behind. 'I'm sorry, Oz,' he said awkwardly. 'I –'

'It's not your fault, Nev. It's them bastards,' said Oz with what he obviously considered to be true nobility.

Dennis grunted sceptically. 'Come off it, Oz,' he said. 'You've only got yourself to blame, man.'

Oz rounded on him in anger and astonishment. 'How?'

'Because,' Dennis told him calmly, 'you're always soundin' off about the Germans. And they're a canny bunch of lads. They're just like the rest of us.'

Oz brooded. 'Not bloody Ulrich.'

'He's a hardnose, but that's his job.'

'We could put his job in the clarts,' said Oz, taking a good swig of beer. 'If you lot'd back me up, that is.'

Wayne, who had been quietly eating his cheese sandwich, looked searchingly at Oz. 'How d'you mean, back you up?'

Oz shrugged. 'Walk off. In protest, like.'

'Over his unfair dismissal. Confrontation with management,' agreed Barry, putting on his *Panorama* presenter's voice.

Dennis shook his head. 'What good d'you imagine that'll do?'

'Leave him short,' Oz said triumphantly, scanning the little group for support. 'Then how'll he get the work done?'

There was an embarrassed silence. Dennis, as usual, spelled it out.

'Oz,' he said with heavy patience, 'he'll call an agent and order another six Brits. He's got plenty to choose from. There's three million unemployed back home!'

'Well, it shouldn't be allowed,' blustered Oz. 'We've got our rights ...'

Dennis sighed. 'We haven't any rights, Oz. We're on the lump, man. We're workin' black. If you want workers' rights, then register with the Germans and pay them income tax and insurance. But you can't have it both ways.'

'In other words, what you're sayin' is, you won't back me up. One of your own mates.'

'Oz,' Dennis said, and his tolerance was wearing more than a bit thin, 'I'm sorry you got paid off. We all are. But we can do sod all about it.'

Oz looked accusingly at Dennis. 'You talked Ulrich into letting Neville stay.'

'Yeah, well,' Dennis said sharply. 'There was other factors helped Neille. A, that bomb he found. And B, your big mouth.'

'What!'

Dennis's eyes narrowed. He had been saving this up for a while, and it came out in a torrent.

'Kidda,' he hissed, 'I've seen blokes come and go like you all the times I've been here. Never been out of the U.K. before, never drunk foreign beer, never eaten foreign food. Like fish out of water without the wife or mother to lend a guidin' hand.' He paused, took a sip of beer, was in full flow again before Oz could interrupt. 'After a week,' he said, 'they've lost their passport, most of their money, and become ridiculously nationalistic on behalf of the home country that can't bloody offer 'em work in the first place!'

There was a shocked silence. It was clear the lads found Dennis's sudden outburst impressive as well as alarming. Even Oz seemed cowed.

Neville coughed. 'Er ... should I get another round in?'

Oz was still staring at Dennis. He shook his head slowly.

'Not for me,' he told Neville. 'I know when I'm not wanted.'

Then he downed the dregs of his Pils, turned on his heel and stalked out of the bar.

Dennis watched him go, shaking his head.

'He'll never learn, Den,' said Bomber.

Dennis nodded wordlessly, turned away to drink his beer in peace.

Within seconds, Barry had appeared at his elbow. 'Den?'

'Yeah?'

'This group needs someone of your eloquence to lead them.'

'Barry ... PISS OFF!'

*

The start of the next day came, supposedly Oz's last. He'd had twenty-four hours' grace to pack up and say his farewells. Even the time for those had passed by early the following morning. All but Neville had taken their leave and gone off to start work as Oz moodily stuffed the last of his clothes into his tatty canvas grip bag.

Neville wandered shyly over to Oz's bed.

'Will you post this letter for us, Oz? When you get back, like.'

Oz took the letter. 'Aye.'

'Cheers . . .' Neville looked embarrassed. 'I'll miss you,' he said after a while. 'Good laugh, you are, Oz.'

'No one else seems to think so,' said Oz with a sigh. 'I don't know why everyone's against me. I really do fail to understand it.'

'Oh, they're not Oz, honest.'

But Oz was not to be robbed of his martyr's crown. 'Aye, well,' he said, still looking hard done-by. He zipped up his bag viciously, reached down onto the bed and handed a packet to Neville. 'You want these winegums?'

'Oh . . . ta.'

'And there's some books on me pillow.'

'Cheers.'

They stood together for a moment, unsure what to do or say.

Oz broke the stalemate. 'I'll be off away, then,' he said firmly.

Neville dived for his work jacket that lay on his bed. 'I'll come with you, Oz,' he said.

They parted outside. A quick handshake.

'I'll see you, Oz.'

'Aye, Nev. Unless I see you first.' Oz chuckled none too convincingly.

'Good luck.'

And that, so it seemed, was that.

Except that, at the same moment as Oz and Neville parted, Dennis walked into the admin hut. He paused inside the door, waited until Ulrich decided to register his arrival.

'They told me you wanted to see me?' he said.

The chargehand nodded. He looked none too happy. 'Yes. You seem to be the lead person.'

'I'm not really,' said Dennis sourly, though he was getting used to it by now.

'No matter.' Ulrich was playing with a pencil. In fact, he looked as though he'd like to snap it in two. 'The point is that you can get Osbourne back. He can stay.'

Dennis was genuinely astonished. 'Really? Well, thanks. That'll be a relief to him.'

Ulrich nodded curtly, got up from his desk and spent some time putting on his coat and finding a work-manifest from the piles on his desk. He did not speak to or look at Dennis again until he was almost at the door.

'I hope he changes,' he snapped. 'For the better. Excuse me.'

He went out, shutting the door hard behind him.

Dennis scratched his head, puzzled by the whole business. Nothing – from the decision to Ulrich's attitude – seemed to add up. He made a gesture of helplessness to Dagmar the secretary, who smiled.

'I should tell you that he is very angry to give back the job,' she said.

'Oh, aye. Then why did he?'

'It was the Germans,' Dagmar told him. 'They say it makes them look not good if English get sack because of argument with German.'

'Really?' Dennis was so chuffed, he could hardly contain himself.

Dagmar nodded. 'Is true. They say, he not come back, they not work.'

Dennis broke into a broad smile. 'Ta, love.' And then he headed out onto the site.

Dennis's first stop after leaving the admin hut was the part of the site where the scaffolders were working. He arrived at the foot of the scaffolding, cupped his hands over his mouth and yelled for all he was worth. A face appeared, staring down at him from forty, fifty feet up. As chance would have it, it was the Eric who had been involved in the original row with Oz in the Club.

'Thanks!' bellowed Dennis. '*Danke schön*!'

'*Bitte*?'

'I heard you got our mate his job back! Much appreciated!' He gave the scaffolders a thumbs-up sign to emphasise his point.

The German exchanged a few words with his companions, who had joined him to look down at the Englishman. He laughed, grinned at Dennis.

'*Ja. Ist gut.* Okay!'

Dennis nodded enthusiastically. 'Tonight, after work,' he said very slowly and clearly, 'come over to our hut. Have a drink!' He mimed downing a glass of Pils.

The Erics had no problem with that one. There were a few shouts of 'Okay!' and a forest of thumbs-ups.

The next one, Hut B, should have been the crowner, but it wasn't. Dennis steamed into the hut, ready to shout the glad tidings, and saw Oz's bed empty and stripped, his bag and the rest of his stuff gone.

Within moments, he was outside yelling for Barry.

On Barry's motor bike, and not necessarily keeping to the German speed limits, they caught up with Oz's bus after about seven or eight minutes' feinting and weaving in the Düsseldorf traffic. Barry, taking his life in his hands, pulled out until they were riding along parallel to the bus. Dennis half-stood on the pillion, jabbering like a lunatic. 'Get off the bus!'

When Oz noticed, his reaction was more like one of tolerant puzzlement than anything else. It was clear that he hadn't yet recognised Dennis; he obviously thought that this was some bizarre German initiation rite, or a robbery. A few seconds later, the truth dawned. He got off at the next stop.

'What's goin' on?' he asked as the bike drew up by the kerb.

Dennis grinned broadly. 'Come back, Oz. All is forgiven.'

*

'That's it. Perfect,' announced Bomber, stepping back from the dartboard that he and Moxey had just hung in a place of honour on the far wall of the hut.

A scattering of cheers, some desultory clapping.

'We could've done with a stronger bulb,' Moxey said. He was a perfectionist where darts were concerned.

Wayne shook his head. 'We can angle the light on the board, right? It'll be fine.'

Neville and Dennis had just finished humping four crates of Pils onto the table in the middle.

'You reckon we've got enough, Den?' asked Neville.

'If we haven't, it's easy enough to get some more.'

Oz had appeared. He nodded wisely. 'Aye. They drink, them Jerries. Almost as much as us.'

Dennis winced. 'Now listen, Oz ...' He decided this needed an announcement, so he clapped his hands to get everyone's attention. 'Look, it's because of "them Jerries" that Oz is still here. That's why we're having this do. And I don't want anyone to forget it.' He waited until there was a reassuring murmur of agreement. 'So when those German scaffolders get here, I want you to make them welcome and make sure we all have a good night. Okay?'

'Okay!' they all chorused back.

'And you especially, Oz,' he said to Oz.

Oz put his hand on his heart. 'Absolutely.'

'And this darts match,' Dennis persisted, 'isn't the World Cup or a replay of World War Two. It's just meant to cement the harmony and goodwill between the Brits and the Germans. Right?'

'Right!'

'Good.' Dennis relaxed, satisfied he'd got his message over.

They were about to start cracking open a beer or two when Oz suddenly piped up: 'Mind you, it might only be darts, but we English have to make certain we thrash the Germans.'

Dennis couldn't bring himself to speak. Wayne stared at

84

Oz. 'Why, for Gawd's sake?' the cockney chippie asked.

'Why?' said Oz, as if Wayne and the rest of them were too thick to see the obvious. 'Because they're the bastards that bombed my granny!'

SIX

The nights were drawing in a bit. And tonight was chillier than most. For one thing it was a Friday, and for the other they hadn't yet been paid. The agent usually came at about six in the evening, but Pfister hadn't shown up yet. Ulrich, of course, had just said 'This is not my responsibility' and hopped into his nicely-upholstered Opel. Eventually most of the lads had wandered back into the hut to pass the time. Most of them had no money till the agent came, anyway. Only one man, a Scouse hardcase called Magowan – built like the Berlin wall, only twice as thick – had stayed outside, grimly waiting for Pfister and leaving no doubts as to what he'd do to the bastard if, or when, he arrived with their wage packets.

Oz was standing at the window, peering into the night. He turned back into the room, scowled.

'The bastard's not shown up yet.'

'He won't come now,' said Neville gloomily. The youngster was already penning an explanatory postcard home to Brenda.

Oz glanced out again. 'Magowan's still there.'

'Best he don't show up, then, if that hard case is waitin' for him,' Bomber said.

Wayne had washed his improbable hair, as he did every Friday, and was busy drying it at the table.

'Eh, Bomber,' he asked. 'Your agent did a runner once with your scratch, you were saying. What happened?'

Bomber smiled ruefully. 'We went short,' he explained. 'We could've tracked him to Berlin with that blonde floozie of his, but that would have cost us more than what he owed us.'

The trend of the conversation was beginning to get Neville seriously worried.

'That's a disgrace. Have we no protection against that kind of thing?' he asked plaintively.

'Course we haven't,' said Dennis. 'We're on the lump, Neville.'

'But what'm I going to tell the wife?'

Bomber stroked his beard. 'Tell her what I told mine,' he suggested. 'The truth and nothing but.'

'I s'pose so ...'

'Mind you, she didn't believe me.'

'Great!' Neville shook his head. 'She counts on her money, every Monday morning.'

Oz wandered back into the room. 'Wish I could on mine, every Friday night.'

'It'll be here tomorrow,' Dennis assured him. 'Look at it this way. If you stay in tonight, you'll have saved that much more.'

Barry approved. 'Very true, Dennis. Saving money's the reason we're all here, isn't it?'

'Not for me it isn't,' said Oz defiantly.

'It is for me.' Neville had finished his postcard. 'Brenda understands that,' he said without any great conviction.

'Here,' said Oz, changing his tack. 'Barry's not married. What's he saving for?'

Barry looked distinctly snotty at that question. 'I'm the sole source of income in my family,' he said. 'My old mum relies on my wage packet since my dad passed on, she does. And what's left goes into the Droitwich and District Building Society for my future.'

Bomber chortled. 'The way you drive that motorbike of yours,' he told Barry, 'I don't reckon you've got much of a future.'

'Well, I'm not concerned with the future,' Oz said. He was beginning to get bored and bad-tempered, like a caged animal. 'I'm concerned with Friday night. Which is now, in case any of you lot have noticed!'

'All right,' said Dennis. 'So you'll miss one Friday night's bevvying. You can send the wife a little extra.'

Oz seemed strangely amused. 'A little extra! I don't send her owt to begin with.'

Suddenly the entire hut had fallen silent. Everyone was staring at him.

'You don't send her *anything*?' said Neville.

Oz shrugged. 'Look,' he said quickly, 'it's like Den said. We're not working officially. So my Margery still cops the social security. If I start sendin' money home, I'm going to jeopardise her benefits, aren't I? So what I make I spend on Friday and Saturday. *But* ...' He made them wait for it. '... If I've got anything left over, course I pocket that for Monday.'

Most of them turned away in disgust and derision. Wayne smiled in a very superior way.

'You should learn to control the cash flow, Oz,' he said, wagging a finger. 'If you had a more sensible fiscal strategy, you'd make your bread last the week and you'd be off down the Altstadt now, like yours truly.'

'I don't know you manage it,' Dennis said. 'What with the number of women you take out.'

Wayne looked even more pleased with himself.

'Ah well,' he told Dennis, 'this one's got her own car, which saves me the cab fare. Also she has her own place, in which she likes to prepare candlelit dinners for two, so all I've got to fork out for is a bottle of plonk.'

Barry's face was lit up with a kind of awe. 'We can learn a lot from you, we can, Wayne.'

'Fiscal strategy, son.' Wayne twirled his green flash one more time, stood up to leave. 'Here, Den: if Pfister does turn up, take care of my wages, would you?'

'Yeah, yeah.' More responsibility.

'So long, then.'

When Wayne had gone off for his date, Bomber sighed. 'Have to reconcile ourselves to a night in, I suppose.' He looked around him and smiled sardonically. 'In our little home away from home.'

Oz stared down at the figure that had been hunched over a steaming bowl of eucalyptus, its head draped with a threadbare towel, ever since they had come in from their vigil.

'Christ, it's more like a hospital ward since Moxey moved in,' he snarled. 'All you can smell is Vick's vapour rub and liniment.'

Moxey's voice drifted up from under its cover. 'I heard that!'

'Oh, you're in there, are you?' said Oz savagely. He leaned over and pulled back the towel, made a brutally unsympathetic face at Moxey.

The scouse flinched. 'It ain't funny, havin' inflamed bronchs.'

'It's even less bloody funny sleepin' next to them. Or tryin' to. You sound like an asthmatic pit pony.'

'Get out of my face, Oz,' Moxey said.

Barry moved in. He and Moxey had become sort of mates. Mainly because when all else was equal, people had a tendency to avoid spending too long with either of them.

'Now, fair's fair,' he coaxed. 'If it weren't for Moxey, we wouldn't have a dart board. Which'll help to while away the time this evening, won't it? Anyone for a game?'

Just then there was a knock on the door. A moment later, Pfister, the agent, walked – or more accurately staggered – into the hut, holding his head back and dabbing with a handkerchief to staunch the flow of blood from his nose.

Several of the lads got to their feet, concerned.

'Mr Pfister,' said Neville. 'Are you all right?'

'*Ja. Ja*,' Pfister insisted, though he looked anything but. He lowered his head and lurched over to the table, still holding the handkerchief to his nose, while with his free hand he clutched his precious briefcase.

'I have today many problem with autobahn,' he explained feebly.

Dennis moved to help him. 'Well, sit down. Get some hot water, Nev,' he said, then turned back to Pfister. 'What happened? Did you have a car crash or something?'

Pfister shook his head automatically, then groaned. Not such a good idea.

'*Nein, nein,*' he said after a short pause. 'This was your friend, Magowan. I think he does not like that I am late ...'

Well, at least they could buy themselves a Pils in the Club come Saturday lunchtime. But that wasn't all there could be to life. Dennis and Neville were discussing that particular fact at a corner table, and the young lad was looking a bit sick.

'It can't cost that much, Neville,' he said.

Neville shook his head gloomily. 'It's in Belgium, Den. That's another country.'

'It's not that far. Look at the map. No farther than from Sunderland to Wembley, say.'

'There's no chance of Sunderland gettin' to Wembley.'

'Maybe,' said Dennis. 'But they *are* going to Liège, and we should be there. It can only be two hours by car ...'

'We haven't got a car, have we?'

'Then we'll go by train.'

'But we'd need passports for Belgium.'

Dennis's patience was wearing thin. 'We've got passports, Neville,' he said slowly and deliberately. 'That's how come they let us into Germany, son.'

Neville blushed. 'How much would the train cost?'

'I've no idea, but it can't be all that much.'

'Mid-week game, though,' said Neville, obviously torn. 'We'd have to knock off early. Probably end up staying overnight. Bound to lose a day's wages.'

'Sometimes it's worth it, Neville. All we've done since we got here is lay bricks. We're entitled to the occasional fling.'

'Don't tell Brenda that.'

'We won't tell Brenda at all ...' said Dennis with the true relish of the married worm on the turn.

It was then that Oz kicked the door open. He seemed to be concealing something bulky behind his back.

'All right, close your eyes,' he boomed.

91

'What?'

'I've got a surprise, haven't I? Turn your backs, you lot. I know you, you'll peep!'

They all duly turned to face the bar again. Oz lumbered forward, plonked a cumbersome portable stereo set on the counter with a flourish.

'Dah-dah!' he fanfared, pleased as punch with himself.

'And whose is that?' asked Dennis suspiciously.

Oz grinned. 'It's mine now. Just bought it. Tape deck. Radio. Twin speakers. And ...' He turned it so everyone could see the *pièce de résistance*. '... a miniature telly.'

'Bloody hell,' Neville gulped. 'Where'd you get it?'

'Bought it off that Scots lad, Ferguson,' said Oz, signalling to the barman for his usual. 'He's goin' back tonight, and he wanted to have some cash to give the wife, I suppose.'

Neville frowned. 'That's more than you'll ever do, Oz.'

'Listen,' said Oz loudly, 'I'm the one who's here in Stalag bloody Thirteen, and I'm entitled to some creature comforts.'

'Well don't you think your wife's entitled to the same?'

Oz made a dismissive gesture, drank some beer and smacked his lips in satisfaction. 'She'll reap the benefit one day,' he said complacently. 'I'll take it home and she can play all her boring Barry Manilow tapes on it. Here, just look at this ...' He grinned like a kid, turned on the television. The screen came to life – after a fashion – in a roaring snowstorm of static.

Attracted by the commotion, Bomber temporarily deserted the space invaders machine. He peered at Oz's prize. 'Great!' he guffawed. 'What's the film: *Scott of the Antarctic?*'

'Worked fine when Fergie showed it to me,' muttered Oz, dealing the hapless machine a fierce but totally ineffective clout. He looked around accusingly, noticed that Bomber had just put some more money into the space invaders. 'There's obviously a lot of interference in here,' he said. 'Turn that space invaders off, It'll work champion then.' When no one responded, he thumped the stereo set again, harder.

Dennis sipped his beer quietly, shook his head. 'You're a lunatic, Oz,' he said. 'You've only been here three weeks and already you're in hock. Must've cost you a week's wages, that.'

'No it hasn't,' Oz denied vehemently. 'I'm more responsible than you think. I know I've got commitments. I mean, I wouldn't spend all me money without puttin' somethin' aside for the really important things in life. Like the Sunderland-Standard Liège game, for instance ...'

Alan had fixed the sink and was about to fix little Kevin's bike – Dennis might have run his own business as a builder, but he never seemed to do a darned thing about the house in the old days. Vera had put the kettle on. She and Alan were having a bit of a giggle and a cuddle. Then the door bell rang.

'Who can that be?' Vera said, patting her hair back into place and pulling away from Alan. She was in her early thirties, and the worry lines had started to show, but a feller like Alan, who had a bit going for him, could still fancy her. That proved something.

Alan chuckled throatily. 'Can't be the Jehovah's Witnesses. We had them last night.'

Vera walked through into the hall, glimpsed a female figure through the glass of the front door. She unlocked it to see a woman a few years younger than herself standing on the step. The visitor was, to put it mildly, a little brash in her appearance: brilliant lipstick, mascara, and a blonde rinse under the headscarf. But she looked a nice enough lass, if a bit pushy.

'Are you Vera Patterson?' she asked.

'Yes.'

'I'm Margery Osbourne.'

Vera smiled with embarrassment. 'I'm sorry. Who?'

'Oz's wife. He's with your old man in Germany, apparently.'

Vera noticed the 'apparently' with interest. She had to make up her mind quickly about whether she wanted to get involved.

'Oh yes ... Well, better come in, pet,' she said. Decision made.

Margery Osbourne looked shy and a touch vulnerable in response. 'Well ... just for a minute,' she said, following Vera through.

With apologies for not having a fire in the living room, Vera led her guest into the kitchen. Alan was spooning coffee into two mugs when they entered. Vera was amused to see how Margery Osbourne's eyes flitted quickly over the suit jacket on the chair – Alan had come straight from work – and then to the other telltale signs such as Alan's stockinged feet.

'Better make that three cups, Alan,' said Vera.

Margery smiled coyly. 'I'm not ... interrupting anything, am I?'

'No, no,' Vera said with a little too much haste. 'This is Alan. He's just round here fixing my boy's bike.'

Alan said: 'How d'you do,' in that polite way of his.

'Margery's husband is out in Germany with Dennis,' Vera explained to him.

'Oh. There's not been an accident, has there?'

'Oh no, nothing like that ...' Margery looked around, obviously uncomfortable with the situation.

'Well, sit down, Margery,' Vera said. 'Take your coat off.' She shot a glance at Alan, making it clear that this was girls' talk time and that he should make himself scarce.

'Aye, well,' he said. 'I'd better get on with the bike, then.'

After he had slipped his shoes back on and disappeared into the garage with a torch, Margery took off her coat. Vera finished making coffee for her and got out some chocolate biscuits to make her feel welcome.

'So ... what can I do for you, Margery?'

Margery stared gloomily into her coffee. 'I don't know who else to turn to,' she began reluctantly. 'I got your address from the Steward at the Club. Your Dennis and Oz used to play snooker there, didn't they?'

'They may have done, yes.'

94

'Yeah. The thing is, they've been gone – what is it? – a month now.'

'It must be.'

Margery sighed. 'And I've never heard from him once. I didn't even know he was in Germany until I went round the Club one night for a drink and that steward said: "Oh, I've just had a postcard from your Oz".' She shook her head in disbelief. 'And I says to him: "That's more than I've had." Mind, it doesn't surprise me. He spends more of his life round there than he ever does at home ...'

'They're in Düsseldorf,' Vera told her.

'Oh, that's nice to know.'

'Did he not discuss it with you before he left?' Vera asked gently.

'No,' said Margery. There was anger fighting with despair somewhere inside her. 'The bugger did a flit. I didn't think much of it at first, because it's not the first time it's happened, Vera. But he usually crawls back when he's got no money and a stack of dirty laundry ...'

Vera nodded. 'They earn good money out there. That's why Dennis went.'

'Well, I've not seen a penny of it,' snapped Margery. They drank their coffee for a moment.

'I don't really know what to say, Margery,' Vera murmured after a while. 'I mean, I can give you their address.'

Suddenly Margery looked as though she was going to burst into tears.

'I wish you would,' she said. 'I've been beside myself. Just tryin' to keep me head above water, y'know. With a house and the bairn.'

'I can imagine.'

'And just before he left, he puts a down payment on a car. Now the bloke's round every other day wanting the balance ...'

'I don't know how you make ends meet, pet.'

'I don't. I can't.' Margery looked searchingly at Vera. 'How good is the money out there? Really?'

Vera avoided her eyes. 'Dennis sends me ... enough for my needs, you know.'

'You're lucky to have a man like him then, aren't you?' said Margery with feeling.

It was Vera's turn to be vulnerable. She picked herself a biscuit, drank some coffee. But she knew she ought to explain. It was only right, what with Alan's being here. No point in pretending.

'We're getting a divorce, in fact,' she said, and wished the saying of it had made her feel better. She had hoped it might, but it didn't.

Margery was a bit embarrassed, but not much. She'd been around. She was still attractive, Vera thought. In a pretty common sort of way.

'Oh ... oh well,' said Margery after a little thought. 'That's your business, pet. Certainly none of mine. I've often thought of leaving Oz meself.' She smiled wryly. Her sense of humour – like her ability to look after herself – was born of bitter experience. 'But then, of course to leave someone the bugger's got to *be* there in the first place ...'

Three days later, Oz got his first post from home. The morning had started normally enough. A bit of backchat about Oz's miraculous stereo – the TV still didn't work, and now Fergie was back in Aberdeen and well out of reach – but otherwise amiable enough. Until Barry came in with a bundle of letters and started handing them out. One for Nev ... two for Moxey ... one for himself, for Bomber, and ... one for Oz.

'What?' Oz, who had been feeding batteries into the back of his beloved machine, looked up in amazement.

'Letter for you,' Barry insisted.

Oz looked at him as if he must be having a legpull. 'C'mon. Impossible. No one knows I'm here.'

Barry peered at the envelope, nodded. '"Tyne and Wear" it says on the postmark. Indisputable.'

'Final demand from the rates office,' Dennis chimed in with a laugh.

Barry, never one to catch on quickly, was still staring earnestly at the envelope. 'No, no. Handwritten. It's a woman's hand, if you ask me.'

With that, he handed it to Oz. A look of panic-stricken horror came over the burly Geordie's face.

'No. It isn't ... It's from the wife ...' He looked around, at first as if pleading for someone to tell him it wasn't true, then with growing anger. He tore open the envelope, muttering: 'Who gave her this address, that's what I'd like to know.'

'Probably your probation officer,' chuckled Dennis.

Life seemed to move on. Oz was scanning his unwanted letter, Moxey was complaining about the lack of milk, Barry was rabbiting about the lack of firm leadership in the hut that led to the lack of milk, Neville was reading snippets of Brenda's news from home aloud.

Without warning, Oz leapt to his feet. He stomped over to Dennis and waved Margery's letter furiously under his nose.

'This is all your bloody fault, Dennis!' he bellowed.

The entire hut broke off and stared at the pair of them in astonishment. Dennis met Oz's eye with total innocence.

'What is?' he asked.

'This!' Oz shrieked. 'She got my address from your wife!'

'How?'

'She went round there!'

'Why?'

'To find out where I was! And your bloody wife told her! They're bosom pals now – goin' out on the town later in the week, apparently. She had no right!'

Dennis didn't move or change his expression. 'Oz,' he said slowly, 'your wife must be pretty desperate to look up a perfect stranger to find your whereabouts.'

'Course she's desperate,' Neville said. 'Cos he never sends her any money.'

'Yeah!' Oz rounded on the others like an animal at bay. 'Only now she knows 'ow much we're making over here. 'Cos she knows 'ow much you lot are sendin' back!'

Barry put on his superior face. 'She don't know how much *I'm* sendin' back. Unless by some amazin' coincidence she has access to my passbook at the Droitwich Building Society.'

Oz muttered something filthy-sounding under his breath, didn't even nod to acknowledge Bomber's entry into the room.

Dennis said hello to Bomber, then got back to the fray. 'No good sounding off at people, Oz,' he told his fellow-Geordie crisply. 'You brought this on yourself. You treat your wife like shit. Then you're put out when she complains.'

'Oh yes,' hissed Oz. His eyes were slits, malicious. 'You lot put your wives on pedestals. I don't know why you bother, Dennis. Your Vera's well provided for both ends ...'

Dennis bridled at last. 'What's that supposed to mean?'

'She says she went round to your house an' there was a bloke there with no shoes on,' Oz said with a triumphant sneer, waving his letter at Dennis.

Dennis knew everyone's eyes were on him. He was suddenly very calm.

'I expect it was Alan,' he said.

'Aye, Alan,' agreed Oz after checking the information in the letter.

'Well, as he's Vera's boyfriend,' Dennis said matter-of-factly, 'he's round there most nights.'

It was obvious that Oz was disappointed not to get a real rise out of Dennis. 'That doesn't bother you, then?' he asked.

'It used to, but unless you've forgotten, I'm in the middle of a divorce, aren't I?'

'And maybe you wouldn't be if you took a firmer hand with your women.'

That brought Dennis back on the boil. 'If I take a firm hand with anyone, it's goin' to be you, Oz,' he growled, moving forward.

Bomber saved the situation yet again. He had finished sorting his stuff out on his bed and wandered into the

98

middle of the room. 'Oh dear,' he bellowed cheerfully. 'You can tell it's Thursday. End of the week, no money left and tension's rife!' He grinned benignly at the two of them. And loomed just enough to make his point.

Dennis picked up his jacket. 'Look, Oz,' he said, still fighting to keep himself under control, 'I don't tell you how to handle your life, but since you've stuck your nose into mine, I'll just say this. If a bloke's got a wife and a bairn, the least he can do is send back some of his scratch instead of squandering it on secondhand junk that didn't work to begin with.'

He looked pointedly at Oz's new stereo, then stalked out of the hut.

No one said anything for a while. Then Bomber coughed and said gently: 'I never knew you had a kid, Oz.'

'Aye. Well.'

'Boy or girl?' asked Barry.

'Boy.'

'How old is he?'

'Five,' Oz said abruptly. Then he shook his hed. 'Or mebbe it's six.'

'You're not certain?' said Neville, incredulous.

'Six. He's six.'

'And what's he called?'

Oz reddened slightly. 'Rodney.'

'Rodney?' echoed Barry.

'So?' Oz took refuge in aggression.

'Oh, nothing. It's a very nice name,' said Barry quickly. '"Rodney Osbourne" has a very nice ring to it. "Arise, Sir Rodney Osbourne..."'

Oz grunted. 'It's really Rod. The wife named him after Rod Stewart.'

'What's he like?'

'I can't stand him,' Oz said with a shrug. 'But the wife were crazy about the feller, before she got on to Barry Manilow ...'

Bomber looked heavenwards. 'I meant the kid,' he said.

'Oh, aye. The kid. He's a canny lad, he is. Always into

trouble,' he added with a faint smile, 'but he can handle it, y'know.'

Oz wandered over to his locker, trying to pretend he didn't mind all the accusing eyes fixed on him. Then he looked up from fiddling in the bottom space of the locker and nodded guiltily.

'All right, all right,' he mumbled. 'I'll be sending some money home. I can't this week, 'cos I bought *that*' he nodded accusingly in the direction of the stereo '– and I want to go to the match. But I will do. I just want to buy some time.'

Meanwhile he had found what he was looking for, a well-used, mangled roll of sellotape. In full view of everyone, he carefully stuck the envelope down again and then handed Margery's letter to Neville.

'Do us a favour, will you, Nev?' he asked coolly. 'Just write: "Not known at this address".'

Come the day of the match, of course things had changed. For Neville, anyway. When he'd got his pile of mark pieces and gone faithfully over to phone Brenda, as was his weekly habit, he'd had his ear bent to the effect that she knew what they all got up to over there, and Neville should pull himself together and think of her and the house and the future and their marriage and ... Turned out she had been out for a drink with Vera and Oz's wife, Margery, at the weekend, and she'd been shocked to hear from Margery the kind of life the men lived out in Germany, playing around and gambling and night-clubbing. So if Neville had been considering a little extravagance in the case of the Sunderland-Liège match, that put the kybosh on it well and truly.

Instead, come Tuesday, he sat with Wayne and Bomber in the hut, fiddling with the famous stereo and trying to get whatever station was running the football from Belgium. Dennis and Oz had gone to get a train in the afternoon, lucky buggers. They'd tried to change Neville's mind, but all he could think of was the wrath of Brenda. Hell hath no fury ...

Bomber, who was darning socks over on his bed,

watched Neville placidly. When the lad had been playing with the wavebands for a while, he suggested mildly: 'I reckon VHF's your best bet.'

But just at that moment, Neville found something. 'I've got ... well, whatever. Listen ... this is a match!'

Through the static, the three of them heard the vague sound of a crowd and an excited commentator.

'Could be boxing,' said Bomber.

'No. No. It's football,' Neville insisted. 'Listen to them klaxons. That's your continental football crowd.'

Wayne put down his copy of the *New Musical Express* and cocked an ear to the radio.

'What language is that?' he said. 'Should be Belgium, shouldn't it?'

'Well, it's not German. This must be it, this must be the game,' said Neville.

Wayne laughed. 'You still can't understand who's doin' what to who, and when, can you?'

'No. But it's my team, on the radio. It's exciting.'

'I don't know why you didn't go with Dennis and Oz if you're so keen.'

Neville looked defensive. 'Better things to do with me money, Wayne.'

'You mean, Brenda's got better things to do with your money,' said the young cockney with a sly grin.

'It's got nothing to do with Brenda. It was my decision. I love football, but the fans these days are ruining it. Especially abroad, it makes you ashamed to be British. I've no wish to rampage through the streets of Liège with a bunch of drunken savages ...'

Wayne answered Neville's prim little speech with a silent, mocking handclap. Bomber laughed.

'Oz should feel at home, though,' he mused.

'Oh yeah,' said Wayne. 'At the forefront, he'll be. "Oz the Barbarian".'

Neville gestured to them to shut up. The crowd noise was reaching a peak. Or the static was getting worse. It was hard to tell.

'What is it?' said Bomber after a moment.

Neville shook his head in disappointment. 'I thought it

was a goal. No ... I reckon it's a corner.'

Bomber carried on: 'Tragic what's happened to our national game,' he said to no one in particular. 'When I were a lad, the terraces would be packed. Jammed together like sardines we'd be at Ashton Gate, but never a cross word. My mother would go, and me sisters. She won't even leave the house now when City's at home.'

They had all forgotten about Barry, who was in bed with his eyes shut. Until a disembodied voice wafted across the room: 'It's not the fault of football as such,' the voice said. 'It's a social problem. Unemployment, urban frustration. These lads have simply chosen the football stadiums as their arena of protest.'

Someone blew a raspberry in the direction of the motionless form on the end bed.

'Go back to sleep, Barry,' said Wayne.

'It's a goal!' Neville sat bolt upright in his chair, looked around at the others, eagerly seeking support.

Sure enough, the clamour and the klaxon noise were deafening.

Must be their lot if they're that chuffed,' Wayne said.

Then the commentator's voice came over more clearly. Something about Ajax one, Borussia nil.

'Ajax?' Neville repeated dully. 'They're Dutch, aren't they?'

Wayne chuckled. 'They are, too. You've got the wrong game, son.'

The little bar was packed, heaving with lads in red and white gear and beers in their fists, half of them busy guzzling the stuff down, the other half yelling in broad Geordie dialect at the harrassed Belgian landlord and his wife. These supporters weren't your young hooligans; most of them were in their twenties or even older – like Dennis.

Beers were appearing through a narrow gap in the crowd. Dennis took one, swallowed gratefully. Belgian beer wasn't so bad.

'Cheers, er ...' he said to the nearest one of the bunch he'd fallen in with after the match.

'Ernie.'

The Geordie fan Dennis was drinking with was a big feller, but good-natured enough with it. Must have been twenty-seven, twenty-eight.

Dennis nodded. 'One good thing about a draw,' he said, raising his voice to make himself heard. 'You lot won't take out your triumph or your defeat on the innocent bystanders of Belgium.'

'We're not like that, man,' said Ernie, mildly offended. 'Just come for the trip, have a good time.'

His mate, Brian, chipped in: 'No, no bother. Mind you, there's always a lunatic fringe somewhere. I'd avoid that lot over there ...' He pointed to another rowdier group in the corner. Dennis could clearly see Oz right in the thick of them.

'How did you lads get here?' he said then, to change the subject and avoid having to look at a drunken Oz for too long.

'Plane,' said Ernie. 'They ran three charters from Newcastle. Forty-two quid all in. Not bad, eh?'

Dennis admitted it wasn't. 'You lads all working, then?'

'Me and Brian are. Just. I was in the shipyards. Riveter. Now I'm drivin' a furniture van.' Ernie grinned crookedly, as if driving wasn't a real man's job.

'Desperate up our way, man,' said Brian.

Dennis nodded. 'Why do you think I'm over here?'

'You like it, do you?'

'No choice,' Dennis said with a humourless laugh. 'I had me own business, see. Jobbin' builder. Worked me bollocks off for five years. Made no difference in the end. Went under. Still owe the government V.A.T.'

Brian looked sympathetic. 'I thought of goin' on the oil rigs for a while,' he said. 'Good money if you don't mind spending your time off in Aberdeen.'

'I spend mine in Düsseldorf,' was Dennis's answer. 'Much the same on a Monday night.'

'Good crack, though?'

'Oh aye, it's worth it, despite the drawbacks.'

Oz lurched through the mob at that moment. He was

already glassy-eyed with booze and looking like he intended no good. He stopped, laid a hand on Dennis's shoulder, grinned.

'Hey, Den!' he slobbered. 'Me an' some of these lads is goin' to find some action. Comin'?'

Dennis shook his head. 'No. I'm quite happy here.'

'We've only got one night. No point in stayin' in one place,' Oz protested.

But Dennis was insistent. 'You be at the station at eleven-thirty,' he told him. 'The train won't wait for you, and nor will I.'

Oz stumbled off with a bunch of banner-wielding piss-artists who looked as though they had a collective I.Q. of about ten – and that was when sober.

'Who's he?' said Ernie warily.

Dennis sighed. 'He's one of the drawbacks I mentioned,' he said.

Oz wondered where the droning hum was coming from. He didn't open his eyes because he had a feeling that if he did, he was going to be sick. Nevertheless, that noise bothered him. And so did the strange, distant chorus of voices wearily singing: *Tie A Yellow Ribbon* ...

He was about to drift off into unconsciousness again when someone shook his shoulder roughly. Coming to with a start, Oz found himself staring stupidly down at a cloth cap containing an assortment of notes and coins. He looked up blearily, was astonished to find himself packed into a narrow corridor in a sort of high-backed armchair, along with a whole lot of other chairs. The man who had shaken him was staring down at him, mouthing something.

'Howay, wake up, man!'

Oz gaped. 'What, what? What's goin' on?'

'We're having a whip round for the driver.'

'Driver? What driver?'

The bloke frowned. 'Well, the pilot, like.'

'What d'you mean, PILOT?'

Oz jerked upright and stared wildly around him. Then the awful truth hit. 'I'm on a soddin' plane!' he wailed.

'Aye,' said the bloke with the cap. 'And we're just comin' in to land. So fasten your safety belt, extinguish all cigaretes, and cough up!'

He shoved the cap right under Oz's nose, shook it to jangle the change.

'What do you mean, we're landing?' said Oz slowly, ignoring the cap. 'Landing where?'

'Why Newcastle, man. We're home.'

Oz groaned, shoved the cap away and put his head in his hands. 'Home?' he said. 'I'm not home. I live in Germany!'

An hour later, he, the lad with the cap and another Sunderland fan were wedged into the back of a minicab, heading away from the airport and towards the fine city of Newcastle. There was a hint of dawn on the eastern horizon. There was more than a hint of suicide in Oz's gloomy, puffy features.

'Why did you bring me with you?' he said to the cap man, whose name was Andy.

Andy shook his head. 'Dunnoo. Couple of the lads carried you on. You were wearin' a scarf. They thought you must be one of us.'

'But I didn't have a ticket.'

'We were all on a group ticket,' said Andy with a yawn. He elbowed away his mate, who had lapsed into drunken unconsciousness again. 'And there's always more seats comin' back than goin'.'

'Oh?' Oz showed a flicker of interest. 'How come?'

'We always leave a few behind. We went to Sportin' Lisbon last year. Three of the lads have never been seen since.'

Oz nodded, looked at his watch. 'Oh God,' Oz moaned. 'I'm supposed to be at work in an hour. In Düsseldorf.'

'Sorry, man,' Andy said. 'Where shall we drop you off? Do you have family here?'

'No,' Oz answered, staring morosely out of the window. 'Only the wife.'

Margery Osbourne opened the front door of her flat, put

out the milk bottle, stood for a moment looking out over the early-morning panorama of Tyneside. It was an impressive view. There were times, or had been, when Margery convinced herself that the view made up for the fact of living in a pokey flat on the eighteenth floor of a ten-year-old highrise that had become an instant slum. Those times were few and far between these days. She straightened up, pulled her nylon housecoat around her in the early-morning chill. He was hovering just inside the door, she could tell.

'Twenty past six,' she said out loud without turning round. 'Can't wait to get off, can you?'

Steve came out in the open. He was carrying his suit jacket, looking shamefaced. She had met him the night she'd gone out with Vera and Brenda. Saturday, that had been – when Brenda had got so defensive about her Neville's having nothing to do with the goings-on in Germany. Well, Margery knew bloody well what Oz would be up to if *he* got the chance, so when Steve had given her the wink and told her he'd be in the pub Monday night as well, she'd been in there like a shot. Why should those husbands get away with it? Trouble was, it all seemed to turn to dross ...

'Aw, it's not that, pet,' Steve said, squeezing carefully past her onto the balcony. 'I'm on the early shift this week. I've got to get home, have a shave and be at work by eight.'

'All right,' she said, doubtful but not wanting to let him know it, in case it put him off. 'Will I see you again, then?'

'Aye.' He grinned, moved away. 'I'll be in touch. Tara.'

'Aye. Well.'

Then he was off towards the lift and she went back inside the start clearing up before little Rodney woke up.

She set to reluctantly, taking the dirty ash trays, glasses and general trash through into the kitchen. The bottle of Vodka from the night before, which was still half-full – they'd got on to more interesting things before it was too late and they were incapable – she put away in the cupboard in the living room. Then she found Steve's tie draped over an armchair, clucked affectionately, held it for a moment. He wasn't such a bad bloke. She'd met worse, and the worst of all was four hundred miles away, thank God ...

When the bell rang, she was about to put the tie aside for safe keeping. Instead she smiled, walked lightly to the door, opened it expectantly. The smile disappeared quickly. Instead of Steve, there stood a big, hungover, puffy and pale Oz.

'Hello, Margery,' mumbled the apparition. 'Let us in, then.'

Half of Margery was telling herself she was having hallucinations; the other, thinking half told her to stick that telltale tie in her housecoat pocket pretty ruddy pronto. Not that Oz noticed. He just shoved past her, shambled in like he'd just got back from buying some cans of beer. She was too astonished, confused and overcome with guilt to stop him. It occurred to her that Oz and Steve had probably met by the lift. If Steve *hadn't* had that early shift ...

'W-what are you doin' here, Oz?' she asked when she got back the power of speech.

Oz grunted. 'I had no choice.'

'Oh. Didn't you?'

'No.'

Margery nodded vaguely, but inside she was trying to work out what he'd heard and from whom. She needn't have worried.

'I got your letter,' continued Oz, looking like a big kid. 'And I was so upset. I said to meself: get yourself over there, son. So I took the first available flight.'

'Because of my letter?' Margery asked carefully, just to make sure.

'Aye.' He seemed surprised she should question his motives.

'Nothing else?'

'What else could there be?'

'Oh, nothing.'

'Well, we've obviously got things to talk about, pet. But first things first. Put the kettle on.'

107

She moved through into the kitchen. He peeled off into the living room and sprawled in the best armchair, waiting for his tea to be brought to him. He hadn't changed a bit. Margery brought the pot and two mugs in to him, poured him a reviving cuppa. As she did so, a thought occurred to her.

'Here,' she said. 'You haven't had the sack, have you, Oz?'

He registered hurt surprise. 'Why would you think that?'

'Well, you've had it plenty of times before,' she said with a bitter little laugh that spoke volumes for her experience of being married to him.

'No, no, Margery. But it's not easy over there. Y'see, the German gaffer, he's got it in for me. So I'm not makin' the scratch that Dennis and Neville are.'

Margery looked at him shrewdly. 'Then he won't be pleased you're not at work today, will he?'

'Aye well,' Oz recovered fast. 'That's his hard luck. I told him: I said, "there's more important things than work," I said. "It's more important that I straighten things out with my missus."'

'I'm touched, Oz. But me an' Rod could've used the money you've spent on the air fare, y'know.'

Oz shrugged, drank some tea. He looked thoughtful, almost dreamy as he stared into Margery's eyes. 'Isn't it money well spent if we can patch things up?' he said. 'When I read your letter I just knew you needed some gesture of reassurance. I felt I was ... losing you. And I didn't think twice. I just got meself over here. I suppose it was impetuous, like ... but I didn't stop to count the pennies.'

'No,' she admitted. Why else would he turn up like this? And God knows, there had been a time – a long while ago – when there'd been romance of a sort between them. Rod was the evidence of that, poor little bugger. 'No, I appreciate that, Oz.'

Oz nodded gratefully. 'Mind you,' he continued in a slightly more practical tone, 'while on the subject, I will need a bit to get meself back.'

Margery tensed. 'Where's that supposed to come from?'

'Howay, I know you, Margery,' he said with a nod at the mantlepiece. 'You always put a bit aside in that pot your mam got us from Whitley Bay, don't you?'

'For Rod's birthday and things like that, but not for air fares,' Margery said firmly. She might be susceptible to a spot of soft soap, but she wasn't *that* stupid.

Oz seemed to accept her decision. He nodded, stared around the room as if getting his bearings. 'How is the lad?' he asked after a short pause.

'You can wake him up in a minute or he'll be late for school.'

'Right. Does he miss me?'

'Naturally. You're his dad, aren't you? And you buggered off without a word ...'

Oz put up a hand for silence. 'There's a reason for that, Margery,' he said smoothly, with a hint of an appeal for understanding. 'I figured if you knew what I was doin' you'd try to stop me.'

'Well, you could have at least let me know where you were. That's why I had to go round to Vera's.'

'You know where I am now,' Oz told her. 'I'm in Düsseldorf.' He sighed. 'Tryin' to earn a bit for the three of us.'

Margery could feel herself melting slowly. She hesitated, wondering whether it was true that confession was good for the soul. In the end she said:

'Well, I'm no saint either, Oz.'

'Few of us are, pet.'

'No.' She smiled nervously, then went on. 'But ... if we're trying to make a fresh start and clear the decks, I'd like to make a clean breast of things.'

Oz grinned lecherously, put out one big hand and fondled his wife through the material of her housecoat. 'Aye, well I've never had any complaints in that department.'

'Not now,' she scolded, though she was flattered. It felt good to be found attractive, even by Oz. Maybe especially by Oz. After all, they'd been through thick and thin together. 'C'mon. We've got to get Rod off to school. Then we can talk.'

'All right,' Oz agreed. Nothing was too much for him. It was incredible. Literally. 'Tell you what,' he added, 'you go and make me some bacon and eggs and I'll wake the kid.'

'Fair enough.'

Margery got up, went through to the kitchen. Oz waited, made sure she was out of sight, made quickly for the mantlepiece and stuck one paw into the teapot next to the clock. He groped, frowned, began to shake the pot irritably.

'Forget it,' came Margery's voice from the kitchen. 'I don't keep it in there anymore!'

Oz could accept that. The problem was that he couldn't get his hand out of the ruddy teapot, no matter how hard he tugged. It was like a ship in a bottle: you could get it in but you couldn't get it out. In the end he was forced to go and wake up Rod before Margery came back into the living room and caught him.

The kid's room was tiny and, like the rest of the flat, untidy. A few gimcrack plastic toys lay around the bed. There were some crayon drawings that Rod had done at school sellotaped to the wall. Oz trod gently, leaned over the bed.

'Hey, Rod. Wake up, son. It's your dad, look.'

The boy's head emerged from under the blankets, two small eyes stared blearily at Oz.

'Oh,' said Rod. 'Where's me mam?'

'She's gettin' your breakfast. Give us a kiss, then.'

The boy gave Oz a clumsy, reluctant peck.

'You all right?' Oz asked.

'No.'

'What's the matter?' A bit defensive on Oz's part.

The boy grimaced. 'Got a pain.'

'Where?'

'Don't know.'

Oz shook his head. 'Now, don't be daft.'

'Well, it was in me tummy.'

'Probably just a lavatory pain,' said Oz sagely. He

wagged a finger. 'You're tryin' to get off school, that's what you're doin'.'

Rod couldn't say much to that. He had woken up now, and he was looking his dad in the eye. 'Have you brought me a present?' he said suddenly.

'No, I haven't, son. I came home a bit unexpected, like.'

The boy was looking past Oz. 'Then what's that behind your back?' he asked.

Oz was forced to bring the teapot hand out into the open.

'Oh, this,' he said, trying to pretend he'd forgotten all about the pot until the boy had mentioned it. 'Just a joke, son. Bit of a laugh. First thing in the morning I'm going to buy you somethin', though. Honest.'

The boy stared at Oz levelly. 'Mam doesn't keep her money in there anymore,' he said.

Margery could hear Oz chatting with young Rod while she got the breakfast things together in the kitchen. The sound of father and son talking like that gave her a sort of a warm glow, though she couldn't make out what they were discussing exactly. She'd find out, she thought as she picked up the tray with the toast and marmalade and the fresh tea and started to move through to the living room. Right on cue, the morning post popped through the letter box, just like in the TV plays. Margery smiled, set down the tray and fetched the letters. Bills, bloody bills – let Oz have a look at them while he was home – and circulars asking you to spend even more of the money you hadn't got in the first place. And a familiar-looking envelope with something scrawled beside the address ...

'OZ!'

Oz shimmied through into the living room wearing an expectant grin.

'Breakfast ready is it, pet?'

'Never mind breakfast,' said Margery quietly. 'So you came back 'cos you were so upset about me letter?'

'That's right, pet,' Oz said, not yet sensing the ominous calm in her voice. Or determined to bluff things through.

'I've got to admit it brought tears to me eyes – '

Margery boiled over. 'You lyin' toad!' she shrieked. 'You never even bloody read it!'

'Of course I read it!'

Margery held up her letter to Oz and stabbed one red-painted nail at the bit where it said: NOT KNOWN AT THIS ADDRESS.

'Then how come it's been sent back with this written on it?'

She was already stooping to pick up crockery from the tray, taking aim.

'You're not even *in* Düsseldorf. God knows where you've been!'

'Don't you trust me, Margery?'

Oz threw up his hands to plead and defend all at once. This time he really had forgotten about the teapot. He stared down at it, confused and horrified. The pot smashed when the first cup hit. Margery was what you might call a bodyline bowler when it came to crockery.

'Who's Nev talkin' to?' asked Barry, looking up from his cards. 'Bit of skirt, is it?'

Wayne chuckled at the thought, checked out Neville's body language as the Geordie stood at the phone in the corner of the bar in the Club.

'Na. Don't be daft,' he said. 'Look at the expression on his boat. Guilty, apologetic ... hang-dog. Talkin' to the wife, in't he?'

'But he always rings his Brenda on Mondays,' Barry said. 'And tonight's Thursday. And he's a creature of habit, is our Nev.'

'True.' Wayne leaned back in his chair, grinned. 'But fink back, son. Conversation last Monday ended a bit acrimonious, didn't it? Lots of 'eavy dialogue. He's bin broodin' about it for three days. So he's now givin' her a bell to make amends – bit of the old "Sorry if I upset you, darlin', I didn't mean it, et cetera, et cetera." Your move.'

Barry refused to settle back to their game of cribbage. 'Such a cynic you are, Wayne.'

The cockney sat like a barrister who had rested his case. 'No I'm not,' he assured him. 'I'm just a trained observer of married men. 'Elps to stop me ever takin' the plunge meself.'

'You won't hold out forever,' said Barry comfortably. 'It's natural for a man to want a mate, Wayne. Some day you'll succumb.'

'P'raps you're right, son. As the poet said: "A man without a wife is like a fish without a bicycle."'

'Glad you see it my way.' Barry smiled happily. Then his face clouded and he frowned. 'But a fish –'

Luckily for Barry's overtaxed brain, Neville had come off the phone and was headed for their table.

'Hey,' he said. 'I just been talking to Brenda.'

'Yeah?' Wayne hammed up the surprise something rotten.

'Aye. And you'll never guess what she told me.'

Wayne relaxed. 'I know, she's sold all the furniture, had 'er hair dyed green and run off with a roadie from The Clash.'

'What?'

Barry shot Wayne a dangerous look. 'Ignore him, Nev. He's so sharp he'll cut himself one day. What is it?'

Neville beamed. 'Oz,' he said deliberately, 'is in England!'

The next day, they waited as usual come knocking-off time. Herr Pfister had got just a shade more punctual since his run-in with Magowan. And the site's resident hardcase always got his pay packet first these day by some strange coincidence. When Pfister had only one packet left, a silence fell over the Brits.

'Osbourne?' asked Pfister. 'Where is Osbourne?' He looked up from his register in irritation.

'You'd better take care of this, Den,' Barry said, digging Dennis in the ribs. Dennis glared daggers at him, but he stepped forward.

'I'll take Osbourne's, Herr Pfister.'

'It is for only three days this week,' said the agent. 'Why is this?'

Dennis shrugged. 'He's sick.'

'Toxic shock syndrome,' chipped in Barry. He'd read about it in the paper. It was the latest trendy illness. Just right.

Dennis scowled. 'Leave this to me, will you, Barry?'

Barry grinned delightedly. Dennis had accepted the mantle of leadership, and that was enough for him.

'And does he come back next week?' asked Pfister.

'Hard to tell with this thing. It can linger on a bit, y'know.'

'If not, I must replace him,' Pfister told Dennis. He showed no particular emotion. He was paid to provide this or that number of workers on site per day, and that was what he did.

Dennis nodded. 'I'll let Herr Ulrich know, Monday morning. But I'll take his pay packet ...'

'Sign please,' Pfister said with a shrug.

As they walked back to the hut, Neville fell into step with Dennis.

'Why d'you think he went home, Dennis?' he said. 'D'you think he was worried about his missus?'

Dennis smiled cynically. 'Not Oz. You know what I think? He had a few jars with those Geordie lads in Liège and scored himself a cheap trip home on a charter.'

'I thought maybe we got through to him,' Neville said, hopeful in the face of the evidence. 'I mean, and he'd gone home to sort his marriage out.'

'Don't kid yourself, Nev. He never thinks beyond his nose, does Oz. If you ask me, we've seen the last of him.'

And they went over to the Club for a few Friday night jars.

Light, the special, grey but penetrating light of a Monday morning, was starting to come through the windows of Hut B. Moxey was first up, in his pyjamas and an old donkey jacket, hacking and sneezing a welcome to the day as he shuffled across to the hot plate to put the kettle on.

Moxey darned near keeled over when the door was flung open.

'Morning campers!' bellowed a voice they all knew

and feared. 'Rise and shine! Hands off cocks, on socks!'

Moxey just stood in silent horror. Neville stirred. 'Oz...?'

'It's not the Duke of Edinburgh, man.'

'Ugghh. I was fast asleep,' moaned Barry.

Oz was relentless. With a look of malicious glee, he strode over to Dennis's bed. Dennis's feet were protruding out the end; Oz tweaked them expertly, booming all the while:

'Time to get up! Monday morning, work to be done ... Come on, Dennis. Rise and shine, bonny lad!'

Figures started to stir and writhe all over the hut, groaning and muttering curses and prayers.

'We ... we thought you'd gone for good,' said Moxey at last. There was something a bit strange about the way he spoke. Hesitant. Holding something back, maybe.

'You don't get rid of me that easy!'

Bomber emerged from his blankets, took one quick look and his bearded face creased in an expression of disgust. 'I'm dreamin',' he mumbled. 'I'm havin' a nightmare that Oz has come back.'

'Why aye son, certainly,' said Oz with a grin.

'Where've you sprung from then?' Wayne asked.

Oz looked chuffed. 'Been back home, 'aven't I? Copped a free flight with the lads after the match. I thought, why not? Go down to the club, see me mates. Look up the wife.'

'Oh, you saw her, did you?' said Dennis, sitting up in bed.

'Naturally. I thought while I was there I might as well sort *her* out.'

'Aye. We heard you'd been back home,' Neville said.

'Oh, how?' Oz's eyes narrowed a fraction.

'I spoke to Brenda. She told me.'

'Aye well, from now on we'll just keep the wives' Mafia out of our affairs, shall we?' Oz said. "Cos one of the good things is, Margery is convinced I'm not in Düsseldorf. In fact, this is the last place she'd think of lookin' for me.' He bowed to his mates, pretending to drink their applause for his latest, greatest achievement.

'I'm not here! The Invisible Man, that's me!'

Bomber commented that he couldn't think of anyone less invisible than Oz. But the returning prodigal had now reached his bed and was starting to look puzzled. He turned back to face the rest of the hut.

'Hey,' said Oz. 'Where's me stereo?'

Wayne exchanged glances with Neville in the next-door bed. 'Oh ...' he said reluctantly. 'I've got that, Oz.'

'Aye well, ask next time, eh?' said Oz, wandering over to retrieve his precious.

Wayne shook his head. 'Er, no. It's mine now.'

'What?'

'I bought it, Oz.'

'Not from me you didn't ...'

Suddenly Oz's air of brash self-congratulation had evaporated.

Barry looked at Dennis, as usual.

'I think, er ... explanations are in order,' said the Brum lad.

Dennis bit back a barbed reply, turned to Oz.

'Well, Oz, it's like this,' he said. 'Us lads thought, like, that you'd gone home for good. I mean, we thought we'd seen the last of you. So we ... we said to ourselves, what shall we do with his stuff?'

'So what *did* you do?'

'Well,' continued Dennis, 'we went through your locker, because we thought you'd need the money. And the only things we found of value were your stereo, your digital clock and your donkey jacket.'

With his usual sense of drama, Oz flung open his locker and rounded on the others when he saw it was empty of his most prized possessions.

'Hey, they've gone an' all!' he protested.

Dennis nodded. 'We had an auction, Oz.'

'An auction?'

'It was democratically decided,' murmured Barry. 'I bought the digital clock.'

'I'm wearin' the jacket,' Moxey told him.

Wayne grinned. 'And I copped the stereo.'

'What bloody nerve!'

'Now wait a minute,' Dennis said quickly. 'We weren't sellin' you short. We raised two hundred and thirty quid. That plus your three days' wages came to over four hundred!'

Oz's manner changed again. He looked pleased, relieved. 'Oh well, that's not so bad. 'Cos I had to borrow a bit to get back here.' He turned to Wayne. 'I'm buyin' that stereo back, mind. Where's the money?'

They all looked at each other awkwardly. Wayne suppressed a chuckle.

Dennis shrugged. 'The thing is, Oz ...' he began, 'thinking you'd need the scratch, like ... we sent it home.'

For a moment Oz looked at him incredulously. 'Home?' he echoed bleakly. 'But I'm here, man. What's goin' to happen to it?'

Neville could hold out no longer. He was smiling, nodding.

'Oh, Oz,' he said. 'I should think your wife will find a use for it, don't you?'

SEVEN

They were lying on their beds one lunchtime. The mail had come late, so there were letters being read.

'One from my second youngest,' said Bomber cheerfully. 'Or is he the third youngest? Never mind. Anyway, he went to Bristol City Saturday last. Real humdinger of a game, he says. Only lost three to one. Obviously City's on the mend. Eh, Den?'

But Dennis was too engrossed in one particular letter that had come for him that morning.

Barry exploited the pause. 'Should keep this stamp,' he told the world in general. 'Bet it'll be rare one day.'

'An Edgbaston Penny Black. I expect it will,' Bomber chortled.

Barry peered at the envelope, then at Bomber. 'No,' he said gravely. 'Saudi Arabia. This letter's from me cousin Dudley, who's workin' out there on the pipeline.'

'Good crack there, I'll bet,' Moxey said wistfully.

'Yes, but your social life's severely curtailed. Nothing to do but play draughts or kick a ball around. And it's too hot to kick a ball.'

Neville came into the hut, closely followed by Oz.

'Any mail for me?'

Dennis jerked a thumb vaguely at the pile on the table. He still seemed very distracted. 'On the table.'

'Nothing for you, Oz,' said Barry.

'Didn't expect it. No news is good news, far as I'm concerned.'

He moved off to lie on his bed. Neville was reading his letter. Barry coughed.

'Got a letter from me cousin, Nev,' Barry said. 'He's in Saudi Arabia.'

'Oh yeah?' muttered Neville, already thoroughly occupied with his own mail.

'Lots of money, like. But naff all to do,' Barry persisted. 'The regime's very strict, you see. Can't even drink.'

Neville glanced up, smiled politely. 'Yeah, I read about that somewhere.'

Oz looked appalled. 'Can't even drink?' he growled.

'No. Against their religion, like.'

'But your cousin's English,' Oz said, genuinely puzzled. 'Well, Brum – it's almost the same.'

'Makes no difference, Oz. You have to abide by the laws of the regime. That's why booze is *verboten* ... Against their beliefs or something. One light ale: well, public flogging, at least.'

'Never!' Outrage was replacing astonishment on Oz's beat-up face.

'That's right,' said Moxey. 'Well-known fact.'

'One light ale, and you get flogged?'

Barry nodded. 'In a market place, Oz.'

'I expect a Newcastle Brown's life imprisonment,' Bomber said.

'But Barry's cousin's *British*,' Oz continued, determined to see this bizarre line of reasoning right through to the end. 'I mean, he's like us lot over here with the Erics. Like, without us, where are they?'

'Still got to abide by their say-so,' said Barry.

'Bollocks!' Oz scoffed. 'If we did something wrong over here, we wouldn't be subject to Erics' rules, would we?'

'Course we would,' said Moxey. 'It's their country. Their laws an' that.'

But Oz was unaffected. 'I'm just sayin'. Don't give them the right to flog us in market places, does it?'

There was no answer to Oz. Not this time or any other.

Neville and Dennis left the hut together. The younger man sighed as they walked.

'Brenda's gettin' all edgy again,' he confessed to Dennis. 'I really don't know what she imagines I get up to over here.

She's obviously torturing herself with fantasies of my dissolute life.'

Dennis laughed harshly and indicated the hut. 'Send her a polaroid of this dump. That'll reassure her.'

'When she sees the crack I'm sendin' home, she must realise there's precious little left for me to enjoy a lavish lifestyle ...'

'She's lonely, man,' Dennis cut him short. 'It's been a few weeks now. Worst time.'

'I suppose so. I miss her, God knows. And home.'

Dennis looked thoughtful. 'I'm going back for the weekend. I'll drop in.'

'Are you?'

'Have to. See the solicitors and sort things out.'

'The ... the divorce is going through, is it?' asked Neville.

'Aye, bar the shouting.' Dennis smiled crookedly. 'Or in her case, the cheering.'

Neville shook his head. 'Oh, come on. I don't reckon your Vera's any more happy about this divorce than you are.'

'Who knows?' Dennis stopped, gestured in the direction of the admin hut. 'I'm goin' to use the capo's phone to check flights. See you.'

Dennis moved off quickly, his stocky frame bent into the chilly wind. He was resilient all right, was Dennis. But then maybe he made life a bit of a struggle for himself, too, when you thought about it. Neville watched him go, then looked down at the letter from Brenda that he was still holding in his own hand and yelled out on impulse: 'Maybe I'll come with you!'

Towards the end of the break, Neville saw Helmut, as he did from time to time. They had a chat together. He was a good lad, was Helmut, Neville had decided; the kind of fellah he'd drink with at home and never mind the lingo problem. They chatted together in a halting mixture of German and English on their way back to the part of the site where they were both working. Until, twenty or thirty yards short of their objective, they saw a section of scaffolding collapse. A couple of blokes had fallen – or

121

jumped. And Neville could hear Oz cursing loudly in his inimitable style. Bomber was helping him up from where he'd gone headlong when the scaffolding had come down.

'You okay, Oz ...?'

The Geordie was already shaking his fist at the two German brickies who had been standing on the scaffolding before it went.

'You naffin' arseholes!' he bellowed like a wounded animal.

'All right, boyo. All right. No harm done.' Bomber was still holding on to him – to restrain him rather than to help now.

'Bastard miracle there wasn't!' Oz oathed.

One of the German brickies shouted something down.

'What did you say?' roared Oz. He saw Helmut hurrying up with Neville, asked: 'Come on. What did he say?'

Helmut blushed. 'He say, er ... accident ... and –'

'Accident, bollocks! It's 'cos you lot are incompetent arseholes!'

'Sharrup, man, Oz. No one did it on purpose,' said Neville.

Oz's eyes blazed. 'Oh, you'd take their side, we might expect that. You should decide which shoe fits, you should.'

'Should what?'

Oz indicated Helmut and sneered. 'You've got more mates among the Erics than among us lot!' he said.

'No, I haven't!' Neville protested quickly. 'You're my mate, Oz. More than –'

Suddenly he realised what he had been about to say. He turned in his excruciating embarrassment to Helmut, who shrugged, pointed at Oz. 'You are ... welcome to such friends,' the young German said, and strode off.

'Hey, Helmut!' Neville called out. But his friend did not look round.

Next day at lunchtime, Dennis was sitting on a tip, reading a newspaper and enjoying a beer, when Neville came and sat beside him. He unwrapped a sandwich and said:

'I've made me mind up. I'm coming with you.'

'Fine,' said Dennis, glancing up briefly from his paper.

'Just getting too much around here. Especially with that Oz. Anyway, I need to see Brenda, put that right.'

Dennis nodded. 'Have you not forgotten somethin'?'

'Like what?'

'That incriminating masterpiece on your right forearm,' said Dennis with a sour laugh.

Neville gasped, clutched his arm. 'Oh! I'd got so used to it, I'd forgotten all about it!'

'Aye. Good job I mentioned it, then.'

Dennis moved off, unable to suppress a smile. Neville stayed where he was. After a moment he rolled up his sleeve, stared at the tattoo. If he had hoped the thing would go away, or at least become less noticeable, he was disappointed. Neville gritted his teeth. The evidence of that drunken Friday night was going to be with him forever, and he'd have to learn how to deal with it . . .

Friday night rolled round again. The rest of the lads were shaving and getting themselves into their good clothes, generally poncing themselves up, while Dennis and Neville packed for their first trip home.

'Where is this bar, then?' Bomber was saying. He had on his double-breasted navy blazer, his Friday night kit.

Wayne grinned. 'It's sort of in the Old Town but not quite. It's like across this square, opposite that bar on the corner where all the Micks go . . .'

'What's it called?' asked Oz impatiently.

'I forget. I just come across it by accident. It's packed with strumps though,' Wayne assured any doubters.

'That'll do Bomber!' the big man crowed. 'Rump and strump.'

'Yeah, well. I promise you it's full of it.'

Oz, who had been combing his hair, suddenly looked suspicious. 'Not one of them student bars, is it?' he asked. 'Can't stand them student bars . . .'

Wayne shook his head, pretended scout's honour. 'No. All kinds get in there. Good music, too. Van Halen, Styx, AC/DC –'

'No chance of Eve Boswell, I suppose,' said Bomber.

'You what?'

Bomber laughed and began to sing in a tuneless but stentorian baritone: '*Sugarbush, come dance with me ...* Don't that ring a bell?'

'Can't say it does, son,' Wayne told him, half admiring, half incredulous.

Dennis shut his case and snapped it to. 'He likes the old ones, does Bomber,' he said.

Bomber grinned. 'I'll tell you who else Bomber used to like. Yana. Remember Yana, Dennis?'

'Vaguely.'

Bomber's eyes took on a dreamy look. 'I can't recall any of her records,' he mused. 'But she had enormous tits and lived somewhere near Brighton.'

The door opened. Neville and Barry came padding in from the showers.

'Howay, Nev. Shift yourself,' said Dennis, tapping his watch.

'Sorry, Den. Wanted to shave. Not be a minute.'

The lad packed away his sponge bag and few remaining things in his suitcase.

'Doc fixed you up, then,' asked Wayne.

Neville smiled. 'Yep. Good idea, that, Wayne. Cheers.' He pulled up his shirtsleeve to reveal his tattooed arm. It had been heavily bandaged so that nothing was visible of Lotte or the rest.

'I read this book once,' Oz told them, 'where this bloke brought the plans through in a plaster cast. Pretends his leg was broken, like, and he come across the border with the microfilm shoved down the plaster. Clever that. Except he was caught and shot.'

'That's great, Oz,' Neville said.

Dennis looked at his watch again. 'Right. I'm ready.'

'Here, have a pint of English bitter on me,' Moxey said.

Dennis shook his head. 'They don't call it bitter where we're from, lad.'

'No,' chimed in Wayne mischeviously, 'they call it sheep-dip.'

Oz bridled. 'Best beer you can get.'

But Dennis wasn't going to be sidetracked. Neville was

ready now, too. 'We'll be off, then,' he said. 'You lads look after yourselves.'

Wayne told him to bring back the Sunday papers if they had time. Oz told Nev to give his Brenda one for him. And just as they were going out through the door, Bomber said gently:

'Hey, Dennis ... hope it works out, boyo.'

Dennis nodded his thanks and left without another word.

Peace settled in. Then Moxey asked Bomber: 'What d'you mean – hope it works out?'

Bomber looked a little embarrassed on Dennis's behalf. 'Goin' about his divorce, isn't he?'

No one else had known except Oz.

'Didn't realise that,' said Moxey.

Wayne shrugged. 'Yeah. News to me.'

'He's definitely gettin' divorced, is he?' Barry asked.

'Sadly, yes.'

They all looked at each other solemnly in honour of Dennis's lost marriage. Oz nodded sagely, sighed.

'Lucky bloody Dennis,' he said.

Not that long before noon the next day, Dennis turned up at Neville's place. Neville answered the door, brought him through into the small, brightly-decorated kitchen and offered him a cup of tea.

'I was passing, like,' said Dennis. 'Have you just had your breakfast?'

Neville looked sheepish. 'I only woke an hour ago. Slept like a log.'

'Where's your Brenda, then?'

'Hairdressers. We're goin' out for a meal tonight. I'll make some fresh tea.'

Dennis looked at the time on the kitchen clock, then raised an eyebrow. 'No, don't bother,' he said. 'Let's go and have a jar down the Magpie.'

'Oh, right you are,' said Neville.

'I've got an hour to kill,' Dennis explained. 'I'm picking up the bairns at one and taking them out for the day.'

'Nice.' Neville started ferrying the crockery and cutlery over to the sink to wash.

Dennis sighed. 'It could be. If I knew where to take them. Where would you suggest?'

'Dunno,' Neville answered. 'Bit cold for the beach.'

'Too cold for the beach in August here!'

'Aye. And they're a bit young for the match.'

Dennis laughed drily. 'They'll need to be quite a bit older before we inflict that special misery on 'em.'

Neville laughed too. Some jokes never lost their appeal, particularly when you'd had a chance to appreciate them in their absence.

Dennis looked at Neville's shirtsleeve. 'How's your arm, by the way?' he chortled. 'On the mend, is it?'

'Oh! What a close shave I had!' the lad breathed. 'Brenda wanted to change the dressing!'

'Never! How did you get out of that?'

Neville grinned in recollection. 'I said they'd put on this special ointment, which had to be allowed to set.'

'Set?' echoed Dennis, laughing fit to bust. 'What did you say it was, aeroplane glue?'

'Aye, well. I had to say something.'

Dennis nodded. 'Well, it's not much of a deception compared with what she imagines you're up to, bonny lad.'

'Oh, I've put her mind at rest about all that,' Neville said proudly. 'You have to be firm with them, Dennis.'

'Really. I can see I should've sought your advice earlier,' said the older man, amused.

Neville remembered the reason Dennis had come home. 'Oh, you were down at the solicitors today,' he began. 'So what –'

But Dennis just looked at his watch in a way that was heavy with meaning. He obviously had no intention of discussing solicitors or divorces at the moment.

'C'mon, get your skates on,' he said with forced cheerfulness. 'Let's have that jar, Nev.'

'Your health, old chum,' Bomber toasted.

Moxey nodded, raised his own glass of Pils. 'Cheers.' He

126

sipped his beer thoughtfully. 'Just think: Den and Nev'll be in their local now.'

Bomber smiled. 'Doubt if Brenda will let Neville out.'

'Aye. Well, Den's got no trouble on that score any more, has he?'

'True,' said Bomber. 'Poor Den. He don't say much – he keeps it all inside – but he takes this divorce kind of hard. It'll knock him off kilter, you'll see.'

Moxey nodded sadly, looked around the near-empty Club. 'So how long have you been married, Bomb?' he asked.

'Longer than I care to recall, boyo. By which I don't mean to cast aspersions on her. I'm referring to time's winged chariot.'

'She's okay is she, your old lady?'

Bomber nodded emphatically. 'Fine woman,' he said. 'Can't have been easy lookin' after Bomber and five kids. No,' he shook his head then, as if there couldn't possibly have been an argument about it. 'I reckon I done all right there. It weren't exactly a union blessed in heaven. But since that night it were consummated in a caravan outside Bridport, it's managed to last the distance in fair nick.'

Moxey leered. 'In spite of your affection for Yana, was it?'

'Ssshh ...' said Bomber with a wink. 'She don't know nothin' about that side o' my life.'

He half-turned to see who was coming in the door. It was Helmut and another German brickie, both dressed in their working clothes.

'Must've been workin' their Saturday,' Moxey said.

Bomber agreed. 'Would've put in a bit myself if I hadn't had such a hangover.'

'Good club Wayne found, weren't it?'

Bomber nodded, turned to greet the two Germans. 'What'll it be, lads?' he asked.

Helmut and his mate exchanged glances. 'Is okay,' said Helmut dismissively.

'Look, don't harbour no grudge about yesterday,' Bomber said with sigh. 'That Oz don't speak for the rest of us. Have a drink roit?'

It looked as though Helmut might be weakening a bit, but when he shot an enquiring glance at his mate, the other bloke shook his head.

'*Nein, danke*,' Helmut told them, and signalled to the barman for two beers.

Bomber shrugged. 'Suit yourself.' He turned away, dropped his voice. 'It would appear,' he said softly to Moxey, 'that relations are strained pro tem.'

'Oh to be in England,' said Moxey, showing an unaccustomed literary bent.

Church bells were pealing in the distance as Neville came into the kitchen with a wad of Sunday papers under one arm.

'Mind if I take the papers, pet?' he said. 'For the lads.'

He looked well fed, happy, secure, and clean. It was amazing what thirty-six hours in his own home could do for a man.

Brenda nodded contentedly. 'Leave me the *Express*. I like to read Roderick Mann.' She was cutting and buttering bread.

'What's the great smell?' asked Neville, sniffing appreciatively.

'I've got a leg of lamb, love.'

He shook his head wryly. 'I eat rubbish out there. All fried – or out of tins.'

'You should try and get the right foods, pet. Fruit's important,' Brenda told him. 'I've packed you a lot of oranges. And I'm making you up some sandwiches for tonight, when you get back.'

There was a short, heavy silence.

'Wish I didn't have to go back.'

Brenda stopped buttering and looked at him tenderly. 'No?'

'No. I know you're convinced we're all raving it up over there. But honestly, it's not like that at all. Not for me, any rate. I stay in most of the time. Or just go over the local.'

'You must go out sometimes though,' Brenda said, probing. 'To discos and that.'

'Why? Do you?'

She considered for a moment. 'Only on Thursdays,' she answered.

'What happens Thursdays?'

'The girls and me go to Tuxedo Junction.' She smiled disarmingly. 'Girls get in free that night.'

Neville frowned. 'What's Tuxedo Junction?'

'It's very exclusive. Lot of footballers get down there . . .'

'Oh, do they!' said Neville with an edge to his voice.

Brenda giggled, turned and put her arms round his neck, obviously delighted at his display of jealousy. 'Don't you trust me, then?' she asked huskily.

'As much as you trust me.'

'That's okay then, isn't it?'

And they both laughed and kissed. By the time they'd finished, the lamb was well done.

'I could've had another four hours with them,' Dennis said. 'The plane doesn't go until four.'

Vera stopped patting her hair and looked away from the hall mirror to where Dennis stood, four-square outside the living room door with a *Sunday Mirror* in his hand.

She shook her head. 'Dennis, I know. But how often do they get a chance to get to the country? Alan's going to run them up to Rothbury.' A self-pitying edge was coming into her voice, but she couldn't stop herself. 'After you've gone, what are they going to do but sit in front of the telly as usual? The kids need it, Dennis.'

'Aye. And does it ever occur to you that I need them?' Dennis said.

'Oh, Dennis. Let's not start –'

Kevin and Angela came crashing down the stairs, and that was another argument averted – or perhaps another chance to settle things destroyed. Vera used the opportunity.

'Kevin,' she scolded mildly, 'I told you to put a warm coat on.'

'I'm not cold, mam.'

'You will be up on those moors.'

Angela was eight, dark, serious like her dad. When

Kevin had dashed off upstairs to get his coat, she showed off her light coat.

'Can I wear this, mam?' she said, with one eye on her dad.

'Yes, but put this scarf round your head,' said Vera mechanically. She smiled wearily at Dennis. 'She's never without a cold, this one.'

Angela made a face. 'Why's me dad not coming?' she asked.

'I've got to go back to Germany,' Dennis told her gently. 'I'd come with you otherwise, you know that.'

Kevin landed at the bottom of the stairs again, this time covering his *Fun Boy Three* T-shirt with a shapeless anorak.

'Can I take me ball?' he panted.

Vera clucked in exasperation. 'You won't need it, Kevin. Just this once you won't need your ball.'

Dennis grinned, leaned over to ruffle his son's hair.

'Play for United one day, won't you?' he said.

'Yeah. Me an' Derek Greenwell are goin' to sign up together.'

They all heard the blare of a car horn outside in the street. It started and it didn't stop.

'Come along,' said Vera, trying to sound cheerful, and matter-of-fact. 'There's Alan.'

She opened the front door a little hastily, waved to a Ford Cortina that was parked across the road. Dennis bent down to give the kids a last hug.

'So long, pets,' he said. 'You look after your mother, won't you? You're big enough now, you know.'

'Tara, dad,' said brother and sister almost together.

Dennis smiled sadly. 'I love you,' he said quietly.

'He's got a great car, has Alan,' Kevin told him, shifting from foot to foot in his excitement.

Dennis's smile froze, but he kept going. 'Has he, now? Better get off then.'

The kids dashed out of the door and down the path. Vera called out for them to be careful, then turned to Dennis.

'How will you get to the airport, then?'

'I'll share a cab with Neville.'

Vera nodded. 'Give him my love, and Brenda if you see

her. Say I'll pop round. I owe her a visit.'

'Sure. Take care, then.'

'You too.'

They stood awkwardly opposite each other for a moment. There was either too much or too little to be said between them. Finally Dennis kissed her coolly on the cheek. Vera nodded, as if acknowledging something, and started off down the path. Twenty seconds later, she was inside Alan's nice flash Cortina and moving away out of Dennis's life. Along with his kids. Jesus.

The hut was empty when they got back at about nine that evening. Except for Moxey, sniffling away while he brewed up a cuppa on the electric ring. Both Dennis and Neville stood for a second, viewing the scene in Hut B through the eyes of men who'd just spent two days back in the civilised world.

'Lo,' said Moxey. 'Good time, lads?'

'Could've been better,' grunted Dennis.

Neville smiled ruefully. 'Great, thanks.'

They chucked their stuff onto their beds. Dennis raised an eyebrow enquiringly. 'Where is everyone?' he asked Moxey.

'In town. Wayne's away with some new bit of splash.'

'And what's up with you?'

Moxey sneezed. 'Full of cold. Want some tea? Nev?'

Neville was sitting forlornly on the edge of his bed, getting more miserable by the moment. He was really suffering from the old culture-shock, wasn't he?

'No thanks,' he said dully. 'God, it's depressing here. Sunday night in a hut in Düsseldorf.'

Moxey nodded. 'Especially after home.'

'Too true.'

Dennis made no comment. To him, this place had its advantages. Like he didn't have to stand by and watch some other guy take off with his wife and kids. But he agreed it wasn't the most salubrious place in the known universe.

'Do you know exactly where the lads are?' he asked.

'They'll be at this new bar Wayne found. It's right across

131

the square opposite the Mick pub.'

Dennis looked at Neville.

'What d'you say, bonny lad? We'll go suicidal if we spend the evenin' here.'

Neville nodded solemly. 'Yeah. Couple won't hurt, will it?'

Little did he know, as the saying goes.

EIGHT

The bar was long, narrow and dimly-lit, and on a Sunday night it wasn't too crowded. Apart from the Brits, the main customers were a bunch of German kids with untidy manes of hair and leather jackets, heavy metal music fans. The young krauts were drinking beer steadily, but they were wired up on something else as well.

Bomber got the beers in, as usual. 'There you go, my dears,' he thundered. 'Welcome home!'

They drank a toast. Never mind the 'home', but it was good to be with the lads.

Oz, of course, had to spoil it. 'Velcome back to ze Fazerland,' he bellowed at the top of his voice. 'Ve told you escape vas impossible!'

Everyone groaned, cast embarrassed glances around the room.

'Keep your voice down, Oz,' muttered Neville.

Dennis grimaced. 'He'll get us ruddy murdered one day.'

'You've been back no time,' said Oz in a hurt voice, 'and already you two are on me back!'

Dennis ignored him, turned to Bomber. 'What's so special about this place, then?' he asked, casting a jaundiced eye around the bar.

'It were chockablock last night, and Friday,' Bomber said. 'Couldn't move for strumps.'

Barry nodded fondly. 'Like the Playboy Mansion it were.'

Dennis still seemed unimpressed. 'Here both nights you were, then?'

'Too right.'

'That explains it, then.'

'What?' said Oz.

Dennis grinned. 'You've frightened 'em all off.'

'I told Oz not to use his charm,' laughed Bomber.

'Bollocks!'

Barry looked defensive. 'Sunday, isn't it? Never anyone about on a Sunday. 'Cept a bunch of piss-artists like us. And them young degenerates.'

An argument seemed to have erupted just across the room between one of the young German rock fans and a pretty young blonde in tattered jeans and leather jacket who looked as though she might be his girl. The Brits registered the mild fracas with interest, and Neville moved over to the bar to order another round. He had his back to the blonde as she deliberately left the group of German lads and sauntered over to the counter. When he looked out of the corner of his eye, she was staring at him, smiling appealingly.

Neville looked away quickly. But she said something in a soft voice in German and touched his arm.

'Sorry,' he said shyly. 'Nix spreck Deutch. English.'

The girl's smile widened. She was dressed scruffily, but she had big eyes and a cheeky mouth. She knew what she was doing, all right, and she had the wherewithal to do it.

'Okay,' she said in quite good English. 'I have no money. You buy me drink?'

Neville gaped. Without realising what was happening, he found himself nodding. 'Awright.'

'Beer.'

'Right.' He added another Pils to his order, handed her the first glass that came his way, made to turn away with a heedless, sophisticated smirk. But she wasn't having that.

'Your name?' she said.

'Oh. Neville.'

'*Bitte*? Neville. I understand.'

'Yup.'

Neville turned away again. He had seen one of the kraut kids staring poisoned daggers at him, and he was starting to understand the situation. She took his hand this time.

'Me. Bettina. My name,' she said smokily.

Barry was the first to notice. He let out a hiss of surprise. "'Ere,' he said. 'Our Neville's pulled.'

Dennis whipped round. 'What? Neville?'

'The jammy Arab,' sneered Oz.

'An' he was only with his wife a jif ago,' commented Barry.

Meanwhile, Bettina had refused to let go. Bomber was ferrying the beers over while Neville stood rooted to the spot, like a rabbit with a ferret. He was flattered – she was a hell of a nice bit of crackling – but he was scared, too. The situation was unpredictable, not Neville's style at all.

'Sorry,' he said when he could find the strength. 'I must go. Leave . . .' He pointed in desperation to the door. 'Sorry . . .'

She shrugged, Neville noticed with relief. He began to move away, but then she held on to him.

'Where you go?' she said.

Neville told her where the site was.

'Taxi?'

'Yeah. Well, must be off . . .'

'It is on my way. I share. Wait.'

In no time, she was back with her handbag, ready to go. Neville, subjected to some ribald advice from his mates and naturally polite, didn't dare pull out now. He'd drop her off at her place, then head on home. He felt tired, didn't he? The lads could think what they wanted . . .

The cab pulled up outside a cluster of apartment blocks in a part of town Neville didn't know. Bettina dug into her handbag. Neville thought she'd say she had no money, and in any case it went against the grain. 'No. No. I pay. Really,' he said.

She smiled. 'Please. You walk me . . .' She pointed at the apartment blocks, pouted prettily.

'Walk?'

'Is dark . . .'

Reluctantly, but compelled by the good manners he'd had drummed into him over the years, Neville agreed that he would see her to her door. It did look pretty intimidating out there for a lass on her own, he told himself. And so he paid the driver and followed Bettina out of the cab. She

135

took his hand, smiled, led him through the first forecourt and on into the heart of the high-rise development.

Finally they arrived under some sodium lighting. Bettina moved on a bit into the shadow, drawing Neville after her.

'Well, there you go,' he said quickly. 'I'd better find meself another taxi –'

But her arms were already snaking round his neck and her lips were moving up to make contact with his. Before Neville knew where he was, he was being kissed by a very hungry woman – and she wasn't just saying thank you. He stood unsurely, his arms dangling down by his sides, until she released him. She was panting.

'You can stay,' she hissed.

Neville moved back a pace. 'What?'

Bettina pointed at a nearby block of flats. 'With me. Only my sister also lives there. She will not mind.'

'I can't. I –'

'Yeh,' she insisted. 'It is okay ...' Bettina smouldered. 'Come ...'

She grabbed his hand, and he pulled it away. Maybe he was starting to get a bit scared. '*Nein*,' he said. 'Ta very much all the same ...'

She looked at him quizzically. This obviously hadn't happened to her before. 'No?'

'Sorry.'

Bettina hissed something in German that obviously cast aspersions on his manhood.

'I'm married,' said Neville uncomprehendingly, as if that made it all okay, even for a girl like this.

Bettina just spat something else, pulled away. Then she headed for the apartment block. She didn't look back.

It took Neville a few minutes to get back to the main street intersection and start hailing cabs. In the meantime, he saw a jeep scream past and hammer down towards the apartments where the girl lived. He thought: 'Someone's got a bee in their bonnet.' And he was damned right.

'I was only tryin' to extricate meself,' Neville said, slipping a fresh blade into his razor.

Barry waited until he had done the underside of his chin, then grunted.

Neville took that for agreement. 'I mean, I didn't want to get involved, so I said I was going. Then blow me, she says: can I share a cab ...'

'Bit of a dilemma,' said Barry, who obviously wished he could be lumbered with Neville's kind of problems.

'Last thing I wanted,' Neville went on. 'I'd only just got back from Brenda!'

'Quite.'

Barry wiped the lather from his face and frowned into the shaving mirror.

'Mind you,' he continued, 'she obviously fancied you. It was clearly on if you'd so wished. I mean, you could've done, couldn't you?'

Neville shrugged. In retrospect, maybe he could enjoy it a bit. 'Oh, yeah ...'

They walked back to the hut. The rest of the lads were busy getting ready for another day. Oz greeted Neville's arrival with a leer.

'You haven't told us the outcome of last night yet. Eh?' he boomed.

Bomber joined in. 'Obviously over in a flash,' he said with a wink. 'He wuz all tucked up when we got back.'

'You bet. Quicksilver Nev,' said Oz.

Wayne looked round from combing his hair, raised an eyebrow. 'Ullo, what was this, then? Nev get jumped?'

Neville blushed furiously. 'Nothing. It's nothing. Honest ...'

Just then, the door was flung open and to general astonishment Ulrich stomped into the hut.

'Please. All outside. Now!' the chargehand bellowed. He looked worried.

They all filed out after him, followed him towards where a couple of cars were parked. POLIZEI, eh? There were some other Brits waiting there. Some Germans and Turks were hanging around too, but Ulrich waved them away as he approached. 'British only ... *Nur Engländer* ...'

'What's goin' on?' Dennis asked one of the Brits who had obviously been there for a while.

The Brit, a Scotsman, shrugged. 'No idea, pal.'

Ulrich was talking to a bloke in plain clothes who was standing with three uniformed German cops. He was telling them that all the Brits were present and correct. The uniformed cops moved towards them, indicating that they should form a line.

Wayne nodded. 'Bleedin' ID parade, innit?'

'What a liberty!' said Oz, scowling defiantly at the Germans.

They were still forming up while one of the plainclothes men split off and went towards one of the cars. He opened the rear door, helped a girl out. Blonde, scruffy, nice looker...

Some of the lads recognised her. Neville certainly did, because he looked amazed and more than a bit put out as soon as she clambered out of the patrol car. Dennis shot him a glance that was both a warning and a question.

It didn't take long, though. The plainclothes cop started to say something slow, careful and official to the girl, but she cut him short, stepped forward and pointed out her man straight away. And who else did she pick out but Mrs Hope's little lad, Neville?

Dennis stood with his arms folded, staring angrily at Grunwald and Ulrich in the admin hut. His rational mind told him that it wasn't their fault young Nev had been dragged off to chokey, but somehow it was hard not to feel that they were also responsible because they too were German.

'The police,' Grunwald said haltingly. 'The police say zat the girl, she ... er ...'

'She was assaulted. Beaten up,' Ulrich filled in for him.

Dennis snorted in derision. 'Anyone could see that! But what's that got to do with Neville?'

'You saw what happened,' Ulrich said. 'She pointed at him! Last night, she say, he beat her up.'

'That's bloody madness, man! You know young Neville, you know he's not capable of a thing like that!'

Ulrich shrugged.

'Don't you?' Dennis persisted.

Ulrich wavered slightly. 'It would surprise me, yes. I admit.'

'So it bastard should.'

'Is in police hands. All right?' said Grunwald, looking at his watch.

'No, it's not all right!' Dennis stormed. 'Look, Neville's down that cop shop. He's alone and he'll be scared stiff. He'll need a lawyer. Let me ring the consul, or get down there, or something ...'

Ulrich put up a hand for silence, then launched into a short, intense discussion with his boss. Herr Grunwald didn't look too happy, but he listened to what the chargehand had to say. After a while, Ulrich turned back to Dennis.

'Okay. He should have help,' he said.

Dennis smiled, and then to his astonishment Dagmar, the secretary, stood up and reached purposefully for her handbag.

'Wait for me!' she said.

Another sharp exchange in German and Ulrich climbed down.

Dagmar smiled at Dennis, took him by the arm. 'I am your help,' she said. 'I am coming with you.'

'Ta, love,' said Dennis. And he meant it.

'Did they let you see him this time?' asked Wayne as Dennis walked into the hut, weary and grim.

Dennis nodded. 'Yeah. Poor sod.'

Bomber frowned. 'Won't they let him out? They have to let you out unless they charge you.'

'They've charged him,' Dennis said dully.

Wayne started. 'With what?'

'I don't know what the Germans call it. Assault, I think. That's what Dagmar said.' He sighed. 'A grand lass, that. And at least Nev's got a lawyer now. I suppose it's the equivalent of our legal aid. Apparently he's a good enough bloke, but how can we tell?'

'Well, what about bail?' Wayne said. 'Don't they have that here?'

'Aye. They want three thousand marks – and his passport.'

Bomber whistled. 'Three thousand! How are we goin' to manage that?'

'God only knows,' Dennis murmured. 'Have to have a whip round. Where are the lads?'

'Over the club. But we're all skint, and it's only Tuesday.'

Dennis subsided onto his bed, shook his head. 'What a bloody mess ...'

By the morning, though, they'd collected a bit. Not enough, but a start. The lads from Hut B trudged off to another day's work in the knowledge that at least they were trying.

Dennis and Bomber were working in the same area of the site. They were almost at the job when Bomber nudged Dennis meaningfully. Alerted, Dennis spotted Helmut and two other Germans coming towards them, and they looked purposeful.

'Shit,' said Dennis to himself. Relations had been pretty poor before the business with Neville and that girl. Now the Erics were well supplied with ammunition. The three Germans stopped. Dennis and Bomber stopped too. 'Look,' Dennis said, 'if you lot want to make somethin' of this, forget it. You should know Neville better –'

Helmut put up a hand, peace signal of sorts. 'Please,' he said firmly. 'We know him, as you say. Therefore we wish to help.'

Dennis didn't know where to put himself. He found himself grinning idiotically. 'You do?' he answered eventually.

'Ya. We do.'

The other Germans nodded gravely.

'By jove, and they don't have much cause,' Bomber said, impressed.

Dennis nodded. 'Cheers. We're goin' to need bail,' he told the Germans. Helmut, their interpreter and spokesman, looked puzzled. 'Er, money,' Dennis explained. 'To get him out of jail ...'

Helmut had got the message. He was talking earnestly to his mates. After a short while, he turned back to Dennis.

'Okay,' he said. 'We all ... put in.'

Meanwhile, on another part of the site, Oz was late for work as usual. He was sneaking past the admin hut on his way to his job when Ulrich stuck his head out.

'YOU!' he bellowed in English.

Oz looked around with exaggerated curiosity, as if wondering who the chargehand could be addressing in English. Then, when it was obvious Ulrich meant him, he feigned shock. 'Now what?' he said. 'Just 'cos I'm two minutes late, man!'

Ulrich shook his head. 'No. Come here,' he barked.

Oz shrugged, moved towards the hut. 'What's wrong?'

'There is telephone. From England.'

'It can't be for me!'

'Please, take it,' said Ulrich simply.

Oz shambled into the hut, gingerly picked up the phone that was lying on the desk.

'Hello?'

He took a moment to realise who it was on the other end of the line. A woman, asking him who he was. He told her, and she confirmed his worst fears. It was Brenda Hope.

'Oh!' Oz said, then tried to sound normal and relaxed. 'Oh, aye.'

'Is he there, please?'

'Er, no,' said Oz. 'He's not at the moment, pet.'

A pause. 'Is he all right?'

'Aye, he's fine. Why?'

'Well ... he always rings me on Monday nights. Mondays and Fridays. Without fail. But he didn't call last night.' Brenda's voice was getting a little catchy. 'I had this number for emergencies, see, and well –'

'Yes, I see,' Oz cut in a little too eagerly. 'Well, there's nowt to worry about.'

If he'd hoped to put Brenda's mind at rest, he had gone the wrong way about it. She had her antennae full out, and she'd picked up his concern. Her voice betrayed panic.

'He's had an accident, hasn't he?' she babbled. 'I know it ...'

'No, no,' Oz soothed. 'He's fine in himself. It's just –' This was the hard bit.

'Just what?' Brenda asked tearfully. 'Why can't he come to the phone?'

Oz coughed. 'Well ... he's had a spot of bother, like ...'

Ten minutes later, he arrived at the place where Dennis was working, to be greeted with surprising good humour.

'Hey, Oz!' Dennis called out. 'The good news is that the Erics are havin' a whip-round for Nev's bail. We'll have him out in a jiff.'

'Oh,' said Oz gloomily.

'Isn't that great?' Dennis caught Oz's mood, looked at him quizzically. 'What's the matter?'

Oz shuffled from one foot to the other. 'Well,' he said, 'the bad news is ... Brenda's comin' over.'

Dennis looked at Bomber. Bomber looked at Dennis. 'WHAT!' they both bellowed together.

Dennis sat smoking his fifth ciggie in the corridor of the police station. Helmut sat next to him in silence. They both knew why they were here, and there wasn't much to be said. Until the swing doors opened and a busy-looking man in his thirties appeared, carrying a bulging briefcase. He saw Dennis and Helmut, stopped and extended a hand in welcome.

'Hello!' he said in good English. 'I'm Hans Bauer.'

Dennis got to his feet, shook hands. 'Dennis Patterson,' he introduced himself. 'You're the person I spoke to on the phone. You're Neville's –'

'Yes, I am his defence lawyer, if things go that far.'

Dennis nodded, impressed. 'Thank God you speak English as well as you do.'

'Thank you,' Bauer laughed. 'The Düsseldorf judiciary knows this only too well. They give me many Englishmen. Oh, and Scots too! Football hooligans, my butter and bread ...'

'I brought a German friend, just in case,' Dennis said, referring to Helmut. Helmut introduced himself too, and he shook hands with the lawyer. They sat down together.

Dennis cleared his throat and began: 'What did you mean – "if it goes that far"?'

142

Bauer shrugged. 'I think there is not a case,' he said. 'I have now seen copies of the girl's statement, and also the report from the police log. I will give you translations, and you will see there are many holes. But I must do some homework of my own, just in case: see witnesses, verify facts.'

'I'll bring all the lads in whenever,' Dennis said.

Helmut spoke to the lawyer in German, waited, nodding, while Bauer replied. Then he turned to Dennis.

'He says let's talk *after* we release Neville.'

'Good idea.'

'Okay. You have brought the assurety?' Bauer asked.

Helmut grinned shyly, removed a plastic shopping bag from under his coat and handed it to Bauer. The lawyer looked at it suspiciously until he glanced inside and saw the crumpled masses of notes.

'It's all there,' Dennis said. 'It'll just need a lot of counting.'

Bauer chuckled. 'Did you win it in a poker school?'

'We had a whip round.'

Bauer frowned. 'I'm sorry?'

Helmut filled in with a German translation, and explained a bit more besides. The lawyer was clearly moved.

'Ah!' he said. 'Then Neville must have many friends.'

Dennis nodded slowly. 'You know, Mister Bauer,' he murmured. 'I think you're right there.'

It all went very quickly. In what seemed like a matter of minutes rather than hours, they were seated in the rear seat of a taxi, with Neville sandwiched between them. The lad was pale and tense and still scared, but at least he was back among friends.

'You want to stop for a drink?' Dennis asked gently.

'No,' said Neville. 'Just let's get back.'

'We would've had you out sooner if we'd had the readies,' Dennis explained.

'I know. Mr Bauer said you'd had a whip-round.'

Dennis glanced at Helmut. 'You can thank our mate here for that, and all the other Erics.'

Neville's lower lip was trembling. 'I can't . . . can't thank

143

you enough,' he said. Then the floodgates opened and he started to sob.

'It's all right, bonny lad,' said Dennis. 'You get it out of your system. Then you can face the lads. They're all dying to see you.'

Neville nodded. 'I never ... thought ... I'd ... miss Oz,' he sniffed.

The hut was like a courtroom. Dennis, Neville and Helmut stood round the table, backed up by the rest of their lads in their work clothes, looking down at some photostated sheets that Dennis had brought with him from the meeting with Bauer.

'Bauer's right,' Dennis was saying. 'This stuff's full of holes. Look,' he muttered, jabbing a finger at one photostat. 'According to this police report, they saw the girl – this Bettina – in the street near where she lives. A patrol car saw her, noticed she was in distress, stopped, but she ... RAN AWAY. They chased her on foot and caught up with her.'

Oz's brow furrowed with the effort of following it all. 'I don't see –'

'She RAN AWAY!' Dennis exclaimed. 'Don't you see? She didn't go lookin' for the cops, she didn't go and report it, or register a complaint, or whatever they call it over here ...'

'Right,' said Wayne. 'And when she saw the Ol' Bill, she tried to do a runner.'

'Absolutely.'

Barry shook his head. 'The prosecution would argue that the girl evaded the police because she didn't want the aggro, loike. Most rape cases are never reported, you know, because the victim don't want the stigma.'

'Oh, aye,' said Oz, intrigued.

Dennis pursed his lips. 'Fair enough. But the other alternative is that she was tryin' to protect someone.'

'The boyfriend!' Neville said suddenly, as if coming out of a dream.

'Boyfriend?' Bomber looked puzzled.

'Well, the bloke she was with in the bar.'

144

Bomber frowned. 'There were a few shaggyhaired louts hanging round her, 'tis true. That was as far as it went.'

'No, Nev's right,' said Barry firmly. 'There was one particular she was havin' a ding-dong with. Looked very beady, he did, when Nev and her went off.'

Wayne grinned at Neville. 'That's obviously why she pulled you. To get up the other geezer's nose.'

'You mean it weren't Nev's irresistible charm?' said Bomber.

That got a laugh all round. Even Neville joined in. It was a release for him. Normality of a kind.

Helmut laughed as loud as the rest. Then he became serious. His amiable face was hard. 'Listen,' he said quietly, 'I have friends. We find these ... boys who you look for.'

'Aye,' said Oz. 'Let's find the bastards and sort 'em out!'

Helmut swallowed hard. 'Er, no,' he said. 'Thanks, but I think best if you not, er ...'

Dennis saved his blushes. 'So do I,' he said. 'You stay put, Oz.'

'But –'

'Pipe down, you prannet,' growled Bomber at Oz.

Helmut continued: 'We know the bars, speak language, ask questions.'

'Need someone to identify 'em, won't you, though?' said Bomber thoughtfully.

Barry nodded. 'You an' me'll go, Bomb. We'll recognise them.'

'Roight, by jove!'

'They had a jeep,' Neville recalled.

Helmut clapped him on the shoulder, turned to the two Brit volunteers. 'Come!'

They exited to a chorus of goodbyes and good lucks. The rest of the party, if that was what it was, started to break up. Moxey went off to make some coffee, while Wayne went for a shower preparatory to dragging Neville out for a beer or two.

'Thing like this ...' Neville said with feeling, sitting himself down on his bed, 'makes you realise who your friends are.'

Dennis nodded agreement. 'It does that.' He padded

over to Neville's bed. 'Listen ...' He hesitated. '... There's something I have to tell you ...'

Oz, who had been hovering, suddenly glanced at the door. 'Er, I'll just be over the Club,' he said. 'Not be long.'

Neville watched him shoot out of the door. He was deeply puzzled. 'What?' he asked Dennis.

Dennis made a decision to let him have it straight. 'Brenda's comin' over,' he said quickly. 'She knows.'

'WHAT!' bellowed Neville. 'How the hell –'

'You didn't ring her Monday. She panicked, called the site. Oz was passing the office at the time.'

'Oz!' Neville snarled. 'I might have known!'

'It's not entirely his fault,' Dennis said mildly. 'He was caught on the spot. He couldn't explain why you weren't available without her thinking you were ill or something. I called her back, but she was adamant. She'd missed today's flight. She'll be over in the morning.'

Neville slumped on his bed, put his head between his hands. 'They should've kept me inside,' he moaned.

'Why, lad?'

'Because,' said Neville. 'I'm gonna kill Oz ...'

Dennis, still weaving his spell, got Dagmar to meet Brenda from the airport and take her down to the modest hotel where she was putting up. And then he headed there himself, choosing a time when Neville was still tied up agreeing formalities with the lawyer.

He knocked politely. Brenda opened the door, peered slightly suspiciously into the narrow corridor, looked a bit brighter when she saw who it was.

'Hello, pet,' said Dennis.

'Oh, Dennis.' Brenda gave him a warm hug as soon as he was through the door.

'I know pet, I know,' he said gently. 'Howay, there's no need to fret. It's all over with.'

She broke away and looked up at him, her eyes glistening. 'What?'

Dennis smiled. 'He's a free man. Well, he's concluding formalities, but all charges are dropped. They've got the other bloke.'

'Honest?'

'Sure. Why, don't look so surprised, lass. You didn't think Neville was guilty, did you?'

'Course not.'

'Some of our German mates found the bloke,' Dennis explained. 'They turned him in. I think they extracted their own confession. He didn't look too healthy, anyway.'

He laughed, but Brenda seemed sombre.

'What exactly happened, then?' she asked.

Dennis had been hoping the question wouldn't arise. He prevaricated just a bit. 'Well, er, this bloke was the boyfriend, like,' he said. 'Got the needle like, when he saw . . .'

'Neville get off with her.'

Dennis shook his head. 'The boyfriend beat her up just outside her place, see. The police saw her condition, and she fingered Nev.'

'So he did take her home, didn't he?'

'Brenda, the point is –' said Dennis in exasperation, but she gave him no time.

'*That* is the point, Dennis. Of course I knew Neville didn't do the things they said he did, but he took that girl home! He went with her.'

'He didn't, pet. She imposed herself on him. She shared his cab. You know Nev – he's so polite, he'd give Hitler a ride.'

Brenda sat down on her bed and stared up at Dennis like a pretty, defiant child. She wasn't to be swayed, said the jut of her chin and the fire in her green eyes.

Dennis looked straight at her. His eyes were blazing, too.

'You're going to make me angry, Brenda Hope,' he told her.

'I'm what! *Me*?'

'Aye,' he said, not taking his gaze off her. 'If you really can't see how much that Neville cares for you, then you're a very silly lass. He cares so much it hurts. It hurts him to be away from home, it hurts every minute he has to spend over here sacrificing everything he wants so's you can enjoy something better in the future.' He threw up his hands. 'He's the only bugger in Germany who *isn't* on the pull!'

147

'You're his friend,' she said accusingly. 'You –'

'– And you're his wife, and you don't seem to know him as well as I do! The reason he got into trouble was because he *didn't* go with the girl. If he'd been like the rest of us, he'd have gone with her, done the business, she'd have been content and no one would've been the wiser. But he's not like the rest of us. He gave her the elbow, she got vindictive, and the rest – as they say – is history.'

This time when she looked up at Dennis, Brenda was crying just a little.

'Suppose so,' she sniffed.

Dennis softened. 'Sorry,' he said. 'I didn't mean to sound off at you. It's just that you two have a marvellous marriage, and I appreciate that all the more 'cos my own's down the toilet.'

'You're right, Dennis,' she said. 'What happens now?'

'Simple.' Dennis smiled. 'Let's go and fetch the lad.'

Brenda smiled back. 'I'll just put some lipstick on.'

There were cheers as Brenda and Neville embraced outside the police station, and the odd ribald comment. The happy couple were surrounded by Brits, Helmut and his sidekicks, and some of the witnesses from the previous Sunday night in the bar. Plus Bauer, the lawyer.

'Thanks for everything,' Dennis told him.

Bauer shrugged amiably. 'For me it was a change from defending Britishers who have broken up bars.'

Neville dragged himself away from his Brenda for a second, shook hands with the lawyer. 'Yeah. Thanks very much.' He widened his gratitude to include everyone else. 'And you, Helmut, and your mates. I don't know how you nailed him so quick!'

Oz shook his head. 'Didn't surprise me.'

'Oh, how's that?' said Dennis.

Oz pointed at Helmut, stood to attention. 'Zey haf vays of making you talk!'

Groans all round, except from Helmut, who seemed to think Oz's Nazi act was hilarious.

Then they all fell silent. A police car pulled up. Out of the rear door came a detective and . . . Bettina. The girl was still wearing her scruffy jeans and her bruises. She looked at

148

Neville, then looked away. Neville stepped forward, but Brenda, with great presence of mind, took him gently but firmly by the arm.

'Never mind, pet,' she said softly. 'She's not worth it.'

Then Bettina was gone. To break the awkward moment, Bauer stepped forward. 'I give you a lift to the hotel, all right?' he said.

Neville nodded eagerly. 'Oh, cheers.'

After the goodbyes – which lasted a moment or two – Neville and Brenda followed the lawyer to his car. Suddenly, Neville turned. Someone was hailing him.

'Nev, can I have a word!'

It was Barry. Neville looked puzzled, then shrugged. 'Just a minute, pet . . .' He hurried over to where the lad was standing. 'What is it?'

Barry seemed very solemn. 'You'll be goin' to bed sooner or later, you and your Bren,' he said.

Neville nodded. 'Aye. But that's no business of yours.'

'Well,' said Barry, 'I think if that's the case you should take precautions.'

Neville looked as though he might be about to get violent. 'Do you mind,' he snapped. 'Brenda's on the pill!'

'I still think you should wear this, though,' Barry chuckled. Out of his pocket he produced the soiled arm bandage that Neville had worn during his trip home. 'Bit of a life saver, eh, Nev?' he said.

It was a quiet day in the admin hut. Whether by accident or design, Dagmar was alone at her desk when Dennis came in, carrying a box of chocolates.

'Hi,' he said. 'I got you these.'

Dagmar took the chocolates. They were good ones. 'Oh, you are kind!'

Dennis grinned bashfully. 'Well, you've been a lot of help, like. I appreciate it.'

'There was no need. But thank you.' She pouted very prettily indeed.

'Thank *you*.'

Dagmar laughed throatily. 'And the happy pair?'

'Brenda's stayin' over. See the old town, have a meal.'

'You will go with them?'

'No,' smiled Dennis. 'What d'they need me for?'

'Then maybe you should take *me* out?'

Dennis's eyes widened. 'Yeah?'

'Or are you another married man?' Dagmar asked him impishly.

'I'm afraid so, yes.' For a moment Dennis was crestfallen. Then he considered and brightened. '... But only just!'

NINE

'Where is everybody?' said Neville bleakly. It was Saturday morning, and weekends were the worst time for him, with nothing to take his mind off his loneliness and futility.

Wayne had come back from the shower hut to fetch his razor. 'Moxey's gone back to the U.K., hasn't he?' he said. 'Bomber's gone fishin' with some of the Erics, and Barry's in the bog. Very regular, is Barry,' he chuckled, delivering a fair imitation of his victim's lugubrious drone.

'Aye. But where's Dennis?'

Neville frowned. Wayne had disappeared again. He stared around the hut for a few moments. Then a bleary Oz spoke from his bed.

'I saw Dennis earlier,' he mumbled.

'Earlier?'

'He woke me up, clumpin' around.'

Neville's curiosity had been aroused. 'Where's he gone, then?'

'I don't know,' said Oz. 'He had a rolled-up towel, but he was fully dressed.'

'Yeah?'

Oz yawned and nodded lazily. 'Aye. Looked like he was goin' swimming.'

'Swimming?' Neville echoed. Saturdays were not his brightest days.

Oz hawked. 'Well, he wasn't goin' sunbathing, was he? Not in this craphole. Is there some tea going?'

Neville told him the kettle was on, moved back towards his own bed, cogitating. Suddenly his face began to light up.

'Hey, Oz!' he said, turning round. 'What a great idea!'

'What is?'

Neville beamed. 'Swimming! Never thought of that. Let's go to the baths!'

'Why?'

'Be a change. Get some exercise. Something to do, at least ...'

Oz clambered out of bed, scratching himself all the while. He wore a pair of particularly unsavoury Y-fronts and a vest that was more holes than nylon.

'I've got to fetch me laundry,' he said.

Neville persisted. 'Okay. But afterwards let's go to the baths. Keep us entertained, man.'

'I suppose so. But I don't have a cossie.'

'We'll buy 'em when we're in town.'

Oz shrugged, coming round to the idea. 'Awright. C'mon, kettle ...'

'Funny how Dennis never said anything,' said Neville, pulling on his jeans.

'He's a cagey lad, is Den,' Oz mused. 'Plays everything close to his chest.'

Neville nodded. 'Lately he seems even more so. He went out Thursday night, and I says to him – just casual, like – where you off too, Den? Well, he tells me to mind me own business.'

'He's still frettin' about the divorce, Nev. That's it.'

'No. He wasn't doing a moody.' Neville looked concerned. 'He seemed quite chipper, really. That's why I was so took aback.'

Oz pursed his lips disapprovingly, poured some water from the kettle into a barely-washed mug. 'He's not really one of the lads, Den. He's too straitlaced.'

'He says he wants his own place,' Neville told him. 'Says if he has to stay out here a while, then he's goin' to find a flat. Can't take the hut any more.'

Oz, squatting on his bed in his hideous underwear, clutching a chipped mug in on hand and a tin of condensed milk in the other, unshaven and unwashed, looked around the hut. He seemed genuinely surprised at what Neville had said.

'So what's wrong with this place?' he asked.

Barry was holding forth on his lack of success with women. To Wayne, of all people. They were standing outside, getting ready for a trip into town on Barry's bike. That was when Wayne saw Dagmar come out of the Admin Hut and lock the door.

'Cor,' he said. 'Clock her, eh?'

'That's Dagmar,' Barry informed him. 'Nice lady.'

'Yer. Tasty, isn't she? Never really taken much notice of her before.'

Barry nodded. 'Keeps herself to herself.'

'Come on then,' said Wayne. 'Head her off.'

Barry laughed self-consciously. 'Lesson one in pulling the birds, eh?'

He kicked the bike into spluttering life. It bounced the hundred yards or so over to where Dagmar was, then came to a halt once more.

''Ullo then,' said Wayne cheerfully.

Dagmar looked at him a cool, level way. 'Good morning.'

'Puttin' in some overtime, eh?'

'*Bitte?*'

'You don't usually work Saturdays.'

'Sometimes. Accounts.' She was glancing towards the car park, obviously wanting to get out of this situation.

Wayne kept at it, though. 'I'd have thought a girl like you had better things to do than accounts,' he said. 'I'd have thought a girl like you would be spending Saturday with her boyfriend. 'Cos a girl like you must have a boyfriend.' He smiled winningly. 'Don't you?'

'Perhaps.' Frosty.

'Only perhaps? So there's hope for us yet, is there?'

Dagmar measured him up and smiled in a way that made it clear she found him wanting.

'I would not live in hope if I was you,' she said firmly.

With a smile that said only too clearly, 'Come back when you're grown up,' Dagmar turned and headed towards the car park.

Barry started to smile. His smile got wider and wider. Then he began to laugh.

153

'All right,' said Wayne, rounding on him. 'What's so bleedin' funny, then?'

Barry watched Dagmar get into her car and drive away. 'Lesson One?' he said. 'Presumably that was how *not* to do it. When do we start with the real thing?'

Wayne fumed. 'Just wait, son. C'mon. Into town ...'

They biked into the centre of Düsseldorf, parked and strolled around in the late summer sunshine. It wasn't long before the topic of the day came up again.

'In the sexual jungle, you're a predator, you are,' Barry said to Wayne as they walked along a sidestreet, looking for somewhere to have a cup of coffee and a snack.

The cockney shrugged. 'I work alone, if that's what you mean,' he said. 'Don't go in mob-handed like the rest of the lads. All they do is booze and talk about it ... by the time they've worked up the nerve to do something, they're all too incapable.'

Barry thought about the implications of that. 'Have you no desire to form a permanent attachment?' he asked.

'No.' Wayne's answer was crisp and firm.

'Have to one day, though.'

'Maybe.'

They walked along in silence for a while, surveying the shops and the passing scenery, including some of the local talent. Barry seemed to be building up to something.

'I got engaged once,' he said suddenly. 'I think I still am, in fact.'

Wayne shot him a sidelong glance. 'Don't you know?'

'Oh, we never broke it off, officially, like. And she's still got the ring.'

'D'you still see her?' Wayne probed, fascinated. To him, Barry was obviously a strange, alien life form.

'No.'

'Do you write?'

'No.'

'Does she write to you?'

'No.'

'Do you care?' Wayne asked, almost at the end of his patience.

'No,' Barry considered. 'Don't like her very much.'

'Then why did you get friggin' engaged, then?' Wayne exploded.

Barry was completely unperturbed. 'I forget,' he said calmly. 'I think it was 'cos her dad had a spare season ticket for West Brom.'

Wayne mimed a silent scream. 'Oh well, obviously that could make a young lad's heart sing,' he said sardonically.

They saw a pleasant-looking little coffee house and turned into it. The place was quite crowded with shoppers resting up after a Saturday morning in the city centre, but Wayne and Barry managed to find a small corner table to drink their coffee.

Barry spooned his coffee dreamily. 'Am I really a radish, Wayne?' he asked.

'Oh, come on, son. Don't have an identity crisis,' growled the cockney. 'Not on me day off. Time's slippin' by.'

'Well, if I'm in your way —'

'No,' Wayne said, softening slightly, but still with a determined set to his jaw. 'I said I'd get us fixed up, didn't I? There's no panic. What you've got to realise is there's thousands of 'em out there. Birds are like the Chinese Army. Once you've jumped a few, you think that's it for a while. But then a whole new battalion comes over the hill.'

'I only want one,' said Barry sadly.

Wayne leered. 'Well, that's where you and me differ, son. I want 'em all.'

'Ah. I've never been that ambitious, myself.'

But Waybe wasn't listening in any more. He was taking in the pair of girls who had just sat down nearby. Nineteen or twenty, nice and giggly; German crackling at its best. He made eye contact, smiled, got a smile in return.

'Barry,' he said quietly, still looking in the girls' direction. 'Our prayers may have been answered.'

'How d'you mean?' asked Barry, who had been staring morosely into his coffee. He had his back to the crumpet, in any case.

'Behind you,' Wayne told him. 'Don't look now! Show some cool.'

But he was too late. Barry immediately swung around

and stared, goggle-eyed, at the girls.

'Yeah,' he said loudly. 'Very tasty. What do we do now?'

Wayne gestured for him to keep easy. 'Not us,' he said. 'You, son.'

'*Me?*'

'Yes indeed,' said Wayne. 'You're the one who has to prove himself. Sooner or later, you got to show what you're made of, son. Now, we've already had a flash ...'

'Have we?'

'Yeah. When they come in. Bit of the old eye contact. Halfway there, ain't we?' Wayne say back easily in his chair. 'So remember, we don't have to promise the world or go through all that boring preamble. Just come straight to the point with a bit of dazzling repartee.'

It took a minute or two for that to sink in. Barry checked over his shoulder. Wayne was right. The two birds knew they were being watched, and they were enjoying the fact.

'Straight to the point, loike!' he said, to give him courage.

Wayne nodded. 'Right.'

Barry took a deep breath, turned to address the girls.

'Hello,' he said.

The girls smiled, giggled. Flushed with his success, Barry smiled back. He didn't intend to beat about the bush. Hadn't Wayne, the expert, told him not to?

'Er ... would you like to come back to our hut?' he said in a firm, clear voice.

Wayne buried his face in his hands. His despair was the deep, howling outrage of a fine musician who sees a beautiful piece ruined by a talentless amateur, the horror of an artist forced to stand by and watch while a clumsy dauber destroys his work beyond redemption ...

Dennis trod water, watched Dagmar move gracefully to the end of the high diving board, spring easily and execute a perfect dive. She surfaced, swam strongly and with obvious pleasure towards the far end of the pool. It was beautiful to watch, and so was she, he reflected, and set off in his steady breast-stroke to join her.

'You're some swimmer,' he said admiringly.

She laughed. 'At school I was even better. I win many prizes.'

'Did you win a prize for English, as well?'

'Yes!'

Dennis was feeling better than he'd felt for months. He laughed with her, enjoying the water, the physical well-being, the closeness to an attractive woman. It was like suddenly realising you'd been asleep for a long time and that now you'd woken up.

'Good job about your English,' he said, 'or we wouldn't have much to say to each other.'

'Oh, I will teach you German.'

Dennis pondered the implications. 'I might have to be around a while for that.'

'So?'

A short pause. Dennis took the plunge.

'Suits me,' he said.

Dagmar nodded. 'Me also.'

'This isn't going to be an easy secret to keep,' Dennis said.

'I think here we are safe,' murmured Dagmar.

They had been moving closer and closer in the water. Their lips brushed as she leaned forward to speak softly, and the moment was indescribably tender. Dennis would remember it for a long time. As he would also remember what happened next.

'GER—R—RON—IM—OOO!'

The whoop was hideously familiar, but it couldn't be, could it? A furrow of terrible doubt formed on Dennis's craggy face. He looked slowly and reluctantly towards the far side of the pool, and his jaw dropped.

It was Oz. Dashing along the side of the pool, his pot belly hanging over the front of his cheap bathing trunks, his eyes wide with delight. As Dennis watched, he held his nose and leapt clumsily into the pool.

'I don't believe it . . .' Dennis whispered to himself before the tidal wave hit him, washing chlorine water into his eyes and up his nose. A few seconds later, when he recovered and stared coughing and spluttering at the outside world

157

again, he could see Neville loping alongside the pool close by.

'How, Dennis!' the lad yelled cheerily.

For a moment, Dennis's mouth worked as silently and comically as a goldfish's.

'What ... what made you come here?' was all he could manage to say.

Neville grinned like a proud schoolboy. 'Oz saw you leavin' with your towel. We worked it out.'

'Oh, terrific,' said Dennis.

At that moment, Oz surfaced like some hideous sea monster from the special effects department at MGM. 'Hiya, Den!' Then, to add insult to injury, his roving eye caught sight of Dagmar. 'Hey isn't that the lass from the office?'

Neville's gaze followed his. 'Oh yeah. It's Dagmar.'

They both looked enquiringly at Dennis.

'Aye,' he said quickly. 'I just bumped into her. Apparently she comes here a lot. Coincidence, like.'

That seemed to satisfy them. 'Great idea this,' said Oz. 'Can't understand why you didn't tell us you were coming here ... Howay, race you, Nev!'

And they plunged back in. Dennis took the opportunity to signal to Dagmar, who had climbed out of the pool on the far side. He mimed making a telephone call. She nodded, laughed to show she understood the ironies of the situation.

Grand lass. Just a question of bloody well getting her alone ...

They arrived back at the club at lunchtime. Oz and Nev got some down quick while Dennis sloped off to the payphone in the corner. Chlorine gives you a thirst. Unless you're Dennis.

'Sup up,' said Oz as Dennis put the phone down and walked slowly over to the bar. 'Another round here, chief, *danke*,' he told the barman.

There was one in for Dennis when he arrived.

'Who were you callin', then?' said Neville.

Dennis took his time reacting. 'Just someone.'

'I gathered that!'

158

'It's personal business, Neville,' Dennis snapped.

Neville looked away, hurt. 'I'm sorry, I'm sure. I didn't mean to pry, did I?'

'Look,' Dennis said with a sigh. 'Even round here it is possible to want some privacy. In fact, it's essential if you want to stay sane.'

They considered the statement during the pause to sup their beers.

Neville broke the silence. 'So that is why you want to ship out?'

'Yes. I suppose it is. That and the probable change in the law,' said Dennis.

Oz shook his head ruefully. 'I don't get it. We were all such mates when we got here.'

'Aye,' Dennis agreed. 'And the best way to stay mates is not to get on top of each other.'

Oz grinned. 'There's no one in our hut I want to get on top of. Arf, arf!'

'Nor me,' said Neville.

'Mind,' Oz continued blithely, 'I wouldn't mind jumpin' that Dagmar.'

Dennis's voice was ominously quiet. 'What?'

'Well, she didn't half look good in that bikini! Nice strong thighs ...'

Neville noticed that there was something a bit strange and none too pleasant about the way Dennis was looking at Oz. As if he was having to control himself, bite something back.

'What's the matter, Dennis?' he asked.

'Nothing. I've got to be off. Goin' into town.'

He walked out of the bar without so much as another look.

'Cor, what's up with him, said Oz. 'Didn't even finish his beer.'

Neville looked puzzled. 'He's is a right mood, isn't he?'

'Well, it's nothin' to do with us, is it?' Oz muttered, and then his eyes lighted on Dennis's undrunk beer. He reached and quaffed it back, happy as a sandboy.

To tell the truth, Barry had had his suspicions when Wayne

asked to be dropped off in the centre of Düsseldorf to do some shopping. But the Londoner had turned up back at the appointed place at the appointed time, as promised, to resume their hunt for crumpet, albeit with much muttering of: 'Would you like to come back to our hut ...', which Barry found embarrassing in the extreme. They'd had another cup of coffee, set out to cruise around a bit on Barry's motor bike. And the break came unexpectedly, as they always do.

They had stopped at a red light. Barry manoeuvred the bike forward until they were alongside a cab. He didn't look at it closely, but Wayne did. He suddenly tapped Barry on the shoulder. The Brum lad turned round to see Wayne staring saucer-eyed into the rear seat of the taxi. In it sat two leggy, ash-blonde girls in airline uniforms.

'There is a God, Barry,' Wayne panted. 'Cop them!'

'What? Oh, goodness. Air hostesses.'

Wayne looked pained. 'Stewardesses they're called these days, you nurk.'

He waved energetically through the window until one of them wound it down and said something in German.

'Don't you speak English?' said Wayne.

The girl nodded. 'Yes.'

'I thought you would, in your job. Where you from?'

The girl glanced at her friend, then back at Wayne. 'Sweden.'

'Ah,' he said knowingly. 'I thought you was Swedish. Something about your flawless complexion told me that.'

'Oh yes. And what is it that you want?'

Wayne looked innocent. 'Me? Nothing.' He pointed to Barry. 'It's just that me and my chauffeur here are strangers in a foreign land, much like yourselves. Only we was feeling very depressed, and then we caught a glimpse of you two and, well, it just lifted our hearts.'

'It just what?' said the stewardess.

'Well, it made us feel ... glad all over,' Wayne told her.

The stewardess turned to her friend and spoke quickly in Swedish. Both of the girls giggled.

'What's happening?' Barry asked.

Wayne shrugged. 'Hard to tell, son. We're dealing here

with the Swedish mentality, which is pretty inscrutable at the best of times.'

Just then, the talkative stewardess leaned out of the window slightly. 'We are very flattered that you feel this way,' she said with a smile.

Wayne nudged Barry in the ribs so hard that it hurt. 'We're away, son!' The lights changed, the cab moved away. 'Follow that car!'

Barry obediently booted the bike into action, but he was a bit hasty. The machine stalled and went dead. Wayne cursed and Barry worked frantically at the kick starter, while in front of them the lights sat tantilisingly on green.

'You friggin' radish, Barry!'

'Stop calling me that!'

As if spurred on by Wayne's cockney oaths, the bike came to life. Just as the lights went back to red ...

By the time they sped through the barrier, the cab containing the sexy Scands was barely visible along the busy street, which curved round past waste ground and opened out towards the ring road a mile or two away among landscaped tower blocks on the left.

'You've lost them!' Wayne hissed.

Barry, goggled and helmeted to the death, shook his head and put his foot down. 'No, they just took a left. Probably headin' for that big building over there.'

'If you lose 'em, I'll hang for you, I swear it ...'

'I'll take a short cut,' shouted Barry, goaded into an act of heroism well beyond his usual capabilities.

Before Wayne could think of raising an objection, the bike swerved right across the oncoming traffic, causing much hooting and fist-shaking from German drivers forced to brake, and bumped onto the waste ground. Barry whooped, feeling distinctly James Bondish. Until he started to look a little sick. The ground really had been laid waste at some stage, and the bumps were small hills. Barry's light bike slid and bounced crazily, and it was a tribute to Barry's unsung skill that they stayed on the damned thing. But they'd done the right thing from one point of view, because Barry could see the cab still, heading straight for a big hotel a quarter of a mile distant. He turned to Wayne in triumph, gave him a thumbs-up, then gulped and went wide-eyed with horror as they careened down a steep slope straight towards an evil-looking small lake that lay at the bottom.

'Oh, no ...!'

The water must have been about a foot deep, filled with black, stagnant rain water, and the bike went through it at about twenty. The tidal wave didn't quite tip it over, but it thoroughly soaked the two riders with liquid, malodorous slime before they emerged the other side and zoomed towards the Hotel Intercontinental in time to see the two Swedish girls disappear through the plate-glass doors, looking even more luscious from a full-dorsal view.

Wayne, his head still resounding with the roar of the bike's engine, blinked, then moaned with longing.

'See,' he said. 'Overnight stop, isn't it? Perfect.'

'Should we go in then, or what?'

Wayne looked at Barry in painful disbelief. 'Go in? Have you seen the state of us? We look like a pair of motorcross riders. Or a couple of sewage operatives. Whichever is the less glamorous, son.'

Barry nodded. 'Roight. Better get cleaned up, eh?'

'Right.' Wayne turned dramatically, still perched on the pillion of the bike, and stared down at the hotel. With his hair streaming in the wind, his ear ring and substantial nose, he looked like nothing so much as an Indian chief in a Hollywood movie. As if realising the fact, he raised one hand in solemn salute. 'We shall return!' he intoned.

'Yeah,' said Barry, laboriously duck-paddling the bike around. 'You said it, London.'

The Club was nearly empty, though it was Saturday night. Moxey had gone home for the weekend, other lads were off on various missions. Dennis had disappeared on another of his mysterious 'walks' and wouldn't say when he'd be back, so all there was amounted to Neville, busy on the pinball machine, and a newly-arrived Oz, who was getting the drinks in.

'How's it goin'?' he asked Neville, putting a Pils down for

162

him by the side of the machine.

'Ta,' said Neville. 'Eighty-three thousand. Don't interrupt. I'm gettin' a good score.'

'Ah. Cheers.' A very short pause. 'D'you hear about Wayne and Barry?'

'Shurrup, man. Eighty-three thousand and fifty ...'

Oz persisted. 'They've pulled. Swedish Air Hostesses.'

Neville went rigid, then looked up, 'Air Hostesses?'

'Swedish,' said Oz bitterly. He was never one for selflessness when it came to women.

'Never!' Neville's attention returned to his game. 'Oh, rats! Lost me free ball.'

Oz seemed miles away. 'Bloody jammy Arabs ...'

Neville decided to give up on the pinball. He turned away, reached for his Pils. 'How did they manage that, then?' he asked Oz.

'Well, they haven't exactly nailed them yet,' said Oz. 'They know they're at the Inter-Continental. Just goin' round there in the hope.'

'Oh, well,' Neville said, looking a little relieved. 'Hardly guaranteed, that, is it?'

'Right. Probably spend all night hanging around the bar for nowt.'

'Then come back and spin some extravagant tale for our benefit.'

'Right,' Oz agreed again, nodding thoughtfully. Then, suddenly, his eyes lit up with a wicked energy. 'Wait a minute!'

Neville had been about to take another swallow of beer. He paused, looked enquiringly at Oz. 'What?'

'I'm sayin', let's get them!'

'How, Oz?'

Oz pulled eagerly at his own beer. 'Stroke I know we pulled at a hotel once before. It were in Sheffield,' he said. 'Night before Newcastle played Burnley in the semi. Great game it was. Supermac scored twice, and on the way back we smashed up a Little Chef on the A1 near Wetherby –'

'Never mind the reminiscing,' growled Neville. 'What was it?'

Oz chuckled, pointed to the payphone in the corner. 'First the number of your Inter-Conti, then the action. Come on.'

A puzzled Neville followed him, like a lamb to the slaughter. Though, of course, the slaughtering was going to be happening to someone else, wasn't it?

'Yeah, well. They must've spotted us havin' our drinkie-poos in the reception, put two an' two together and called down to page us. Has bin known, my son,' said Wayne. 'Who cares. They're up there, eagerly awaitin' us.'

Barry nodded. They were standing in the lift, just on their way past the fourth floor and heading for the sixth. Room 612 the message had said. The girls were waiting for them in room 612 ...

'Do I look all right?' asked Barry nervously.

Wayne glanced at him. They were both neatly dressed but hardly your international sophisticates. Particularly Barry. Wayne had a shrewd suspicion that the hotel reception staff had been planning to chuck them out before the paging message had come over the P.A.

'Did you have to wear your sandals?' he murmured. 'And your socks?'

Barry looked defensive. 'They're comfortable!' he said. Then he turned a bit crestfallen. 'Don't undermine me confidence. Not now!'

Wayne grinned, patted him on the cheek. 'Don't worry. You're adorable, son.' He began to sing to himself: *'Strangers in the night, exchangin' glances. Strangers in the night –'*

The lift stopped on the sixth floor and the doors slid smoothly open. They stepped out onto the thick-piled carpet, looked around appreciatively, began to make their way down the corridor, counting as they went. Six-oh-four. Six-oh-six ...

And towards the corridor's end – not in 612 but in a room not so far further on – Dennis got up from his seat and padded to the door.

'I will be finished soon,' Dagmar called out huskily from the shower.

Dennis smiled. They'd done this on impulse, booking in. Seemed the only way to get any privacy. A drink or two, a spot of dinner, and then –

'No rush, pet,' he answered. 'Take your time over yourself. I'm goin' to look and see if there's any sign of room service. I ordered those drinks an age ago.'

He checked himself in the mirror, decided he couldn't see what she saw in him but what the hell, and opened the door to look for the waiter. There was certainly someone out there just a few doors away, looking disorientated . . .

Two faces whipped round and stared blankly at Dennis as he stepped out into the corridor. They belonged to two men who had been standing in front of the door of room 612, just about to knock, and they looked at Dennis with growing recognition and amazement. The feeling was reciprocated.

'Hello, Den!' stuttered Wayne. He jabbed Barry in the ribs. 'Look, it's bleedin' Dennis, innit?'

Barry smiled foolishly. 'Bloimey, what're you doin' here, Den?'

With seconds, Dennis was back in the room.

'Dagmar!' he hissed.

'Yes?'

'Don't come out of the bathroom. Stay in there.'

'What?'

'Just stay in there, please!'

He checked quickly to ensure that her half-empty suitcase was out of sight, moved back to the door of the room as Wayne and Barry arrived on the threshold.

'What on earth are you doin' 'ere?' asked Wayne.

'Er, well, I just wanted to spend the weekend on my own,' Dennis said hastily, placing himelf firmly in the doorway to block any attempts at entry. 'Thought I'd check into a hotel.'

Barry looked at him curiously. 'What a strange thing to do.'

'Not really. It's warm and comfortable, and I've got my own bathroom. Change from the squalor of the hut, isn't it?'

'I suppose so.'

'Now if you'll excuse me, I'm about to have some dinner...'

Suddenly another figure appeared round a corner in the corridor. A clerk from reception, looking flustered and worried. When he spotted Wayne and Barry, he called out something in German that was clearly questioning their right to be here. So the management really had decided they weren't welcome.

'Naffin' hell!' oathed Wayne.

'Oh, lummy!' Barry agreed.

Wayne's expression changed to one of pleading. 'Bail us out, Den,' he said. 'Get this geezer off our back, will you?' Then, without giving Dennis a chance to respond, he turned and took a few steps towards the clerk. 'What's the problem, squire?' he asked with feigned lack of concern. 'Visiting a friend, aren't we?'

The clerk continued until he was almost at the door, looked quizzically at Dennis. 'These people are wiz you, sir?'

Dennis grimaced. 'Er, yeah.'

'Oh, zen I am so sorry.'

Of course, after that Wayne and Barry had to come into the room, and Dennis had to close the door on the clerk, who was hanging around in the corridor just to make sure.

'Nice room. Very well appointed,' commented Barry, looking around.

Wayne nodded. 'Yeah. You've got a point, Den. Bit of luxury of a weekend. Bit of privacy.'

'Aye, and a fat chance of that with you two here!' growled Dennis. 'What are you doing in this hotel?'

'We haven't actually done it yet,' Wayne said with a grin. 'But we're about to get it together with these two stewardesses. Real darlings, they are.'

Barry nodded enthusiastically. 'Swedish!'

'They're staying here, see. Three doors down. They paged us and we was about to do the business, wasn't we, Barry?'

'I shouldn't think straight off, Wayne,' Barry said, suddenly cautious. 'I'd expect we'd have to break the ice with a bit of charm and a few drinks first ...'

Dennis glanced anxiously at the bathroom door. There was an eery silence from out there. But then again, maybe it only sounded eery because he knew the room contained Dagmar, wet and probably starkers.

'Well, I ... I wouldn't keep the ladies waiting if I were you,' he mumbled.

'Sure. Just wait till that nosey Eric pisses off, eh?'

They stood in uncomfortable silence for a few moments. Then Wayne suddenly brightened. 'Here, Den,' he said. 'Come with us. They're bound to 'ave mates. Obviously the air crews stay here. Place must be crawlin' with uniformed crumpet.'

Dennis shook his head. 'I told you. I'm trying to have a bit of time on me jack.'

'Why? Depressed or something?'

'I just need to sort a few things out.'

'You need your own space, as they say,' Barry chimed in helpfully.

Dennis smiled sourly. 'I wouldn't mind that, yes.'

'Come on,' Wayne said incredulously. 'You can't tell me you'd rather sit in this lonely room watchin' poxy Greman TV than go down the road and strump some Nordic nymph ...'

But Dennis wasn't listening. He was too busy keeping one eye on the main door, one eye on the bathroom.

'Look, lads,' he said absently. 'The coast must be clear by now. Why don't you just shove off and leave me be, okay?'

'Suit yourself. This offer will not be repeated.'

'Yeah,' agreed Barry. 'Let's go. Den obviously wishes to be alone.'

Dennis strode over to the door. 'Bingo! It's sunk in at last.'

He opened the door, motioned to the other two. And in walked a German waiter with a tray on which sat two vodka tonics. The late room service.

'*Ach, danke,*' the waiter said gratefully to Dennis, and walked into the room.

Dennis looked at Wayne and Barry. They looked at him and at the tray. A penny dropped. They exchanged knowing smiles. Even Barry. Dennis signed the tab and the waiter left.

'Eh, you're the sly one, aren't you, Den,' Wayne said when the man had gone. 'You've got an assignation, haven't you? He's expectin' another party, Barry.'

'Looks like it.' Barry chortled, feeling very man-of-the-world. 'You old devil, Dennis.'

Dennis reddened. 'Look,' he growled dangeously, 'why don't you two just bugger off!'

'On your way, son,' said Wayne. 'But come on, tell us. Who is it?'

Dennis was standing at the door, pointedly holding it open. 'Wayne, do you mind?'

But the cockney had the bit between his teeth. 'Here, it's not that Dagmar, is it?' he said.

'Why the hell would it be her?' Dennis answered, a little too forcefully.

'Well, she does seem to like you. Always puts down the welcome mat when you walks in the office. Cold shoulder for the rest of us.'

Barry nodded. 'Yeah. Wayne tried it on this morning. Nothing doing.'

Wayne glanced at him poisonously. The failure obviously still rankled. 'I didn't try it on. I was just being conversational!'

Dennis looked as though he was about to boil over. 'Once and for all,' he snapped, 'I'm not expecting anyone! I wanted a night on me own, and I ordered two drinks to save keep ringing up room service. You're the pair that's on the pull, and I suggest you get on with it before your Swedish birds go off the boil. Right?'

Wayne nodded, still smiling slyly. 'Sorry, squire. No offence. C'mon, Barry.'

'Roight you are, Wayne. Only a bit of fun. All right, Den?'

'Okay,' said Dennis, cooling off slightly. 'No offence taken.'

They were at the door now, passing through ... Dennis sighed with relief. Too soon. They were out in the corridor when Barry threw in one last remark that was presumably also intended to be helpful. And he didn't keep his voice down.

'We know you wouldn't be on the pull,' he said. 'We know how you feel about your Vera.'

Dennis shut the door abruptly, then closed his eyes for a moment. Dagmar would have heard every syllable of that from the bathroom. Then he crossed to the drinks tray, picked up a glass and took a healthy swig.

'You can come out now,' he said after a short while. Dagmar duly appeared. 'I suppose you heard all that,' he continued, hardly daring look at her.'

Dagmar stood a few feet from him, impassive. 'Of course.'

'What can I say?' Dennis shrugged and indicated the tray. 'There's a drink for you.'

'How did they know about us?' asked Dagmar coldly.

'They didn't. They – Dennis's voice trailed off. He shook his head in frustration.

'They mention my name, Dennis!'

'It was a shot in the dark,' he muttered weakly.

'I thought you had wanted not for them to know.'

'They didn't!' He sighed sadly, obviously convinced that the evening had deteriorated beyond salvation. 'I suppose you don't believe me, though. I suppose you picture us all in that hut, boasting about our sexual conquests, or confiding our fantasies.' He smiled, and it had no humour in it. 'I don't blame you, love. That what it's like most of the time.'

'I am sure,' said Dagmar, still cool.

'Honestly, Wayne's remark about you was sheer speculation. Just a coincidence.' Dennis spoke more for her benefit than his own. He just didn't want her thinking he was that kind of bloke, whatever might happen with their relationship.

'Another one?' Dagmar paused. 'And who is Vera?'

Dennis looked at her levelly. 'She's my wife.'

'Oh.'

'Look,' said Dennis. 'Should we just call it a day? I mean, should we have a drink and forget it?'

Dagmar looked down at the drinks tray, thought for a

moment, then leaned over and picked up the spare drink. She sipped it and looked back at him.

'I came here because I wanted to be with you,' she said. 'I still do.'

'Thanks,' Dennis said. In a way he was surprised, and in a way not. During the course of the day he had heard about how she had come back from Hamburg recently to live with her mother after the end of a long, intense affair up in the north country. She had taken the job at the site to fill in time. He had been lucky to find a woman with her style there. He had been a lucky bastard all along, because Dagmar was no ordinary strump, that was for sure. She was exceptional.

Dennis smiled at Dagmar. She smiled back, showing the dimples in her cheeks. He looked at his watch.

'We'll go down to dinner soon,' he said.

'That will be nice.'

She moved across the room until she was close to him. Then they kissed. As he released her, Dennis felt his whole body relax. It was going to be all right. He and this marvellous woman were going to spend the night together.

Fifteen minutes or so later, Dennis locked the door of their room behind them and took Dagmar by the arm, ready to squire her down to dinner. They both looked a treat, despite having to hurry with their preparations because of the interruptions; Dennis in his suit, Dagmar in a very slinky number that was like a foretaste of what they both knew would come after the meal.

'All right?' asked Dennis gently.

'Yes. Finally.'

'No harm done, is there?'

Dagmar smiled. 'I suppose that I still feel the need to look over my shoulder, or round the corner . . .' The smile broadened into a tinkling laugh. 'But never mind.'

'Not to worry,' said Dennis, joining in with her laughter. As it happened, they were passing room 612. He pointed to the door, dropped his voice to a conspiratorial whisper. 'They're happily ensconced in there,' he told her. 'While you and me, pet, have a nice dinner for two, candlelit with

170

several bottles of good wine, and put the events of the past firmly behind us.'

Dagmar stopped, put her arms around his neck and hugged him. 'At last!' They kissed again, and then began to walk towards the lifts with a spring in both their steps. Until, a little way further on, they heard the door of 612 open. Dennis glanced over his shoulder, then stopped abruptly when he saw a couple of Germal hotel employees backing out of the room, obviously addressing its inmates in profusely apologetic terms. One of them Dennis recognised as the clerk from reception who had come up to check on Wayne and Barry. The clerk certainly recognised him, too. No sooner had Dennis turned than the man called out to Dennis in English: 'Please, one moment!'

Dennis looked at him coolly. 'What can we do for you?'

The Germans advanced towards him and Dagmar, and there was something in their body language that told Dennis this was bad news. The clerk spoke first.

'Your two friends,' he said with narrowed eyes. 'The men who were going into your room sooner this night?'

The clerk left the question hanging, as if Dennis should know more. But the Englishman shrugged.

'Aye,' he said. 'What about them?'

The clerk looked at his companion. 'We must know who they are.'

'Why, for goodness sake?'

'Please,' said the clerk firmly, 'if you could come to the Manager's office?'

Barry followed Wayne down the dark stairwell. Fast. They halted just before they got to a pair of fire doors leading out onto a landing. There didn't seem to be many people about or much sign of life in this far corner of the hotel. That had been deliberate on their part once they'd started running. In fact, it had been a bloody necessity.

'Here, wait,' Wayne panted. 'What floor's this?'

'I dunno, why?' asked Barry. He was equally out of breath, and very, very scared.

Wayne looked grim. 'They could still collar us on the

ground floor.' He moved to an outside window. 'Over here, son.'

Barry watched him anxiously. He was out of his depth and he knew it. The whole, horrific sequence of events since they had barged into room 612 ten, fifteen minutes – it seemed like a lifetime – since, kept flashing through his mind. A half-dressed honeymoon couple; and Wayne not catching on fast enough and getting stroppy; and then the bloke of the couple screaming blue murder because he thought he and his missus were being mugged in their room by two English psychos; and then again the nightmare dash through the corridors, a maze of service entrances and bewildering stairs that seemed to go on for ever. Ending up here, not knowing whether there was a bloodthirsty posse of Erics waiting for them on the ground floor . . .

'You've obviously had much more experience at this kind of stuff,' he told Wayne. 'I tell you one thing: I'm never goin' on the pull with you again. Life's too short.'

His words were felt right in the heart, as were Wayne's when he retorted: 'Bloody mutual, that is. You're a jinx, you are, Barry. Should've ruddy well known.'

Meanwhile, the cockney was struggling with the catch of the window. With a grunt, he unclipped it and pushed open the window. Barry slithered over and looked out along with him.

'Jesus.'

'Geronimo, more like!'

They looked down and realised that they were about two floors from the ground. That was the bad news. The good news was that the ground they were looking down on formed the edge of the hotel car park, where Barry's bike was stabled.

'All right?' asked Wayne urgently. 'Ready?'

Barry looked at him in horrified disbelief. 'Ready? I'll break me leg!'

'Don't be daft. We're fit enough.'

'No we're not. We might have been, if we'd gone jogging or swimming with Nev. But as you so despise physical exercise –'

'Leave it out, Barry,' snapped Wayne. 'It's not that much of a jump.'

Barry looked down again to check and closed his eyes. 'Not for the S.A.S., maybe. And I *don't* mean the airline!'

But Wayne was already on the window and was dangling his feet over the edge. 'Come on,' he said encouragingly. 'It's like Butch and Sundance, innit?'

Barry groaned, but he had already resigned himself to the lunge. 'Yeah. And we know what happened to them, don't we?' he said.

Sunday dawned grey in the city by the Rhine. The building site was deserted. A curious early-morning bystander might have wondered why a taxi should draw up by the main entrance and drop a lonely, tired-looking figure to begin his walk across the waste ground towards the huts in the far corner. But then, such an observer wouldn't have experienced the events of the previous night through Dennis's eyes. And, unless he was loony, he wouldn't have wanted to. Exhaustion, disappointment and barely-supressed fury showed in every fragment of Dennis's body as he approached the hut with his overnight bag.

Inside the hut, the pair who had not gone out on adventures the Saturday night were stirring. Oz was standing in his usual early-morning uniform of airtex-and-nylon rags, forking cold baked beans out of a tin and waiting for the kettle to boil. Neville, pulling on some jeans in the early morning chill, had just got out of bed and joined him. They were starting to notice the winter was coming on. They'd been here months rather than weeks now. A chunk even out of young men's lives.

'Tea'll brew in a minute,' grunted Oz.

Neville yawned, nodded. Then he looked around and saw Dennis's bed. Not slept in.

'Hey!' he said, suddenly alert. 'Dennis stayed out all night.'

Oz frowned. 'Old enough, isn't he?'

'Yeah,' said Neville. 'I know, but . . . only this week I gave him a bit of advice, and I reckon he's taken it.'

173

'Eh? What advice.'

Neville grinned shyly. 'I told him he should find another lass.'

'Very sound advice, Nev,' said Oz.

The lad began to look thoughtful, even doubting. 'But I don't know,' he continued. 'When I thought it over, I thought, no that's not the answer. Not for Dennis.'

'Why not?' asked Oz, spooning tea into the pot. Or was he using the bean fork?

Neville crossed to the table. 'I know Dennis. If he had some sort of fling, it would probably do no good.'

Oz was grinning maliciously. There had been high jinks the night before all right, particularly when a certain pair of Don Juans had arrived back at the hut. 'Did Wayne an' Barry no good, that's for sure. Heh, heh!'

Then the door crunched open at the touch of a peremptory toe, and Dennis marched in, wearing a crumpled suit and carrying an overnight bag. To say his face was like thunder would have been an understatement. Like comparing the Krakatoa eruption to a burst pipe.

Without even acknowledging the other two, Dennis stomped over and tossed the bag onto his bed.

'Er, hello, Den,' said Neville. 'Where've you been.'

'Maybe we shouldn't ask, heh, heh!' Oz leered.

Dennis glowered at them, keeping his distance. 'No, maybe you shouldn't. Not that it'll make any difference,' he said bitterly. 'News spreads faster than the plague round here.'

Both of them were genuinely puzzled. The evil grin even faded a bit on Oz's lips.

'What are you on about, Den?' Neville asked.

'What I'm on about, Neville, is privacy.'

'Oh yes. You were on about that just the other day.'

'Well,' Dennis grated, 'at that time I still kidded meself it could exist. I've subsequently found out it doesn't. No chance. With you lot there's no hiding place!'

'Us lot?' echoed Neville.

Dennis snorted in disgust, pointed to the beds where Wayne and Barry lay sleeping. 'Well, those two pricks over there.'

174

Neville looked puzzled. They had heard Wayne and Barry return, enjoyed their discomfiture, but they didn't know the details. 'What did they do?' he said cautiously. Somewhere at the back of his mind a little warning bell was beginning to sound.

Not so in Oz's case. Like a big, playfully malevolent hound, he steamed in at the mention of the unhappy pair.

'Hey, Den,' Oz burbled. 'Their night wasn't owt to write home about either,' he said before Dennis could reply. 'I did them, didn't I? I blew 'em out, Dennis.'

Maybe Dennis was tired, certainly he was distracted. Whatever the case, he just nodded absently. 'In a minute, Oz. Though I'm glad to hear they had a bad time, I can tell you.'

He was intent on the miscreants' beds. He had approached Barry's and was studying where to make his grab. After due consideration, he lunged and caught hold of one of his feet. The blanket flew off, and there was a howl of agony as Barry instantly awoke. Wayne stirred in response in his bed across the way.

'Wassa panic? Oh ... hello, Dennis,' mumbled the cockney.

At least he could speak. Barry was still moaning with pain, clutching his left foot. Dennis and the others looked at it more closely, realised it was purple and swollen.

'That's my foot,' Barry gibbered at last. 'Butch an' bloody Sundance foot! Me crushed an' broken foot! What bastard just tweaked it?'

Dennis, though, was already heading towards Wayne's bed. 'Oh, "Hello, Dennis",' he said in a merciless imitation of the cockney's whine. 'Is that all you've got to say for yourself? After what happened last night?'

Wayne looked confused. 'Last night? We split, didn't we?'

'So how come,' said Dennis with soft menace, 'that I spend an hour and a half in the manager's office explaining who my guests were? A couple of thugs who apparently terrorised some honeymoon couple ...'

'Oh shit,' Wayne murmured. His chipper aggression had collapsed completely. 'Did it all come down to you?'

'Of course it bloody well did! In future, just stay out of my life, will you?'

He stalked off, shaking his head at the futility of it all. Wayne and Barry exchanged looks of genuine embarrassment and horror. Mainly the latter.

Wayne cleared his throat. 'Did you . . . I mean, did you say . . .?'

'No,' Dennis said without turning round, 'I didn't say anything. Told them you were just two blokes I met in the bar.'

He reached his bed, started unpacking his things. Silence fell. Wayne slid gently out of bed, put on his trousers and reached for a towel. He nodded to Barry, worldlessly indicating that they ought to make themselves scarce. Barry, hobbling on the bruised foot he had given himself in the jump from the second-storey window of the Inter-Continental, painfully got together his own things.

'Er, cheers, Den,' said Wayne, making his exit.

Barry limped towards the door. 'Yeah. Ta.'

Wayne paused one more time at the threshold. 'Weren't our fault, Den,' he said firmly. 'Not entirely. We got set up. Some bloody joker.'

Dennis gave him a glance. 'Yes? Well, I'd better not find out who!'

'Same with me, mate,' said Wayne, then decided to finally get out.

In the uncomfortable silence that descended again, Dennis started to take off his clothes. He glanced at Oz, saw that the other man was looking uncharacteristically worried.

'Oh, I'm sorry about that outburst,' he said. Slowly, his anger was evaporating. Dennis was never one to harbour grudges for long. 'Now, what were you saying, Oz, about blowing them two out last night?'

Oz grinned foolishly, shrugged, pretended an interest in something very high up in the roof.

'What? Oh, er, nothing. Nothing, Den.' He looked down at his boots. Anywhere but straight at Dennis. 'I mean, it pales into significance. Jolly japes in the dorm, Den. Irrelevant, really . . .'

And he looked across at Neville in a way that mingled a threat with a plea of: don't you dare say a word.

Oz had survived fights on the terraces, lethally ramshackle cars, the effects of his big mouth in a thousand bars, and even – so far – the challenges of 'abroad' without serious damage to his person. He had a feeling that if Dennis Patterson ever found out who was really responsible for everyone's Saturday Night fiasco, his run of luck would come to an end. Oz knew that there was no wrath like the wrath of a quiet, peaceable man. Dennis would bloody well kill him.

'Here, anyone fancy a swim?' he asked innocently.

TEN

'Can I borrow your thingy?' asked Dennis.

Wayne grinned suggestively. 'I think I'll be needing it, Den.'

A couple of weeks was a long time in the politics of Hut 'B'. Time had all but healed the wounds from the Battle of the Inter-Continental. And Dennis had started going out at nights again, alone, and looking a good deal happier.

'No, I mean your –' He mimed listening to Wayne's Sony Walkman cassette recorder.

'What, now?' said the Cockney. 'Aren't you coming out with me, then?'

Dennis frowned, then looked embarrassed. He and Wayne had been due to go out on a blind date together, a sort of final make-up for the damage done. And he'd clean forgotten. Maybe purposely, if he was honest.

'I thought that was Saturday,' he said lamely.

'No, mate. Friday. Tonight.'

Dennis said nothing, and Wayne was sharp enough to realise that the older man basically wanted out. He shrugged.

At that moment, Oz toddled over from where he had been sitting clipping his toenails on his bed.

'You weren't going out wi' one of his tarts, were you?' he asked Dennis with characteristic finesse.

Wayne looked offended. 'Tarts, nothing,' he said. 'My one's got a nice respectable friend, and I thought of you, Den, because she fancies someone mature and interesting.'

'Sure,' nodded Dennis, uncomfortable but not about to budge. 'Sorry, Wayne. It's just that me and Neville

179

arranged to have a go at learning German. From cassettes, like.'

Wayne sighed. 'She speaks beautiful English, Den. I checked.'

No response. He didn't push the issue.

'Okay, okay,' he said. 'It's on the top of the cupboard there.'

Meanwhile, Oz was digesting the information about Neville and Dennis's German aspirations.

'I'm surprised at you, Dennis,' he said after a pause. 'Never thought you'd fly the white flag in the language war.'

'Fly the what?'

'Well, you dont have to go crawlin' to them. Let 'em speak English, sez I.'

Barry barged in, looking irritated and wet from the shower. Lately he had been on an anti-squalor crusade, and it was reaching its climax. His mum had a lot to answer for.

'The shower!' he announced loudly. 'Blocked with hair!' He pointed accusingly at Oz. 'Yours!'

Oz, who had just finished dressing, looked at him coolly. 'It's this German shampoo. It's loosened me follicles.' Then he took a couple of steps towards Wayne, struck a body-builder's pose, even pulling his gut in, which was a considerable achievement in physical control. 'How's this for mature and interesting, Wayne? You know the song: "Tonight I'm gonna l-u-u-v someone to death!" What's the lucky girl's name?'

There was general laughter. Even Barry couldn't keep a straight face. Wayne laughed too, but he answered quickly.

'Ah, I don't really think she's your type ...'

Oz was unperturbed. It was a long time since he had let such things get to him. In sexual matters, in fact, he had a skin like a rhinoceros. A rhino on heat, at that.

'You've got to take someone along,' he said. 'Else there'll be three of you, won't there?'

Wayne squirmed a bit. He was in a tight situation. 'I don't think you'd fancy her. She's a bit – upper class.'

Oz chortled lecherously. 'Just the lad, then, aren't I? A bit rough.'

'No, no. It's a bit of *class* she likes.'

'Howay, man,' Dennis joined in. 'Give him a break.'

And the message was actually starting to get through to Oz. He was looking distinctly huffy.

'Don't bother. I'll find me own bird. Just tryin' to help you out, that's all.'

Suddenly Wayne relented. 'Okay, then. I'll tell her you're an eccentric millionaire.'

Oz shook his head uncertainly. 'No, sod it. I'm not beggin' any favours.'

That was how it stayed for a few moments until Neville came wandering in, all set up for his German session.

'*Guten Abend, Herr Dennis*,' he said with a shy grin.

'And *guten Abend*, Nev,' answered Dennis.

'Bloody hell!' growled Oz. 'I can't stay here listenin' to that. Come on.'

Wayne wagged a finger. 'Best behaviour now.'

They headed for the door.

'I'm not a bloody kid, you know,' Oz grumbled.

'None of that farting out loud.'

'*All right!*'

'And we'll make up a good cover story for you ...'

Oz agreed to keep occupied with a few marks fed into the Casino's gaming tables while Wayne primed the girls with the piece of fiction they had concocted during the cab ride there.

Oz emerged fifteen minutes after Wayne's meeting with the girls, having gained a decent win or two at roulette, and was pleased to see they were both still there. Wayne was obviously doing a good job talking him up. In fact, he was still at it as Oz made his way over to the table in the bar.

'Yeah, his father owns the company we all work for,' Wayne was confiding to his very attentive female companions. 'Oz'll be taking it over when the old man retires, but first he's got to work for three months as a common bricklayer, so he knows the business from all sides.'

Heidi, the svelte brunette who was Wayne's target, looked at the approaching Oz, pursed her lips. 'He does not look rich.'

'Oh no,' said Wayne hastily. 'He does his best to be just like one of the boys.'

Then the new arrival was at the table. Wayne indicated the brunette. 'Oz, this is Heidi –'

Oz bowed awkwardly.

'– and Uli.'

Oz bowed again, and this time leaned forward, seized her hand and delivered a fulsome kiss.

'Nice to meet you.'

Uli smiled. 'Wayne has been telling us of your father.'

'Oh,' said Oz, his eyes narrowing, 'that bugger.' Then he remembered the cover story and the fact that Wayne can't have been talking about his real dad. 'Oh, *that* bugger,' he corrected himself quickly. 'Aye. Good bloke, my old man.'

While Wayne poured him a glass of German champagne from the bottle in the ice bucket on the table, Oz had a chance to examine Uli, his companion. Blonde. Thirtyish and elegant, but sexy with it. A hint of the mature woman who knew all the tricks and also knew what she wanted from a man. He liked what he saw. Class was right.

'Cheers,' he said. 'Aye. Handing over the firm to me . . . yeah.'

There was a pause while he sipped his champagne appraisingly. Then Oz wrinkled his nose, downed the rest in one.

'Tell you what,' he announced with a smacking of lips. 'I'm as dry as a boat. What about us goin' on to beer?'

Uli, the elegant blonde, smiled indulgently. 'Just one of the boys.'

'Look again, bonny lass,' Oz boomed. 'One of the *men*!'

Their eyes met and Oz knew he was in with a chance. So long as there was the fictional background intact, he could be the rough diamond, couldn't he? She was lapping it up.

They finished the champagne. Oz ordered a beer.

Wayne looked at his watch then asked if he wanted another drink. 'Well,' he said with a glance at Heidi. 'If you'll excuse us –'

For a moment, Oz forgot himself. 'Why?' he asked. 'What have you done?'

'I am baby-sitting for my sister,' Heidi told him.

Oz nodded, but suddenly he had lost his confidence. He leaned forward for a whispered conference with Wayne.

'Wayne, you don't have to go.'

'What? That's the whole idea, innit?'

'Look, suppose I forget my story –'

Wayne was already smiling at the girls. 'Nah. You won't forget your American Express Gold Card. You left it in the safe, didn't you?'

Oz looked bemused and lost. 'Did I?'

'You see?' Wayne said without a moment's hesitation. He was one of the press-on-regardless school, and that was for sure. 'He's used to havin' his social secretary to organise him.'

It worked, too. Uri leaned forward and placed a delicate, reassuring hand on Oz's arm.

'Don't worry, Oz,' she told him huskily. '*I* will organise you tonight!'

Oz's uneasiness was instantly replaced by a warm glow of anticipated conquest.

'Any time, love,' he mumbled, grinning stupidly at Wayne, who was already on his feet, ready to leave. 'You can organise me any time.'

'*Guten Tag*,' said Dennis.

Neville finished spluttering and roaring like a car, mimed putting on a handbrake with appropriate sounds.

'*Guten Tag*,' he said then. '*Benzin, bitte.*'

'*Wieviel Benzin?*'

'*Dreissig Liter, bitte.*'

Dennis grinned, pretended to stick a an imaginary petrol hose into the top of Neville's jeans.

Barry, who had been ironing a shirt, looked up. He was obviously impressed.

'Hey, that sounds really German,' he told them. 'Y'know, it's quite a stimulating environment in here. I mean, seein' you blokes absorbing an alien culture and language, broadenin' yourselves, that's encouragin'.'

'Ta,' said Dennis. 'Well, the word is that one day in the not too distant future we'll have to decide whether we really belong here or not.'

Both Neville and Barry looked at him quizzically.

'The parliament here,' Dennis explained, 'they're discussin' a law that'll mean we can't avoid payin' tax, insurance and all that any more. So there won't be the gravy train any more. We'll have to graft like natives, accept the drawbacks and the benefits, or go 'ome.'

'Who told you that?' asked Barry.

Dennis shrugged. 'I talk to people. I get out more these days, meet the locals. You know.'

'I'd noticed,' Neville murmured. But he was more concerned about what Dennis had said about their jobs. 'Closing a loophole, eh?'

'Yeah.'

Neville sighed. 'In that case, that'll do for tonight. Comin' across the road, Barry?' he asked, clearly indicating the joys of a Pils in the Club.

'No thanks,' said Barry. 'I'd better get through this ironing. Permanent Press seems to have lost its meaning these days.'

Suspecting that they might be getting onto the subject of the hut and its squalor yet again, Neville turned to Dennis. 'Are you right, Den?'

Dennis shook his head. 'Better leave me out, too. I'm a bit skint just now.'

'Aha. We don't have to worry about that,' Neville said with a smirk of self-congratulation. He walking, smiling, over to his bed, whipped aside the pillow with a flourish. Then his face fell. He had obviously been expecting to find something there.

'What's wrong?' said Dennis.

Neville's expression changed from confusion to anger. 'Oz,' he said bitterly. 'He owed me fifty D-marks. "I'll leave it under your pillow before I go out," he said.'

'Ah, Neville,' Dennis said with a shake of his head. 'Fancy lending Oz money. Pearls before swine. And non-returnable, too.'

Barry agreed. 'Yeah. You should've tackled him when you came in.'

'I forgot – and he took advantage,' Neville muttered through gritted teeth. His blue eyes took on a look of steely resolution. 'Well, I'll have to go and get it back then, won't I? Where'd he go?'

'Don't make a big song and dance about it, man,' soothed Dennis, ever the peacemaker.

'There's a principle at stake, Dennis,' Barry said, changing sides. He turned to Neville. 'Him and Wayne went to the Casino bar.'

'Right,' Neville said crisply. 'See you later. With my fifty marks.'

And with that he strode out of the hut.

Meanwhile, Oz had begun to really enter into his role as a playboy capitalist's son. He wasn't yet perfect, of course, but then it was a miracle he'd got this far, some would say. At present he was aiming for a cross between J.R. Ewing and Rhett Butler, and he was holding a few of the lines he could remember from *Love Story* in reserve.

'Fate can play some strange tricks!' he said with an extravagant gesture of world-weariness. He sighed philosophically. 'Who'd have thought that I, who never liked Krauts –'

Uli frowned. She must have misheard him she was thinking. 'You never liked . . .?'

'Ah . . . Crowds,' Oz corrected himself hastily. 'And traffic and all that. I've always liked the country meself.'

Uli smiled in a puzzled fashion. This expansive Englishman was an enigma. Fascinating.

'I, too,' she said thoughtfully. 'But you were saying about Fate.'

'Oh, aye. Whoever would have thought I'd be expanding the family empire to Germany!' said Oz, shaking his head in incredulous consideration of the marvel that had brought him to this place.

Uli glowed at the mention of 'family empire'.

'Where will you live?' she asked.

'In the hut. We couldn't get hostel accommodation on account of the car breakin' down, and – ah, . . .' He checked himself, smiled as if he had suddenly seen the point. 'You mean, where will *I* live? Well . . . In the mountains. Near a river.' Oz pursed his lips thoughtfully. 'A small castle'd be about right. After all, I'm all alone . . .'

He sighed. Uli met his eye and smiled sympathetically. Then Oz pretended to snap out of his poor little rich boy's musings. Suddenly he was all manly resolution.

'Where do *you* live, Uli?'

She looked down at her glass. 'Please ... I would rather not talk about me.'

'Here, you're not married, are you?' Oz asked sharply.

'Divorced.' Uli's voice was quiet, dignified.

'Oh,' said Oz. 'Dennis is getting divorced, y'know ... ah ... he should have been here now instead of me – that's my brother Dennis, that is. Should've come to Germany instead of me. But for his divorce. Payin' a fortune in alimony he is, poor sod.' He slowed down a bit, looked at her searchingly. 'Are you – all right by money?'

Uli smiled gratefully, erroneously believing that Oz was being thoughtful on her account. Oh yes, thank you. I have money of my own. And I have a job as a beauty consultant.'

Oz was impressed. 'Canny, that. You've certainly got first-hand experience of beauty. I bet you're good at it.'

Uli's smile turned slightly sad. 'And I have a boyfriend who is jealous.'

A pause. 'Big lad, is he?' he asked, trying to appear casual.

'Not as big as you, in the sense of importance. I wanted to leave him since a long time. But he is very vigilant.'

Oz glanced around briefly. There were only serious drinkers and couples in the bar. And a pianist in the corner, tinkling out slushy standards. No boy friend, by the looks.

'Oh, well,' he said, turning back to Uli, 'I can be very vigilant meself. When the need arises, like.'

He hadn't noticed Neville come in the door, though. The lad was heading straight through the bar in his jeans and casual jacket, causing one or two raised eyebrows. Oz was staring manfully at Uli, emphasising his vigilance, when Neville arrived at his shoulder.

'Hey, Oz –'

Oz whipped round with an expression of intense panic, as if someone from the Gateshead rates office had just walked in. His mouth moved soundlessly and jerkily, like a puppet's.

Neville, meanwhile, was gazing at Uli in obvious admiration.

'Excuse me, pet,' he said, obviously deciding to be polite. 'I just want to have a quick word with the chief here.'

Uli looked at Oz for confirmation. 'This is one of your men?'

'One of the lads, right,' said Oz, nodding furiously and with an imploring look at Neville.

'Ah. So you're in Oz's company?' Uli said to Neville.

'Aye – day and night!' Then Neville turned to Oz and spoke urgently: 'What about it, Oz? You promised. The money ...'

Oz looked at him, then at Uli. He realised that there was only one way out of this.

'How much would you like, son?' he burbled. 'Fifty do you?' Oz quickly reached into his pocket, searched through his winnings and picked out a fifty-mark note, which he handed to Neville with the kind of grandiose lack of respect that he fancied rich bastards favoured. 'There you are, bonny lad! Any time!'

Neville didn't know whether to be astonished or crease up. In the end he settled for mild sarcasm. 'Thanks, Oz. You're a gentleman.'

Oz could feel Uli's admiring gaze on him. Everything was coming up roses tonight. He could do no wrong.

'Aye, I know,' he said with a complacent smile. 'But there's no need to tell everyone!'

Well, that was the old Oz. But Neville was intrigued to see a new one as well. Something bizarre, unthinkable, and almost frightening was happening here. It told in Oz's gestures, the way he looked at the world, in his voice and the words he used. No. It couldn't be. Not so soon. But the conclusion was inescapable.

Oz, Neville realised in wonderment, was falling in love ...

It only took a day or two before the lads began to notice how Oz had changed. He had taken to admiring German craftmanship – even their ruddy bricks – and had actually been seen to exchange a civil word with Ulrich, the chargehand. He went out on the Sunday on a picnic with Uli, was out a couple more nights. The signs were all there. And it came out in the open a few days later still.

Barry and Dennis were sweeping up the junk that was scattered around the floor of the hut. Neville was going through one of his German tapes. He'd got the bit between his teeth now. Never mind the threat of some law: he knew foreign languages were always useful. Bomber was sitting sewing a button on one of Wayne's shirts. Expertly.

'Where did you learn to do that, Bomb?' asked Wayne.

The big man chuckled, not in the slightest embarrassed. 'I've picked up a lot o' tricks in my time!' And he winked, bit off the thread and handed the mended shirt over to Wayne.

'Thanks, Bomb. You're a mate.'

Enter Oz, back from an early evening assignation. They had got used to that these days since he'd met Uli. So why the stares, the intakes of breath, the low whistles, as Oz strode in?

Well, it was the pullover. Brilliant wool, picture of a yacht covering Oz's chest and a bit of his gut as well. Anything more unlike Oz's previous sartorial style – if that was the description – would have been hard to imagine.

'Cor, bugger!' gasped Bomber.

Barry and Dennis paused in their cleaning work.

'Ah – that's a canny woolly, man,' said Dennis.

Barry grinned. 'We can hang it on the wall when he's not wearin' it.'

'Can you hell!' Oz said huffily. 'This is for best, man.'

Wayne coughed delicately. 'Might we ask where you got it, Oz?'

Oz looked pleased with himself. The triumph was all the sweeter because he knew Wayne had got virtually nowhere with Uli's friend Heidi. 'Gave me a prezzie, didn't she?'

Neville nodded. 'She must think a lot of you.'

The comment was made in a tone of mild disbelief, but Oz took the complimentary part of it for granted.

'Aye,' he said. 'You know what, Nev? They can't tell accents here. I could be talking with the same as the Queen Mother for all she knows.'

Wayne chuckled cynically, winked at the others. ''Course, it's not his money she's after.'

'Oh, no. She does, she loves me for meself,' said Oz airily. 'We might even get married.'

There was a sudden, uneasy silence. The lads looked at each other with wary expressions, as if to say: which universe is this bloke in?

Dennis was the first to say the inevitable.

'Oz,' he began gently, 'what are you talking about? You *are* married, you prannet!'

He had no effect on Oz, not a jot. The big, battered softie just stood there and said: 'Dennis, that's in the U.K. This is abroad. It doesn't count here.'

And it got worse. The next week, they were finishing their tea break, when Ulrich came in sight, heading their way. The normally truculent Oz got quickly to his feet, gulping down the remains of his tea.

'Come on, lads. That's enough lazing around,' he said.

Dennis and Bomber looked at him in astonishment. Dennis was smiling vaguely, until he realised Oz was serious.

'Them German fellows over there have started already,' Oz explained.

Bomber continued to drink his tea. 'So bloomin' what?'

'We can learn a thing or two from the Germans, you know,' said Oz. He turned, saw Ulrich had reached them. '*Guten Tag, Herr Ulrich. Wie geht es?*' he said.

If Dennis and Bomber were surprised by Oz's fluency, Ulrich seemed flabbergasted. He was struck dumb for a moment, then fired back some German.

Oz had to admit defeat early on, but he stayed amiable. 'Aye, well, Herr Ulrich, I haven't got that far with my lessons yet.'

Ulrich smiled and nodded. 'Yes, but you are trying, Osbourne. This is good. And also you are starting back to work quickly.' The chargehand stared meaningfully at the other two. 'In Germany, just because we are allowed a break, we do not always take it, you know.'

With that, he was off.

'That's bloody great!' said Dennis. 'We're on a legitimate

break, and you make it look like skiving.'

Bomber's forehead creased in a rare display of irritation. 'Yus, What's all this creepin' around the Germans, then? One extreme to the other . . .'

'Uli's made me see them in a different light,' Oz said simply. 'They're a fine people.' he gazed across at the Turkish labourers clustered by a brazier across the way. 'Not like that lot over there.'

'Come on. The Abduls are all right, man.'

'Well, they account for half the crime in German cities,' Oz retorted, obviously repeating what he had been told elsewhere. He was sounding more like a parrot with every passing day.

'Cobblers!'

Oz was unaffected by Bomber's vehement disagreement. 'You look around. The only dirty bits in this town are the bits where the Abduls live. Proves somethin'.'

'Proves nothing! That's not *their* fault,' said Dennis. 'Any more than it's our fault we live in a flamin' shed!'

'I've seen it, man, and you haven't.'

'But it's always been the Germans you've been having a go at till now!'

'Aye, well, I was wrong. But I'm big enough to admit me mistakes,' Oz told Dennis.

Bomber chucked away the dregs of his tea, stood up and stretched. It really was time to get back to work.

'Oz,' Bomber said, reaching for his trowel, 'you may be big enough, but you don't have the time for that. To admit all your mistakes you'd have to live to be a hundred and fifty!'

And the bizarre spectacle of Oz in Love continued. There really did seem no end to it. He mooned over the glossy colour photo of Uli that he kept by his bed; he was out most nights; he had really begun smartening up; he spent hours boring the lads with praise of the Federal Republic of Germany, its people and all its works; he was even picking up a smattering of the language. In short, he was undergoing a complete transformation.

So was the hut. Or at least that was the plan. There came

190

an early evening when they were all gathered in the Club – Oz excepted – to discuss smartening their barrack up. Talk was of nicking paint from the site stores and giving the place a lick, though no one seemed able to enforce any sort of agreement about which colour they were going to use. Bomber was the first to decide he'd had enough.

'Well,' he announced with a glance at his watch, 'I'm goin' to cut my losses while the night's got something left to give. Bomber's goin' to get his weary muscles relaxed with a good massage.'

Ironic mutterings all round. Everyone knew what Bomber meant by that. The big man from Someset had very straighforward sexual needs and preferences, and he didn't mind who knew it.

Dennis shook his head in gentle exasperation. 'I'm surprised you're not fed up with that massage parlour.'

'Oh, I don't just go to *one*, Dennis,' retorted Bomber. 'I circulate meself. One of the German lads is taking me over to Essen tonight. He reckons that's where the best places are.'

Just then, Oz strode in and ordered a beer. He joined the main group, mildly disdainful at the talk of bought sex. *He* didn't have to pay for it, was his unspoken message.

"Ullo,' said Wayne. 'We thought you'd be out with Uli, giving her some tips on how to behave with the British upper classes!'

Oz ignored the mockery. 'She's gone to see her mother. Sees her regular as clockwork, being a good daughter. I'm not seein' her until tomorrow.'

Wayne wasn't about to give up the chance to wield his sharp tongue, particularly as his own failure with the equally luscious Heidi still rankled a bit.

'I can see it now,' he pressed on. '"Mother, I have met this rich British aristocrat who is pretendin' to be a poor slob of a briekie!" Cor, and is he ever convincing!'

'You're just jealous,' said Oz philosophically. 'It's no more than I expected.'

Bomber was getting a bit impatient. He had fixed up to give Wayne a lift somewhere just off the Essen road, and their chauffeur would be waiting. The cockney acknowledged they had to go and made for the door.

'I'm not jealous of the rollicking you're goin' to get when she rumbles you, squire,' he said to Oz as his parting shot.

Dennis told Bomber he'd be in the Club later if he wanted to drop by on his way back.

'I'll give you a first-hand account,' said Bomber with a wink. He guffawed. 'Oh, "first-hand" – it's going to be one of me witty evenings.'

When Bomber and Wayne had gone, Oz tuned into the discussion about the paint.

'I don't know why you bother,' he said. 'From what Den's saying, you'll be back in England before you make up your minds.'

'No. We chose yellow. It'll be done as soon as we got a rota agreed.'

'Oz nodded indifferently. 'Well, doesn't bother me. I doubt I'll be here to see it.'

'Why's that, Oz? Your rich dad fetching you home to be Managing Director?'

'No, man.' A dramatic pause. 'Me and Uli have been makin' some plans. She's got a few bob of her own, and we might be going into business together.'

Dennis blanched. 'What: your brains and her money? This is all Wayne's fault. He's actually got the poor woman thinking you could run a business now!'

'Is this before or after you get married, Oz?' asked Barry sceptically.

Oz still didn't give an inch. 'You think I'm kidding, don't you?' he said, then reached into his pocket and fished out a jeweller's box. 'Well, have a look at this.'

They craned over as he opened the box to reveal a wedding ring.

'Blimey! You lashed out there, Oz.'

Oz looked puzzled.

'Lashed out, nothing,' he said. 'This is what she bought for me!'

But Oz didn't stay long. He needed his beauty sleep, he said. Uli kept him busy. The others drifted back and forth between the hut and the Club during the course of the evening. Just before midnight, Dennis, Barry and Neville were having a final nightcap when Bomber walked in, as he had promised he would on his return from the massage parlour.

'Bomber!' said Dennis. 'How was the new place?'

The big man smiled mysteriously, rocked on his heels. 'Quite an experience.'

Neville raised an eyebrow. 'Yeah? What were the girls like?' He'd never do that kind of thing himself, but it was a bit titillating, wasn't it?

'Oh. The most interesting one is the one who runs the place.' A deep breath.

'Tell us, man!' hissed Dennis impatiently.

Bomber shrugged 'I recognised her from the picture by Oz's bed. It's Uli.'

That took a while and some refills to absorb. Bed was forgotten.

'You sure it was her, Bomber?' Dennis asked again.

They were on their third beer following Bomber's revelation. After all, it left them all with a pretty big responsibility. Should they tell, or not?

Bomber nodded. 'Knew her from the photograph straight away. And I did a bit of research afterwards to make sure. Her boyfriend is the bloke who owns the shop. Turkish fellow, nasty piece of work!'

'So Oz was mistaken,' Barry said gavely. 'She's not a beauty consultant.'

'I don't think there's any mistake about it. At least from her side, it was deliberate.'

'Right,' said Dennis. 'She'll be thinking that the gent who own this big building firm would give her the push if he knew she worked in the red light district.'

Neville frowned. 'You can't blame the lass for trying to get herself out of that environment. But it seems a bit rough on Oz.'

'I'd call it poetic justice meself,' said Barry with a venom that he had obviously been storing up for some time.

'Then are you goin' to tell him?'

'No. I'd be more inclined to tell her.'

Dennis shook his head. 'I don't reckon we should interfere either way. Let nature take its course,' he said, to general approval.

'It's a sobering thought ...'

But Bomber cut into Barry's attempt at philosophy before the boy from Brum could get started.

'Bomber's not here for sobering thoughts,' he boomed. 'I want the other kind. Whose shout is it before this place closes?'

The painting project was half-complete when Dennis woke up in the middle of the night some days later. Maybe it was the smell of the freshly purloined and applied paint, and maybe it was the fact that his conscience had been troubling him over the matter of Oz and Uli, but he felt instantly awake and tense. He could have sworn he heard a noise.

The suspicion of a sound made him look more closely across the way. His eyes, gradually accustoming themselves to the darkness, scanned the hut, ending up over by the cage where they kept their tools. Nothing moving. Not a sound. Not even Oz's snore ...

No Oz.

Dennis sat up, checked. Definitely no one in Oz's bed. And what is more, a distinct lack of the clothes and stuff usually scattered around it. Dennis slid out of bed, shuffled across.

There was a note on the bedside locker, and predictably it was addressed to him. He opened it and read quickly by torchlight.

Dear Dennis ... it began. *Just a line to say I am off. With Uli* ...

Bloody hell, thought Dennis. I should've told him. But he read on, fascinated in a hideous sort of way.

Well, that's the way it goes. Some of us have got it and some of us have not ... Oz's childish, spidery scrawl continued. *She loves me and I love her in a very adult way that some may find it very difficult to understand. We will find each other in another time, another place. Do us a favour and drop a line to Margery to tell her my stay has been extended*

... Dennis cursed silently. Clearing up other people's mess as usual . . . *I will come and take you out for a drink somewhere flash as soon as I have got it all sorted. Oz.*

Yeah, thought Dennis. Thanks a lot. I look forward to that. He switched off the torch, briefly considered going after him, because he guessed the noise he heard was Oz leaving the hut. Well, sod Oz. Pretty soon he and Uli would realise that neither was who they pretended to be, and then the solids would hit the air conditioning. Then would be soon enough to get involved – if absolutely necessary.

Dennis lay back in bed, tried to replace thoughts of Oz and Uli with some of himself and Dagmar. Were he and she any different? Was he doing any more than looking for a girl on the rebound from Vera, and was Dagmar after more than a sensible, mature man who would help her heal her wounds? Still, at least there were no lies on either side, no unfinished business that could rebound on them later. Dennis and Dagmar liked each other, and they fancied each other too. What more could a man want in a relationship with a woman? Why didn't he just stay in Germany and enjoy himself, even if they changed the law so that the money wasn't so good? Well, there were two good reasons five hundred miles away across the North Sea, and their names were Kevin and Angela ...

Fatherly guilt was still struggling with sexual longing when Dennis suddenly heard a shriek from the far side of the site. He sat up. The sound was instantly identifiable as belonging to a man in fear and panic. It was quickly followed by more shouts in English and a language that Dennis didn't understand but reckoned to be Turkish. And they were getting close. Whoever the two combatants were, they were running round the site and heading for the residential huts.

Dennis stumbled out of bed and over to the window. The lights were already going on in the Turkish hut, the 'Casbah'. And others in the British hut were coming to as well. There were sleepy mutterings from Bomber and Barry. Neville was getting quite stroppy in his corner.

Then Dennis saw an unmistakable figure come haring round the corner in the moonlight. It was Oz, running for

195

his life. God, you'd never have thought he was that fit. And hard on his heels was a swarthy bloke with a heavy Turkish moustache, though he wasn't one of the Turks from the site. Something was glinting in his hand, and it looked like a knife.

Dennis was about to head for the door of the hut when he saw that some of the Turkish lads from the Casbah had come outside. As he watched, several Turks managed to get between their knife-wielding compatriot and Oz. After some initial protests, the man settled down to having a furious row in Turkish with them. Oz took one look at what was happening, then bolted for the British hut. He came crashing through the door seconds later, wide-eyed with fear.

'Christ! A bloody madman's after me!'

He rushed to the window, followed by several of the now wide-awake lads, barking an order for all lights to be extinguished.

They watched, Oz still breathing heavily, shaking all over, as Chem, the elder statesman of the Turkish labourers, argued loudly with the knife man. After a while, the bad feeling seemed to subside, though. Chem and the outsider suddenly laughed and touched hands in a sort of raffish handshake.

'He's got them on his side!' Oz moaned. 'He'll be bringin' the whole lot with him! Barricade the ruddy door!'

But Dennis put a restraining hand on his arm and indicated the real situation. The group of Turks was starting to break up amid much backslapping and hilarity. The homicidal one was laughing most of all, shaking his head while Chem escorted him away from the huts.

Even when he disappeared from sight, Oz continued to stare out of the window.

'I was goin' to meet a friend,' he said. 'That bloke had a bloody great knife in his hand. He was goin' to kill me.'

Bomber nodded thoughtfully. 'Them Abduls just about saved your life, then, didn't they?'

'What do you mean?' said Oz, turning away from the window at last. 'He's one of them!'

Neville started grumbling about the time – it was half

196

past two – and ostentatiously adjusting his pillows for sleep. Meanwhile, the argument continued.

'I think you owe the Turks a bit of an apology, after the way you've been running them down,' said Dennis.

Wayne agreed. 'Fair do's, Oz. You ought to go round there in the morning and say thanks.'

'Oh aye,' Oz snapped. 'Take 'em a card and a bunch of flowers, too, I suppose. Listen, one Abdul tries to kill me, and another Abdul stops him. Makes it even Stephen, doesn't it?' He looked around for justification. 'Back to where we started.'

Everyone was crawling back to bed in disgust. The lights started going out. Very soon, Dennis and Oz were left alone in the centre of the room. Beckoning to Oz, Dennis went over to his locker and retrieved the note that he had found a few minutes before.

'You've had a lucky escape,' he said quietly to Oz, who flushed with guilt. 'I reckon she has, too ... though if that bloke out there was her boyfriend – she did say he was jealous, didn't she? – then maybe I'm not so sure about that.'

'Betrayal,' said Oz, though he was obviously relieved. 'Nothin' but ruddy betrayal.'

Oz said very little next morning. He toddled into work, kept himself to himself. The same, though, couldn't be said for the Turks. More than once, when Oz appeared on the scaffolding in view of the labourers working below, men would call out in Turkish and laugh. It was unusual, because the Abduls normally grafted away and stayed quiet. Finally, by mid-morning, it had become too obvious to ignore.

'There!' said Barry, looking down at the Turks. 'They're at it again.'

He was right. A gaggle of three or four had gathered. One of them was pointing at Oz, and the others were splitting their sides. Maybe Oz had too much else to think about, because he didn't seem to notice. But everyone else on the Brit side did.

'Aye,' agreed Dennis. 'It's a big joke every time they see him.'

Bomber nodded, waved to catch the Turks' attention, pointed to Oz. 'Hey – what's so funny?' he called out.

Chem, last night's spokesman, was among the group. He was a little better educated than the rest and spoke rudimentary English as well as German. In response to Bomber's beckoning, he walked over to where the Brits were working. He wore a broad grin.

'Why you laugh at Oz?' asked Bomber in measured, slow tones.

Chem chuckled. 'This man, he saying: "Him taking my woman, I cutting him!"'

Meanwhile, Oz had noticed the disturbance and had arrived on the scene. 'What's goin' on?' he asked.

The Turks burst out laughing again.

'And so what did you lads say to this feller, then?' asked Dennis.

'I saying: "No cutting him. Is our friend. Working together",' he said shyly, pointing to Oz. 'But he say, "No. He taking my woman, I cutting him." Very mad.'

'You can say that again,' Oz interrupted. 'Off his bloody rocker.'

'Shut up, Oz,' snapped Dennis, then turned back to Chem. 'So how did you change his mind?' he asked politely.

Chem looked cunning. 'I say quick: "He not taking your woman. We knowing this man. He not taking *any* woman. He have nothing with women."'

It took a moment for Oz to comprehend. 'What?' he said with dawning anger.

'We saying: "He nothing for woman, this man!"'

'Nothing for woman! Me?' Oz was furious.

Barry nodded appreciatively. 'Very ingenious.'

Chem acknowledged his approval. 'So he laugh and go away.'

'It's a bloody lie!' Oz protested.

Dennis grinned. 'Useful, though. Saved your life.'

But Oz was only interested in the aspersions that had been cast on his manhood.

'And I can prove it!' he was saying.

Bomber chortled. 'Not here, I hope.'

'Well,' said Wayne to Chem, 'on behalf of our colleague here – who is by no means a gentleman – we would like to thank you.'

They exchanged introductions and handshakes all round. Then the approach of Ulrich – always attracted by a break in the site's work rhythms – brought the encounter to an end. Oz, though, continued to complain.

'I'm not staying here being a laugh-stock for them Abduls,' he growled.

Barry decided to stir. 'Can't help wondering, though, if there isn't some factual basis for their story.'

'Well, there bloody well isn't!' Oz bellowed. 'Hundred percent man, that's me. Renowned for it!'

'So you keep saying,' chipped in Wayne slyly.

Oz rounded on him: 'Aye. I'm not all talk and no action, like some.' There was an awkward silence. Everyone, including Oz, now knew the truth about Uli's real profession, and the news had hit him hard. There was self-pity in his voice. 'I've had a bad deal from everyone over this,' he continued. 'First Wayne gets me into it. Then *she* lies to me –'

'She warned you she had a jealous boyfriend,' said Dennis. 'Though admittedly she never told you he owned the place where she worked, or what she did for a living . . .'

'Aye, and she never told me he was a bloody maniac!' said Oz. Then he seemed to become thoughtful. 'Still, I've got to own up. It was me own fault, really.'

Bomber looked at Dennis in wondering disbelief. 'I never thought I'd hear him say that!'

'I think maybe this had taught him something,' Dennis agreed.

Oz nodded slowly. 'Aye, it has,' he said harshly. 'It's taught me I should never have trusted a German – just because it happened to be a woman!'

ELEVEN

Dennis plodded over to the Admin Hut with a heavy heart. He'd thought he had it all settled, and then Fate had stuck its oar in again. For God's sake, he was due to spend a second weekend with Dagmar. How was he going to give her the bad news? It was all right for buggers like Oz; they just lied ...

'Hello,' said Dagmar, looking up from her filing when he entered the hut.

'Hi,' said Dennis, trying to look casual.

Luckily, Ulrich was out with Grunwald somewhere. Even Christa, the gorgeous little blonde who had just started work as Dagmar's assistant, was out. It was the right moment – and he was going to have to waste it saying the wrong thing.

Dagmar looked at him quizzically. 'Why such a serious face?'

'Me?' Dennis shrugged. 'No, I'm okay ... well, actually I'm not. It's about the weekend.'

'Oh yes,' Dagmar said gaily. 'It is all right with my mother. The neighbour will look after her, and ...'

Her voice trailed off. She bit her lip nervously, realising that Dennis had bad news and sensing what it was about.

'Or is there not to be a weekend?' she asked.

Dennis sighed. 'No. There *will* be a weekend. I mean, I want that very much. It's not ... just not this one.'

'No?'

'It's Vera,' Dennis said softly. 'My wife. She's coming over Saturday.'

'I see.'

He sighed in exasperation. 'No, you don't. This wasn't my idea. It was hers. There's a few things to straighten out. Formalities, like. I'm sorry.'

'I understand. Perhaps another time.'

Her voice was flat and toneless. The things it implied made Dennis angry.

'Well, so far as I'm concerned there's no "perhaps" about it!' he said aggressively.

'You tell me,' Dagmar answered, still sulking.

'I *am* telling you. Next week for sure. Or the weekend after!'

'But that is when the new regulations come into operation. You and your friends will be leaving Germany.'

'They may be. Not necessarily me.'

Dagmar pouted. 'Oh. But that is your personal business.'

'Look, don't act like this, will you not!' he snapped, lapsing into broad Geordie.

'I am not acting like anything.' In fact, she looked as though she was about to cry.

'You are,' said Dennis gently but firmly. 'You're behaving like you're ... like you're offended. It wasn't my idea, you know. It was hers. I don't know what the problem is, but I owe it to her to find out.'

A slight sign of give. 'I am sorry. Of course you must see her.'

He nodded. 'I want you to as well.'

'Me? You want me to meet her?'

'Yes.'

'Why?'

'You know *she* exists,' Dennis explained. 'I want her to know that you do.'

'Is this such a good idea?'

Dennis leaned forward and put his hands on the desk. He looked her straight in the eye. 'Look, I'm sick of keeping part of my life – an important part – under wraps. Tired of trying to hide it. With the lads, I had good reason. But I seen no good reason for keeping it from Vera – or anyone else for that matter.'

She opened her mouth to say something.

'Including your mother!' he said for good measure.

Dagmar laughed. It was an abrupt change of mood. 'Even her!'

'Aye well, I mean it, Dagmar.'

She smiled ruefully. 'Okay. I will meet your Vera.'

'Champion.' The hooter for the end of the lunch break sounded. 'Must rush. See you before then.'

'Okay . . .'

Dennis made his way back to where he was working, looking considerably more cheerful. At least he had managed to head off the immediate crisis. Vera's letter and the phone call that had followed had thrown him, he didn't mind admitting now.

'You seem more cheerful than a while ago, Den,' commented Bomber. 'Your old lady still making the trip, is she?'

Dennis nodded. 'Aye. She'll be here tomorrow afternoon.'

'Put her up in a hotel, will you?'

'Well, I can hardly put her up in the hut, Bomb.'

The Somerset man grinned and stroked his beard. 'I don't know,' he said slowly. 'Sometimes think our wives should stay in the hut. They should all come over here on a charter. Be an eye-opener for 'em to see how we really live. They might realise what a sacrifice we're making.'

'That's true enough,' Dennis agreed. 'Especially if they saw King Rat.'

'Roight.'

They both laughed. What else could you do? Rats had been discovered in the hut – big ones, too – and at the moment the place was festooned with poisonous baits and traps. A right little home from home. Anyone who had been thinking of staying on after the new regulations were introduced was being given a clear indication of the price they would have to pay.

Meanwhile, Neville, who had been hanging around in the background, moved in as Bomber busied himelf collecting Darbo.

'Had a letter from Brenda today,' he told Dennis,

checking that no one was listening.

Dennis grinned to himself. 'I'd be surprised if you hadn't. What's new?'

Neville pressed on regardless. 'Said she'd been round to Vera's. Said she ...'

'Said she'd what?'

'Said she, well ... couldn't really work out why Vera was so set on coming out here,' Neville said shyly.

'Aye. I'll know tomorrow, won't I?'

The lad nodded, obviously uncomfortable. 'Could be a bit tricky, eh?'

'How?'

'Well, you know –'

'No, I don't,' Dennis stonewalled.

Neville looked desperate. 'I'm a man of the world,' he said, looking about twelve and a half. '... I mean you and Dagmar. It could just be ... a bit tricky.'

Dennis shrugged. 'Not really. She'll be meeting Dagmar when she's here.'

'She will?' echoed Neville thinly, obviously astonished.

'Why not? It's not as if I'm cheatin', is it? Dagmar's not my bit on the side. Vera's got Alan.'

'Yes, but ...'

'No buts about it, bonny lad. That's the way things are, right? And the sooner everyone knows that's the way they are, the better.'

'Oh, yes. Right. I couldn't agree more,' sighed Neville, who couldn't agree less. Not after what Brenda had said about Vera's real reason for coming out to Düsseldorf.

It was later that afternoon that another miracle happened on site. Dennis, a man who had recently had no women in his life, now had two. And another of the Brits, who had always had so many, was drastically narrowing down the field. He didn't yet know it, of course. He just thought he was having a routine go at the new blonde in Admin, but in reality Wayne was about to meet his match. Yes, yer actual Wayne ...

At close to knocking-off time for the office staff, Wayne swaggered into the Admin Hut. He was carrying a bouquet of flowers and his Playboy simpering grin. Both Dagmar and Christa looked up. Wayne ignored Dagmar and glided over to where the younger, blonde girl was working. He stopped dramatically.

'I'd like you to have these,' he said.

Christa had been typing. As he finished speaking, she looked up and Wayne found himself looking into a pair of the most devastating china-blue eyes he had ever encountered. Christa smiled uncertainly, revealing fine, dazzling white teeth. Dear Heaven, she didn't know what she'd got ...

'For me?' she said in her slow, drawling, incomparably sexy English.

Wayne could only nod like a dummy. All the chat he usually had ready had disappeared like the mist with the dawn. He had always laughed at blokes who admitted to romantic thoughts, let alone actions. Now, after catching his first direct sight of those eyes, Wayne knew he would never laugh again. He couldn't take his gaze away from her.

'Yes. These are for you. From me,' he said stupidly. 'Me.'

Confused, Christa looked away at Dagmar, who was just finishing a phone conversation. The older woman saw Christa's plight.

'Wayne?' Dagmar asked with a smile. 'Why are you behaving so strangely? Who do those flowers belong to?'

Wayne didn't even turn round. He carried on staring at the blonde vision in front of him. 'To her,' he murmured. 'As does my heart ...'

So it happened. Wayne beat a retreat, headed back to work. But he returned to the area of the Admin Hut at the end of the afternoon. He stood forlorn and dreamy. Inquisitive and sarcastic remarks from homegoing workmates passed over him. Wayne lurked, casting frequent glances at the entrance to the hut where Christa and Dagmar worked. He was a new man, and he didn't know how to handle it.

Barry and Moxey had just passed on their way to the hut. He had turned down an invitation to go on to the Club, got some strange looks. He didn't care. All he cared about was the moment when *she* appeared through the door, and it happened shortly after.

'Oh, hello. I was just passing,' he panted, dashing forward as Christa moved towards her car, still carrying the bouquet he had brought her earlier in the afternoon.

She stopped, looked at him with a surprising directness. No dumb blonde, this one. 'Why do you buy me these?'

'We ... why did I buy you those,' Wayne repeated dully, totally taken aback. He grinned foolishly. 'I just felt like it, didn't I? Impulse.'

'But they are lovely.'

His mouth fell open. There was no side to this girl at all. When she had something to say she just said it.

'No more than you deserve, is it?' he mumbled.

She smiled, carried on walking towards her small saloon car, which was waiting in the staff car park.

'I'm Wayne, by the way,' he told her, walking quickly to keep up with her.

'I know.' She reached her car, bent down gracefully to unlock the door. She placed the flowers carefully on the passenger seat, turned back to him. 'Thank you, Wayne,' she said huskily.

'My pleasure ... Christa.'

She smiled again, then indicated the bleak group of huts where he and the other less fortunate members of the workforce lived. 'You English, you all live there?' she asked.

Wayne reddened, desperately embarrassed. 'What? Oh, yeah. There. We call it the Stalag.'

'Please?'

'Stalag,' he said nervously. 'Like a prisoner of war camp. You know.'

She said something in German, laughed and nodded. She understood. He joined in, though uncertain why.

'Is it nice?' she asked.

'Nice?' Well, it ain't the Hilton. But it's okay.' He grinned, regaining a little bit of his cocksureness. 'Just one of the hardships we have to endure to stay in your wonderful country.'

She nodded gravely, then closed the door of her car firmly.

'Show me,' she said.

'Show me – I mean, you?' gasped Wayne, astonished at this fabulous creature's clarity of thought and intention. He found it terrifying and adorable at the same time.

'Yes. Show me.'

Wayne stalled frantically. 'It's pretty basic, luv,' he explained. 'I mean there's socks and crisps all over. I don't really think ...'

But she was already heading towards the Stalag, with him following like a slave. Neither of them saw Oz, Barry and Moxey thirty yards or so away, but the Club-bound trio saw them. They stopped, stared in evious disbelief until the girl and Wayne disappeared into the hut. In the hut? With Wayne? A gorgeous female like that? Couldn't be ...

What happened a very short while later was very quick, very confused and at the end distinctly filthy. When they heard Christa scream, the trio dashed towards the hut and careened in, certain that Wayne had comitted some unspeakable act of assault. Oz, in full cry, grabbed the Londoner and hurled him bodily out of the hut and straight into a very muddy patch just outside the step. Barry and Moxey, who got there a moment later, dashed into the hut to find him comforting Christa.

'It's all right, pet,' he told the weeping girl. 'I've sorted out that cockney craphat.'

Christa continued to sob.

Barry leaned over her. 'What happened?' he asked. 'Did Wayne try to ravish you, miss?'

Christa looked up, shook her head. 'Wayne? *Nein!*' She got unsteadily to her feet, pointed at a locker. 'I look in there. I see a RAT!'

And right on cue, Wayne appeared in the doorway, dripping mud. 'And it *wasn't* me!'

The cab swung out of the terminal forecourt and started the several miles' journey towards the centre of Düsseldorf. For a little while, Dennis and Vera sat in silence in the back seat. Then he broke the ice.

'The bairns okay?'

Vera nodded, smiled. 'Smashing. Spoke to them before I

207

left and they were having the time of their lives. They're going over to Holy Island today.'

'Have they got school on Monday?'

'Yes,' Vera said, then glanced sidelong at Dennis. She'd done herself up nicely. In fact, she'd taken a lot of trouble, and she looked tastier than she had done for a good number of years. 'But Helen's going to bring them back and stay over. So she'll get them off if I don't get back.'

Dennis had been musing on the fact that his – soon to be former – wife was still a good-looking woman, when she bothered. Then the implications of her words sank in.

'How do you mean – if you don't get back?'

'Well, I thought I might stay Sunday night as well. I don't go abroad very often.' Vera laughed gaily, then noticed the serious look on Dennis's face. 'Unless ... unless it's inconvenient.'

'No, no. Whatever,' Dennis said hastily.

Vera touched his arm. 'You don't seem very keen.'

'Aye. Well, you've never had a Sunday night in Düsseldorf!' he said, trying to make light of it.

Vera seemed to accept that. She looked out of the car at the passing scenery and buildings. 'Will we pass near where you work?'

'Why, there's nothing for you to see there!'

'I was just interested. To see where you live. You know . . .'

Dennis laughed bitterly. 'Wayne Norris, a lad from the site, he showed a young lady where we live. I think she's in intensive care still.'

'Is it that awful?'

'Poor lass saw a rat.'

He felt Vera shudder. 'A rat?' she murmured. 'How revolting! I never thought you lived in conditions that bad.'

'We don't really. The rat just showed up last week, captivated by some chocolate cake of Brenda's.'

'Oh,' said Vera, glad to change the subject. 'She said she was going to send some things out for Neville. Will I see him?'

'Aye, why not?' said Dennis easily. 'Could ask him to have dinner with us tonight.'

'No,' said Vera with a coy smile. 'I'd rather we just had dinner by ourselves.'

An awkward silence followed. Dennis stared at the floor. Then he cleared his throat. 'Well, there's a problem there. I've asked someone else, like.'

'Who?' She was trying to stay calm and friendly, but there was a clear catch in her voice.

'A friend,' said Dennis. 'Someone I think . . . you ought to meet.'

Vera obviously didn't much like the sound of that, but they didn't discuss the subject again before they got to the hotel, a small but comfortable establishment on the edge of the Old Town. Once he had seen Vera installed, Dennis discreetly withdrew to the separate room he had booked along the corridor from hers and changed. He appeared in the bar in suit and tie. Dagmar was there, as arranged, and she looked composed but a little apprehensive as she sipped an aperitif.

'Hi,' said Dennis. 'You're prompt, pet.'

'Hello. I am German.'

'So you are.'

Dennis caught the attention of the girl behind the bar. 'You want a refill?' he asked Dagmar.

She nodded firmly. 'No, no.'

Dennis shrugged. 'Zwei gin and tonic, bitte.'

They sat in silence for a short while.

'So, how is . . . Vera?' Dagmar asked.

'Okay. She'll be down in a sec.'

'And did you sort out your problems?'

'No problems, really,' Dennis said. 'Just the usual things – money and kids. And we've had a quick look at the Old Town.'

Dagmar nodded gravely. 'So. When you go back to England, where will you live?'

'*If* I go back.'

'Okay, if you go back.'

Dennis thought for a moment, sighed. 'Haven't thought about it,' he admitted. 'Been living day to day lately. I suppose I'll stay at my mother's at first.' He grinned wryly. 'That'll be something. I'll have to remember to take me shoes off when I come in, empty the ashtrays and not rumple the cushions.'

Dagmar giggled, almost despite herself. 'She sounds like *my* mother!'

'Aye. Me mum's so fastidious, she puts a litter tray under the cuckoo clock.'

They both laughed as the girl brought the gin and tonics. Dennis was using the humour quite deliberately to cover up the tension, and they both knew it. He took a hearty gulp of his gin.

'You are now nervous about this evening, yes?' Dagmar said gently.

'I am all of a sudden.'

She reached over and put her hand in his to reassure him. 'It will be okay.'

And that was how Vera first saw them. She had just come into the bar, wearing a smart little outfit and made up with just the right combination of elegance and mature sexuality. Dressed to stun, in fact, rather than to kill. Dennis saw her and automatically removed his hand from Dagmar's gentle grasp. Guilt habits died hard.

'Oh, over here, pet,' he said, trying to appear casual without much success. He ushered her to a stool. 'Vera,' he introduced her, 'this is Dagmar.'

'Hello, Vera,' Dagmar said quickly. 'It is nice to meet you.'

'Nice to meet you, too.'

Both their smiles were more than a little glassy. Dennis hastily handed Vera her gin and tonic. 'Got you one in,' he told her. 'Cheers!'

'Thanks. Cheers.'

More silence to fill. Dagmar was the first to take the plunge.

'Dennis tells me you have already seen something of the city,' she said.

Vera nodded stiffly. 'Yes. It's much nicer than I expected.'

'I didn't show her where we work,' offered Dennis.

'No,' Dagmar said. 'That is not so nice.'

'Bomber reckons all the wives should come out and see

210

it. Make them realise what a miserable existence we lead ...' Dennis answered, eagerly warming to his theme.

Vera, though, just looked around at the surroundings in the bar, then at Dagmar, then at Dennis. This conversation, she decided, was a conspiracy between the pair of them to show her what a tough time Dennis had. Well, she didn't have to take *that* lying down.

'Well,' she said with a fine combination of the sweet and sour, 'you don't seem to live too bad a life by some people's standards.'

Dennis winced. 'Aye, well. Let's have another one, then go and eat.'

'I'm all right for now, thanks,' Vera said evenly.

'Not for me,' murmured Dagmar.

All the signals indicated that battle lines were being drawn up. This was not going to be easy. Dennis looked at the two women, then waved to the barmaid.

'I'll have one, though,' he said. And by golly, he needed it.

Vera's bedroom at the hotel was small. When they got back from the restaurant, Dennis followed her in, watched as she carefully put her handbag and coat on the bed before turning to face him. She looked terrible: nervous and evasive.

'Okay,' Dennis said deliberately. 'Out with it. What's wrong?'

'Nothing.' Her tone betrayed her. It was defiant, accusing.

Dennis looked at her searchingly. 'It was an excellent restaurant, that. But you hardly ate a thing, and you said even less.'

'I told you,' Vera said, this time with an edge of complaint, 'I'm not feeling well. It must've been the flight. You know I don't like flying. You and Dagmar could've stayed and put me in a taxi ...'

Dennis snorted in exasperation. 'Of course we couldn't have stayed!'

'Why? Don't you normally stay with her?'

So now it was coming out, after all. Dennis felt a surge of

211

anger. 'What's that supposed to mean?' he snapped.

She looked away. 'Oh, just drop it, Dennis.'

'No, I won't,' he said firmly. Once he had the bit between his teeth, Dennis was nothing if not persistent.

'I'm tired,' sighed Vera, sitting down on the bed to remove her shoes.

Dennis shook his head. 'You're upset. And you're upset because I brought Dagmar.'

She looked up at him, their eyes met. 'Yes,' Vera said, 'I am upset because you brought Dagmar. Sometimes, Dennis you can be ...'

'I can be what?'

'... Insensitive. About what other people feel. You're stubborn. You get a notion fixed in your mind and you see it through. You don't always *think* it through.'

Dennis looked at her, shrugged. He was genuinely puzzled, it was true. Perhaps Vera had right on her side. 'I just want you to know the way things are,' he said more gently than before. 'No secrets. I know most of what's going on in your life. I want you to know the same about me.'

Vera shook her head, laughed a short, humourless laugh. 'Oh, it's you who don't know the way things are, pet,' she said.

'Oh, really!' exclaimed Dennis. 'Well, inform me, then!' he barked.

Suddenly she looked a bit like a little girl being confronted by a furious father. 'Don't get angry,' she muttered. 'We should've spent all our anger by now.'

Dennis nodded, calmed down. 'I'm not really angry. Confused, maybe.'

And so Vera started, slowly and deliberately. It was truth-telling time, all right.

'You don't see things as clearly as you think,' she told him. 'I didn't come here to "sort things out" – we could have done that over the phone. No.' She paused and took a deep breath. 'I came because our divorce isn't final yet. And ... I'm not sure I want it to be.'

Dennis took a couple of moments to react. 'What?' he echoed, flabbergasted. 'Wait a minute ... this divorce was

212

your idea if I remember correctly.'

'I know it was, Vera said mildly. 'And I know that hurt you. Hurt your pride, anyway. There were lots of reasons for our splitting up – good reasons, some would say – but I don't want to go over all that again.'

'Aye. Well, I wish I knew what you did want, Vera.'

She almost laughed out loud. 'I want you!' she said, looking him straight in the eyes, no longer tired and resentful but fiery. 'I want to forget the divorce, and I want *us* again!'

A heartbeat. 'Bloody hell,' breathed Dennis.

Vera got to her feet, marched the few steps towards the dressing table and a bag full of duty-frees.

'I got some gin on the plane,' she said. 'There's some glasses in the bathroom.'

Dennis nodded, as if mesmerised. It was the best idea he'd heard all evening. Still nodding, he made his way into the bathroom.

It was around midnight, and long after licensing hours ended at home in England, when Dennis stuck his head round the door of the Club. The place was almost empty, except for Wayne, who was standing at the bar. The cockney looked surprised to see Dennis, and maybe a bit embarrassed.

'Hello, Den!' he said. 'What you doin' here?'

Dennis shrugged. 'Nightcap.'

'Yeah, me too. What's yer poison?'

'Scotch.'

'No mistakin' that.' Wayne turned and ordered, then eyed Dennis appraisingly. 'Thought you were staying out tonight ...'

'Changed me mind,' said Dennis bluntly.

Wayne nodded, collected the drinks, suggested they find a table. They moved across to a corner of the room.

'Well,' Wayne said when they were seated. 'Things not work out with Dagmar and your old lady?'

'Disastrous.' Dennis sipped his whisky almost greedily. 'I thought I was just being straight and above board, you know. Vera said I was showing off.'

'Showing off?'

'Showing off Dagmar. Well, she is a smart lass. Attractive. Young. Maybe Vera's right and that's what I was doing.'

'She is a bit special, Dagmar,' Wayne agreed. He looked wistful. 'As is her sidekick.'

Dennis was puzzled for a moment. Then he got the message. 'Oh. Christa! Looks like you and me have collared the clerical staff, haven't we?'

'I wish I had,' said Wayne bleakly.

'Not work out, then? Thought the rat incident had been sorted out.'

'Saw her tonight,' Wayne explained. 'Wouldn't let me get near her.' He stared pleadingly at Dennis. 'Trouble was, I didn't want to, Den. I mean, come on strong. Jump it.'

'No? You're slipping.'

Wayne shook his head. 'I'm smitten, that's what I am. Don't tell the lads, but I can confide in you, can't I? I mean, I can bend your ear for a bit ...'

'Carry on,' said Dennis with his habitual wry smile. 'I don't have a care in the world.'

Wayne leaned forward confidingly. 'See, I'm serious about this Christa,' he said hoarsely. 'It's madness, I know, but I'm really bowled over. Now you won't tell the lads –'

Dennis managed to hide his amusement. Wayne was talking as if he'd got some terrible social disease. 'No, no,' he said. 'My lips are sealed.'

'I get embarrassed just thinkin' about it,' Wayne murmured. 'I'm actin' like an adolescent. Couldn't happen to me, I always said. And it has.'

In fact, Dennis decided, this *was* serious. He took a closer look at the cockney lad, decided it was all there. 'You're really serious, aren't you?'

'Deadly serious. 'Course,' Wayne mused, 'never havin' been in this situation before, it's hard to be certain about the symptons. But I think – well, I'm positive – that this is it. It's devastating, Den.'

'It's not the end of the world, kid. Go for it,' Dennis said sagely.

Wayne shook his head in despiar. 'Can't fathom it. An'

the trouble is, we're shippin' out in a week or two because of the law, ain't we?'

'So?'

'So I might have to decide. Whether to go back or chance me arm here.'

Dennis drained his glass, put it down heavily on the table. 'You're not the only one who has to make that decision.'

Wayne dragged himself out of his own well of self-pity and looked at Dennis with interest. 'You too?'

'Aye.'

'You mean, home or Dagmar.'

Dennis smiled sourly. 'I mean, Dagmar or Vera.'

'Blimey, Dennis,' said Wayne in genuine consternation. 'What are we going to do?'

They eyed each other for a moment. Dennis raised his empty glass.

'Well, I was about to get pissed,' he said quietly. 'Care to join me?'

TWELVE

Dennis slapped the brick down viciously. 'She loves me ...' he muttered sarcastically. Another. 'She loves me not ...' He lined up the brick. 'Now, of course, she ruddy loves me again ...'

'All right, Dennis?' Oz called out.

Dennis didn't look up. 'Wonderful.'

'Yeah?' said Oz, wandering over. 'Only you seem a bit down-in-the-mouth to me, like.'

'No, no,' Dennis said ironically. 'Full of the joys of spring, I am, Oz.'

Oz just looked puzzled. 'That's what you say, man. But I know different. I can tell by the way you're working you're not happy.' He settled on a piece of scaffolding. 'You're all listless. Same with our budgie back home – if he's not nuttin' seven shades out of his bell, we know there's somethin' bothering him.' Dennis showed no reaction. 'Aye,' said Oz, as if it really mattered, 'you can learn a lot about human nature by studyin' budgies.'

'Really?'

'Yeah.'

Dennis consented to look up for a moment. 'All right,' he said heavily. 'Suppose I *was* feelin' a bit down-in-the-beak. What do you do for your budgie that you could do for me?'

'Er, well. It varies,' Oz said, uncertain. 'I mean, sometimes we give him a cuttlefish to chew on, and other times we move his mirror round to give him a change of scene. Usually does the trick.'

'Aye. Well it won't work with me,' Dennis snapped.

'Nah – I suppose not,' said Oz, climbing down.

Neville had joined them while they were chatting, and he was standing around with his 'concerned' look on his young face. Dennis stared at him balefully. 'And what's the matter with you, lad?'

Neville shrugged. 'Oz is a bit concerned about you, Dennis.'

'I mean, are you going back to England or not?' Oz chipped in.

Dennis straightened up, fixed them both with a beady eye. 'What's it got to do with you?'

'Well, you're my mate, aren't you?' said Oz. 'I'd like to know what you're doin' before I decide what I'm doing, that's all. I don't want to stay on in Germany if all me mates are going home ...'

'So you're not really concerned about me at all,' Dennis said slowly. 'Basically, you're concerned about you.'

Oz could say nothing. He just looked a bit shamefaced.

'Look, bonny lad,' Dennis continued, jabbing the air with his trowel for emphasis, 'I'll tell you exactly what I told Vera. I'll make my mind up at the end of the week, and when I do, it's what's best for me that matters. Not what's best for Vera, or for Dagmar, or for you, or for your flamin' budgie! For once in my life I'm puttin' my interests first, all right?'

Then he got back to work, grafting like a demon. End of conversation.

The long-awaited summons to the Admin Hut came a few minutes later. From their various corners of the site, the Brits wandered over to a meeting with Grunwald.

'Hey, Bomber,' said Oz. 'How about you? Signing on for another spell?'

The big man smiled and shook his head. 'Not me, Oz. I'd sooner pay tax in England than in Germany, if that's what it comes down to.'

'Yeah,' said Oz thoughtfully. 'But you've got to have a job before you pay tax, Bomb. And the West Country's nearly as bad as Newcastle.'

Bomber winked. 'Bomber'll be all right. Harvest time's

218

comin' up. I shall hump a spot of hay for a few weeks, then see what's what. I've had a good run here.'

Oz's face fell. 'Another one bites the dust!'

Bomber addressed Dennis, who had been walking silently a little way away, with them and yet not part of them. Sullen.

'How about you, Den? Decided yet?' he boomed.

Dennis just scowled and strode on.

'Touchy subject that, Bomber,' Oz explained.

'So I see.'

They both had to move aside as Wayne suddenly burst through, haring like a lunatic towards the Admin Hut.

'Bloody hell! Is it a bird, is it a Wayne?' quipped Oz.

By the time they arrived at the Admin Hut, the cockney chippie was being ushered out of Christa's presence and into Grunwald's office, and he was struggling every inch of the way. No wonder he had hurried to get there a short while ahead of everyone. A few minutes with his beloved . . .

When they were all in the hut, Grunwald lit his pipe, to give the occasion solemnity, and called for silence. He ignored the fact that Wayne kept dancing around the room, trying to get close to Christa, cleared his throat and began:

'Gentlemen, as you probably know, there have been one or two changes concerning the Federal Government's attitude to *Gastarbeiter* – visiting workers. This is because of increasing unemployment in Germany.' He smiled his wintry smile. 'Yes, we have it also.'

'Ah, but ours is bigger than yours!' called out Bomber proudly.

Grunwald smiled. 'So,' he continued, 'we have to look at ways of keeping jobs for our own people. Now, up till now you have worked here without paying taxes or insurance, and that has been very convenient for everyone.' He paused and looked at them all solemnly. 'From next Monday, however, if you wish to stay and work in Germany, you must apply for official registration and be issued with a licence.'

Oz scowled. 'Does that mean we have to give up British

219

nationality, because I'm buggered if I'm becoming a German!'

'No, no,' Grunwald explained hastily. 'You misunderstand, Osbourne. As members of the EEC, you have a right to work here. But now you must accept your financial obligations to the German state.'

'Why can't we work here and have our tax sent home to England?'

'Don't be ridiculous, Oz,' said Neville.

But Oz persisted. 'I'm not – I just think it's a bit much that we're givin' Germany our skill and our labour, and now it's tryin' to issue us with dog licences and take money off us!'

Neville apologised to Grunwald, who accepted and decided to ignore Oz. He asked for the names of those proposing to stay so that he could deal with the paperwork.

'Well, I can tell you now that I'm going back to England,' said Neville.

'So.' Grunwald made a note in his pad.

'Me too, Mr Grunwald. The family calls,' Bomber told him.

Grunwald expressed regret, noted the names, looked at the others.

'Not sure, yet, Herr Grunwald,' said Barry.

'Me neither.' Moxey was looking unhappy.

Grunwald's gaze flickered, moved across to Dennis. 'Mr Patterson?'

Dennis could feel all Dagmar's attention on him in the next room. 'I haven't decided yet, Herr Grunwald,' he said stiffly.

'Well, it looks as though nobody is staying,' said the site boss.

'I wouldn't be too sure about that, Herr Grunwald,' Dennis corrected him. He nodded in the direction of Wayne. The cockney was standing transfixed, staring through the connecting hatch straight at the lovely Christa, in a world of his own and without the slightest idea of what was being said. All right for some.

*

220

'I'd forgotten all about this, Wayne, until you went and asked,' growled Neville.

He had rolled his sleeve back and was allowing his fatal tattoo to be used as a model for the Wayne/Christa entwined around a heart motif that the chippie was carving into a bit of polished planking.

'Just as well,' Wayne told him, chiselling away cheerfully. 'Imagine what the scene would've been this coming Saturday – you and Brenda are locked passionately together on the sofa over a cup of cocoa. Unable to control your ardour any longer, you slip your pyjama jacket off and – wallop! Brenda's screams wake up half Tyneside! At least now you've got five days to think up a story.'

Neville refused to be comforted. 'Yeah, well – whatever I tell her, she's goin' to believe the worst, isn't she? Have you finished yet?'

'What? Oh yeah. Just wanted to get the general idea. Ta.'

'What is it you're making, anyway?' asked Neville, rolling down his sleeve.

'It's a sort of commemorative plaque, I suppose. Two hearts intertwined for ever – Wayne an' Christa. You know, like Marks & Spencer or Neville and Lotte –'

Neville got to his feet, clearly offended. 'Instead of making tactless jokes, Wayne, why don't you use your rancid imagination to help me come with an explanation for the damned tattoo?'

Wayne gave every sign of thinking seriously. 'All right,' he said, 'how about this: It was your first night over here, you underestimated the strength of German beer, got pissed out of your brain, and woke up the next morning with that on your arm.'

'That's no good – that's what happened,' said Neville, making for the door. 'Thanks a bunch, Wayne,' he added huffily.

Before he could walk out, though, the door opened and in sauntered Barry.

'All right, Nev?'

'Not really, Barry, thank you.' Neville made to leave.

'Oh, Nev.' Barry took his arm and led him to one side. 'What?'

Barry peered around secretively. 'I know I had to bring this up with you once before,' he whispered. 'Now you're goin' home, though, you won't forget about your little t-a-t-t-o-o, will you?' He spelled out the feared word.

Neville glowered at him. 'Barry,' he said with slow-acting venom. 'Get s-t-u-f-f-e-d, will you?'

With that he stalked out, leaving a nonplussed Barry.

'Charming,' said Barry when he'd worked out the spelling.

Wayne chuckled. 'Don't take offence, mate. There's a lot of chickens comin' home to roost this week. The pressure's on. We've had our own private cocoon these past few months, but now real life is howling at the door again.'

Barry glanced at the door, impressed by Wayne's image. Then he came and sat down.

'Y'know, Wayne,' he said. 'I hope you don't mind me sayin' this, but there's a great serenity and wisdom about you these days.'

'That's the power of love, innit?'

'I suppose it must be.' Barry looked sheepish, as if hardly daring to continue. Finally he said: 'What's it like – you know, to be in love? Between you and me, I've never really sparkled in that department. Or in any adjacent ones for that matter. I'm the sort of bloke who sees the three-year expiry date on a packet of nodders an' wonders if he'll use 'em in time . . .'

Wayne shrugged. 'Don't worry, son. Your turn'll come. And you'll know when it hits you.'

'Yeah – but what does it feel like?'

'Well,' Wayne mused, putting down his chisel for a moment. 'Let's have a think. Love . . . love is bein' able to sit in a hut on a German buildin' site, carving two names into a plank of wood and not feelin' a pratt about it. Okay?'

Barry's eyes widened in admiration. 'I know I've had a bit of a viperish tongue where you're concerned in the past, Wayne, but that – that was almost poetry!' he gasped.

'I hope she likes it,' Wayne said. 'It's important.'

'You mean to say, you're goin' to let this Christa woman decide your future for you?' said Barry.

'Yeah, why not?' Wayne seemed unabashed. 'If she wants

222

me to stay, I'll stay. If she doesn't, then I won't want to be around anyway.'

'Cor...' Barry was in awe. 'You see, that's the sort of thing that's beyond my comprehension, really. Deep emotions that can change the course of your very existence. Even when I got engaged, the only major upheaval it caused was goin' to watch West Brom instead of Wolves.' He frowned sadly. 'I think I must be shrivelled inside, me.'

'Now, now,' said Wayne. 'You're gettin' all mournful. You should look on this week as a chance to expand your horizons, drift with the wind, be a free spirit.'

'Yeah – I suppose you're right. I think I might try Saudi Arabia or one of the Gulf States.'

Wayne looked shocked. 'They're no good to you, are they? You can't drink, and anything you touch a woman with gets chopped off!'

'That's the point,' Barry agreed bleakly. 'If I went there, I'd be forced to accept the inevitability of my celibate nature.' His eyes took on a faraway look. 'You know, I think I must've been a Giant Panda in a former life. They don't get much either, do they?'

Wayne, meanwhile, had been working away busily. He grinned. 'There it is,' he said. 'All I've got to do now is saw it off across here and slap a dab of varnish on it.'

Barry looked at the masterpiece. 'Very nice. Here – when you hand it over to Christa, why don' you sing her that old Elvis song, the one in German – "'I Don't Have a Wooden Heart . . .'"'

'That's a terrific idea,' said Wayne, impressed. He slapped Barry on the shoulder. 'There you are, see – you're an old romantic, after all. There's hope for you yet.'

'Yeah. P'raps you're right,' Barry said, brightening. 'Bit of hope.'

But if most of the lads managed to start sorting themselves out, Dennis was the exception. He got worse. That night in the Club, he sneaked off to one end of the bar and launched a solitary attack on a bottle of schnaps while the rest of them indulged in the usual banter. Neville's tattoo was still the big theme.

'Here, what about: "I contributed to a German heart-disease charity, and instead of a little flag in me lapel, they put a tattoo on me arm'?" Neville suggested, only half-joking.

That caused general mockery.

'Even Brenda would see through that one!' Oz guffawed.

Neville turned and stared along the bar in Dennis's direction. 'Well, I'm sure Dennis could come up with something,' he said hopefully.

Dennis didn't even look at him. 'Not a chance,' he growled.

A hush fell among the Brits.

'What's got into him?' Moxey murmured.

Bomber shrugged helplessly. 'I dunno, but it's certainly taken a hold.'

'Well, I'm gonna have a word with him,' said Oz gruffly. 'He'll talk to me.'

He made a move, but Dennis turned on him before he got very far along the bar. 'Stay right where you are, Oz!' he rasped dangerously. He was well oiled, and it hadn't improved his mood.

'Come on, Den. We're your mates!' Bomber said. 'Whatever it is that's got to you, share it with us...'

Dennis laughed. It was not a pleasant or a humorous sound. It was bitter.

'A trouble shared is a trouble halved, eh? That was one of Vera's favourite phrases...'

It was too much for Neville as well. The younger man advanced on Dennis, concern written all over his open, honest face. 'Come on, Dennis – snap out of it.'

Dennis's eyes narrowed. 'Snap out of it! Will you listen to this lad?' He rounded on all of them. 'Have you any idea of what it's like being kicked out of a marriage?' he said, his voice thick with self-pity. 'It's... it's like being asked to take down all of them walls we've been building, brick by brick with your bare hands. Imagine what that feels like, eh?' He paused. His voice fell to a croak. 'Then imagine what it would be like if they came along and said, "now put 'em back up again"!'

'We can help you, Den,' said Bomber, voicing the confusion and concern of the lads.

Dennis shook his head. 'Thanks for the offer, Bomber, but you can't. I can help you with your problems, but apparently it doesn't work the other way round. That's how it is. So just do me the only favour you can – all of you – and leave me alone.'

With that he slid off the barstool, still holding the half-empty bottle of schnaps, and tottered unsteadily out of the Club. They watched him in silence.

Goodbye to Dennis the Rock, the man you could rely on. It was almost like losing a father.

'Mornin', ladies,' said Wayne shyly, edging his way into the Admin Hut. He was carrying something bulky behind his back. Christa and Dagmar exchanged looks.

'Good morning, Wayne,' said Dagmar.

Christa smiled sweetly. 'Hello, Wayne.'

Encouraged, Wayne whipped out the piece of varnished wood from behind him. 'Tarraa! I've brought you a little something.' He handed it to her.

'Oh Wayne!' Christa gasped. 'It's beautiful! Did you make it yourself?'

Wayne nodded proudly. 'My union card says "joiner", but I'm a sculptor really.'

'Dagmar, look,' said Christa. 'Wayne has made me a paperweight.'

That deflated the cockney a bit. 'No – its not a paperweight. Its a plaque, isn't it?' He grinned. 'It's supposed to go on your wall – you know, above your bed.'

Christa's blue eyes twinkled. 'Ah, yes,' she said tactfully. 'Of course. It will look very nice there.'

'That's all right then,' said Wayne, his confidence restored. 'I ... er ... also wanted to fill in one of those forms. If you'll give me a hand.'

'Which forms?' The eyes were still twinkling.

Wayne blushed, found it hard to get the words out. 'You know. The ... er ... work-permit things. Or whatever ...'

'You're staying?' Christa asked with a smile.

'Yeah. 'Bout the only one who is by the look of it,' Wayne blurted. Then he saw Dagmar's sad reaction out of the corner of his eye and realised that he'd goofed. 'I mean, there's a couple of us who haven't quite made their minds up yet,' he added hastily.

Christa, meanwhile, was taking a form out of her desk. Wayne, having said the initial part of his piece, looked on apprehensively. She had become cool, businesslike again. Maybe this was just a bit of work to her. Maybe she was the office tease. Every place had one . . .

'I write it in for you, shall I?' she asked.

'Yes, please. My German never got past the "donner and blitzen" stage.

'Okay. Your full name, please.'

Wayne hesitated. He summoned up all his courage, leaned forward and looked into her eyes. 'Look,' he murmured, 'you . . . you *do* realise why I'm doing this, don't you?'

There was a heavy pause. Christa looked down at the form, and when she looked up again her eyes were shining and she was smiling with warm reassurance.

'I can guess. It's okay,' she said very deliberately.

'Yes. Yes. Well, it's Wayne Winston Norris,' the cockney gabbled, vastly relieved.

In the last ten seconds, his whole world had changed.

And all Dagmar could do was to pretend to work, try to be happy for them, when every word was like a stab in the heart.

The rest of that day passed in relative peace. Dennis, hungover from his exploits the previous night in the Club and God knows where else, kept himself to himself. But the rest of them worked – and worked hard, for the German management was not going to let up on them just because they were leaving. When they gathered in the hut after work that evening, most of the lads were well shattered – except Wayne, who was still on Cloud Nine, of course.

'Cup of Rosie, Bomb?' he offered, doing the honours on the tea.

'Cheers, Wayne,' Bomber said, slumping wearily into a chair. 'Though I reckon I'll have trouble liftin' it. These buggers are gettin' their money's worth out of us before we go back – we've had a foreman stood over us all afternoon. How've they been down your section?'

Wayne joined Bomber at the table, shoved his mug of tea over. 'Sweetness and light, mate,' he told him cheerfully. 'Mind you, I *have* signed the pledge today. Official worker on Monday, me.'

Bomber took a second or two to digest the information that Wayne had so casually dropped. Then he grinned, put out one ham of a hand and they shook on it.

'Well, good luck to you, boy,' he said. 'I hope you make a go of it!' The big man winked, making his meaning unmistakable.

'Ta,' said Wayne simply. No jokes, no backchat. He knew Bomber meant what he said.

Then Moxey, Neville and Oz trooped in, threw their gear into the cage and headed for the stove and the tea. Or rather, Moxey and Neville did. Oz sauntered over to the table and put his feet up.

'Young Wayne's signed on, then,' said Bomber with a nod in the direction of the young cockney.

Oz tutted, shook his head. 'Gonna be stuck with you, then, London?'

Wayne smiled ruefully. 'It's Oz's charm that knocks me out.'

Oz chortled, called over to the tea corner: 'Bring us a tea over, Nev!'

Moxey turned to Neville, who was spooning sugar into a mug. 'He's getting really bossy, isn't he?'

Neville grinned. 'Yeah – Barry's Planet of the Apes theory has gone to his head.'

The monkey reference came, of course, from a comment by Barry. The paperback-reader claimed that with Dennis virtually inoperative as the hut's leader, a succession struggle was beginning, and that Oz was a leading contender. This he culled from his reading of *The Naked Ape* and its comments on the political life of chimpanzees. Accordingly, Neville and Moxey loped over like chimps and made authentic zoo noises as they brought Oz's tea over. Oz, playing up to them, accepted their obeisance with majestic indifference.

Wayne looked on in amusement. 'Of course,' he commented, 'the advantage of bein' a chippie is that you don't have work in the hot sun. So you get to keep all your marbles.'

When the performance was over, Oz sipped his tea thoughtfully. 'This is all Barry's fault, this is. Him reckonin' we miss Dennis's leadership.'

'Well, we're all worried about Den, that's for sure,' said Bomber.

'Yeah,' agreed Wayne. Come on – what are we goin' to do about him, eh? We've leant on him enough over the past months. It's about time we helped the poor sod out.'

'But that's just the point, Wayne,' Neville said. 'He won't let us.'

'Must be his pride, like,' Oz contributed.

Moxey sat down. 'Maybe he doesn't trust us.'

Wayne was just opening his mouth to say something more when the man himself walked in. Dennis didn't acknowledge them, just chucked his gear on his bed, picked up a towel. Then he headed for the door again. But just as he reached it, he turned as if he knew all eyes were on him.

'Oh,' he said quietly, 'just so's we don't have any more embarrassing scenes, I won't be drinking in the Club tonight. I'm goin' into town to get mindless. So you'll be safe where you are.'

Then he was gone without another word. There was a general sighing and shaking of heads among the lads.

'Aye, I reckon that instead of examining our behaviour, Professor bloody Barry ought to take a look at his. I've never seen Dennis so withdrawn,' Oz said.

Neville looked at Oz without much charity. 'Why don't you pool your knowledge of budgies with Barry's knowledge of chimps?' he suggested acidly. 'Between you, you might come up with a solution.'

Oz was hurt. 'There's no need for that, Nev.'

'Isn't there? You don't seem to care about Dennis at all!'

Neville's newfound aggression lit a fire in turn under Oz. The other Geordie, cut to the quick, jumped to his feet.

'I bloody do!' Oz protested furiously. 'And what's more – I'll bloody prove it!'

And with that, he stormed out into the unknown. As Wayne had so wisely said, quite a few things were coming to a head this last week.

The *Bierkeller* was crowded, smoky, reeking of stale beer and staler humanity. Harassed waiters scurried around the huge, dimly-lit cavern carrying trays of foaming Pils. This was a good place to do some serious drinking. It was also a good place to lose yourself in the crowd. Or so Dennis had thought when he picked it. He sat in one corner at a small table, morosely attacking his umpteenth beer of the night and waiting patiently for oblivion. But this evening it was not to be granted him.

'Hello there, Geordie,' growled a harsh Scouse voice.

Dennis looked up blearily. Christ, he thought. It was Magowan. The brutal Merseysider had disappeared from the site and their lives a while back, to everyone's relief. He had jumped bail, in fact, while awaiting trial for an incident involving some Germans in a bar and nasty work with a broken bottle. Dennis was surprised and dismayed to see him here, smirking down at him.

'Magowan!' he croaked. 'What are you doing here?'

'Same as you, by the looks of it. Getting pissed!'

Without waiting for an invitation, Magowan grabbed an innocent German drinker by the collar and shoved him to one side so that he could sit down opposite Dennis.

Dennis frowned. 'Join me, why don't you?'

His sarcasm was lost on Magowan. Perhaps fortunately. 'Thanks,' said the animal.

They sat weighing each other up for a few moments. Dennis broke the ice, if that was the right expression.

'I thought you were supposed to be out of the country, avoiding the law,' Dennis said.

Magowan grinned wolfishly. 'Takes more than some poxy German court to drive me out of town. I just kept me head down for a few days, steered clear of the construction sites 'cos I figured I'd be a marked man.' He looked very, very pleased with himself.

'A reasonable assumption in the circumstances,' Dennis agreed. 'So what are you doing for a crust, then? You couldn't have made much out of selling our dart-board . . .'

The last little dig bounced off Magowan's heavy armour.

The Scouse bruiser had walked off with the hut's board as well, but he wasn't about to give it back, that was clear.

'Yeah. Sorry about that. Left you the darts, though ...' Magowan chuckled, turned and spotted a waiter gliding past with a tray of beers. He stood up, grabbed the man's arm. 'Oi! How about some more beer!' he grunted. When the waiter tried to hand him a glass, he simply grabbed the tray and pushed the waiter away, bellowing: 'No! No! You stupid Eric – leave us the tray. And put it on the slate, *verstehen?*'

He planted the tray on the table. The terrified waiter opened and closed his mouth a couple of times, but nothing came out. Then he ducked off through the throng. Discretion was obviously the better part of valour with crazy Englishmen.

'Should keep us going for a while,' Magowan said.

Dennis shook his head in disapproval, but he took another beer from the tray. 'The one advantage of being with you, Magowan, is that you get decent service,' he said.

What Dennis didn't notice was the fact that Oz had come down the steps into the Bierkeller and had been about to walk over when he had noticed Magowan. Oz was now sipping a beer a way away, biding his time and obviously hoping that Magowan would get fed up and leave so that that he could be alone with Dennis and 'sort him out'.

'So what are you actually doing, then?' Dennis asked, unaware of Oz's presence a few yards distant.

Magowan finished off half a glass of beer and smacked his lips. 'Oh, I'm workin' as a bouncer in a night-club. Any Erics get out of order, I drag 'em off the floor, chuck 'em down the stairs and out into the alley.'

'Voluntary work, is it? Do it for love?'

Magowan shook his head. 'Twenty quid a night plus all I can drink.'

'Must cost 'em a hundred a night, then.'

That did it. Magowan leaned forward menacingly. 'Listen, Geordie,' he said in a voice like iron fillings, 'I'm drinkin' with you 'cos you're a Brit, right? But don't take the piss, or I'll treat you the same way I treat the customers.'

'Oh, they get customers in this club, do they?' said

Dennis. 'Surprised you haven't frightened 'em all off ...'

He was spoiling for a fight, which in Magowan's case meant that Dennis must have a suicidal impulse. The craggy Scouse's eyes narrowed into slits.

'Right,' he snarled. 'Soon as I've finished this tray, I'm goin' to give you a thumping.'

'Thump away, Magowan,' retorted Dennis bitterly. 'What do I care?'

Magowan leered. 'Tired of life, are we, Geordie?'

'You could say that.'

If Dennis was unaware of Oz's shadowy presence, he was also ignorant of the fact that there were some other blokes from the site drinking in the Bierkeller tonight. Not particularly welcome ones, either: they were a couple of German joiners who didn't much like Brits and had chanced their arms with Dagmar and Christa – purely because they were known to be going out with Englishmen. The incidents had been petty, but everyone in Hut B knew and avoided the pair, who were the exception so far as their German workmates went. With all the others, Brits would stand a beer or two when they met by chance of a night, but not with the notorious joiners.

The trouble was, the joiners had been drinking as hard, if not harder, than Dennis tonight, and when they spotted him in the corner they pushed their way over. Dennis was deep in his potentially lethal verbal tussle with Magowan when he heard a slurred voice next to him, making comments in German that were obviously intended for his consumption. He half-understood them, and certainly caught the word 'Dagmar' at the end, and the way it was said.

Dennis looked up, found himself staring into the smirking face of one of the joiners, who immediately made some remark to his mate, pointed deliberately at Dennis and laughed.

Magowan, of course, had noticed the situation and was relishing it. 'Couple of Erics lookin' for trouble, if you ask me.'

Dennis nodded but put up a warning hand. 'Stay out of this Magowan. I'll handle it,' he said without taking his eyes off the two Germans. Then he spoke to the main culprit, slowly and with steel in his voice. *'Nicht verstehen,* bonny lad.'

The German swayed slightly, sneered. 'Go home wiz your wife,' he drawled. 'We will have Dagmar!'

Magowan looked pleased. 'I'd say they were provoking you, Geordie,' he said, their previous argument forgotten. 'Want me to sort 'em out?'

Dennis got to his feet. 'Get lost, Magowan. This is my problem.'

Magowan laughed cruelly. 'You're not hard enough for it, Geordie!'

Without looking at the Scouse, Dennis said: 'Oh, aren't I?' and launched a haymaker punch straight into the stomach of the still-leering German who had made the remark about Dagmar. The German was lifted off his feet and crumpled onto the floor. The punch had had strength, pent-up emotion and, most importantly, real hatred behind it. The punch represented everything Dennis had been longing to do all this tortured week of his life. And it did damage.

'Not bad!' said Magowan, impressed. He looked down with a connoisseur's approval at the injured German, who was still writhing on the ground, wheezing and moaning.

Dennis turned away, having acquitted himself to his own satisfaction. Meanwhile, the other German crouched down to examine his friend. Dennis didn't see him grimace, straighten up again quickly and reach for a beer-glass, his face contorted with murderous anger . . .

Oz did. He had started to move at the first sign of trouble, and when the uninjured German decided to cut up rough, he was only a few feet from Dennis's back, though unseen by his friend.

'Dennis, watch it!' Oz bawled at the top of his lungs, and launched himself forward between the German and Dennis.

With seconds, Magowan was in there too. There was shouting, screaming, and blood flowing on the scrubbed floor of the old Bierkeller – and some of the blood was made in Newcastle.

THIRTEEN

Neville dashed along the corridor, burst into the hospital room, then suddenly stopped, shocked and awed by what he saw. The phone call to the Club, the frantic dash in a taxi, and suddenly here was the reality. A bloodstained Dennis sitting in tatters at one end of the bleak, sterile room, and on the bed an unconscious Oz with one arm heavily bandaged and wired up to a serum drip. Dennis had his head in his hands. When Neville entered, he looked up and gave him a thin smile.

'Bit of a choker, isn't?' he said quietly.

Neville took a step forward. 'Is . . . is he all right?'

Dennis nodded. 'Aye. They've just sedated him to make him rest. They had to give him a blood transfusion. Over two litres.' He shrugged. 'Good job the ambulance got here so quick.'

'What happened, for God's sake?' said Neville, taking in Dennis's battered, distraught condition.

'There was a bit of a rumble with some German lads in this Bierkeller. Magowan turned up and Oz got in the way of a beer glass.'

Neville snorted disapproval. 'Magowan! That bloody madman'd start a fight in an empty house! And Oz isn't far behind . . .'

Something in Dennis's expression made him stop. The older man was shaking his head sadly. There was an uneasy silence for a moment.

'You've got it wrong, Nev,' Dennis began, and the words cost him dear. 'It was my fault. I started the rumble.'

'*You* did?'

Dennis nodded slowly. 'Aye.' He cleared his throat, decided to make the effort and get it off his chest. 'I should've walked away. Normally I'd have done just that – but then things haven't been exactly normal these past couple of days.' He paused and spoke softly and thoughtfully: 'That glass was meant for me – Oz just appeared out of the crowd. He saved me, Nev.'

Neville considered the implications, remembering Oz's hasty promise after their argument in the hut earlier in the evening. 'He must have followed you.'

'What?'

'The two of us had a bit of a row in the hut tonight,' Neville explained. 'I accused him of not caring about you. He said he'd prove he did. I suppose he must have been keeping an eye on you.'

Dennis leaned back in his hospital chair, rested his head against the wall and looked skyward. 'My God, what a mess!'

Then a young woman doctor walked in. Pleasant-looking, but with the kind of brisk, no-nonsense manner that quickly put a man on his best behaviour. Dennis got to his feet.

'Doctor, this is one of Mr Osbourne's colleagues,' he said, introducing the younger man. 'Neville Hope.'

The doctor shook Neville's hand in the German fashion. 'Hello. Your friend Mr Osbourne is a very lucky man,' she told him in near-perfect English.

'I know,' said Neville. 'We're very grateful for what you've done.'

The doctor smiled as she checked the flow of the drip. 'Don't thank me for doing my job, Mr Hope.' She sighed. 'I just wish you men could settle arguments without resorting to violence.'

Neville shifted uneasily. 'It's not typical, doctor.'

'Forgive me,' she said. 'I see a lot of people injured in stupid, drunken fights over football or women. Sometimes I am not so patient with my patients.' A thin smile at her own joke.

'That's very understandable,' Dennis agreed. 'Is he going to be all right, then?'

'Oh, yes. He had lost a lot of blood, but that's been replaced. He is resting. And fortunately the wound is not too large.' The doctor indicated the area of wound by measuring it out on her own arm. 'He will have a scar, of course, but eventually that can be corrected, if he wishes.'

Suddenly Neville's eyes brightened and he snapped out of his gloomy reverie.

'Corrected?' he asked, all attention.

'Yes. Skin graft, cosmetic surgery, whatever you call it.'

Then Neville started to take off his jacket, and Dennis realised what he was up to. He hissed that this was neither the time nor the place, but the lad was desperate. Within seconds he had his sleeve rolled up and was waggling his tattooed arm under the doctor's nose.

'I hope you don't mind my asking, doctor, but – as you're here – is there anything I can do about this?'

Dennis put his head back into his hands.

'Oz wouldn't mind,' Neville said defensively. 'And I've got to do something.'

The doctor peered at the design with interest. 'Who is Lotte?' she asked.

Neville blushed. 'I don't know. But she's not my wife, and that's the trouble.'

'Ah, so this is an unwanted souvenir of your stay in Germany?'

'Very much unwanted, doctor. I've already lied once to my wife about it.' Neville looked shamefaced. 'I bandaged it up, told her it was an injury. I can't do that for the rest of my life, can I?'

The doctor nodded sagely. Dennis could see she was supressing a smile. 'Okay – if you would like to step outside with me, I'll see what I can do . . .'

Neville went out eagerly, ushered through the door by the doctor. And as she followed him out into the corridor she paused to give Dennis a broad wink.

Dennis smiled for the first time in a long while. Left alone with Oz, he stood up and wandered across to the bed, looked down at his mate's prone form.

'Sorry, Oz,' he whispered, patting the motionless hand. 'Sorry.'

'C'mon, he'll be all right,' said Bomber with as much certainty as he could muster.

Wayne nodded. 'Strong as an ox, ain't he?'

'We'd have heard by now if it was bad,' said Barry hopefully.

'Yeah – they're really on the ball in these German hospitals.' Moxey's voice trailed off and he took a gloomy sip at his beer.

The subdued group of Brits ranged along the bar of the Club had been waiting for over two hours now, since Neville had left in a taxi for the hospital. Their mood hadn't improved, particularly in the past half-hour or so. Surely he'd be back soon – or at least phone . . .

'Hey, here he is!' bellowed Bomber suddenly. They all turned, saw a dejected Neville coming towards them.

'What's the word, then, Nev?' Wayne asked.

Neville shook his head. He looked as though he was about to burst into tears. 'They . . . they couldn't do anything . . .' he mumbled.

They all stared at him in frozen horror.

'Dear God . . .'

'Not Oz!'

'He was only thirty-one . . .'

'No, no,' Neville said, pulling himself together sufficiently to remedy the misunderstanding. 'I mean they could do nothing for my tattoo, not for Oz. He's fine, out of danger, very comfortable.'

There were boos and catcalls.

'Sorry lads, I was a bit preoccupied.'

'So what happened then?' asked Moxey urgently.

Neville nodded. 'Well, this lady doctor said I should stop being pathetic and just tell Brenda the truth. That if our relationship was strong, she'd understand. Gave me a right earful!'

Wayne scowled and moved closer. 'Neville,' he growled, 'how about if we ripped your arm off? Would that solve the problem? Tell us about Oz, for Christ's sake!'

'Well,' Neville began reluctantly. 'It looks as though he must have followed Dennis to the Bierkeller – to guard him, like. Anyway, there was a bit of aggravation and Oz got his arm slashed with a beer glass.'

He paused for the collective wince at the thought.

'The thing is,' he continued, 'that Dennis says it was his fault. Says he started the trouble.'

Bomber grunted sceptically, looked at the others. 'Ah, well,' he said. 'Dennis would say that, wouldn't he?'

There were nods all round. The thought was inconceivable. Then they heard Dennis's voice, loud and clear:

'It's the truth, Bomber.'

He had come in a short while after Neville and had been standing nearby but behind them, listening to the last few moments of the conversation. And he still looked terrible. Bloodstained clothes, bruised and cut face, and almost feverishly unhappy eyes.

They all looked at him in astonishment. He made no attempt to come forward, just stood a few feet away and looked back at them.

'Yes,' he continued quietly. 'Because of me, Oz was nearly killed.'

Bomber shook his head incredulously.

Dennis nodded to emphasis the truth of what he was telling them. 'Look, I've acted like a right prick these last few days,' he said. 'Wallowing in me own problems, shutting everybody else out. I'll make it up to Oz in due course, but in the meantime I've got a lot of apologies to make – you lads'll do for a start.' He took a deep breath. 'I'm sorry.'

There was a long pause while he stood there, staring at them, almost as if awaiting their verdict on him. It was like a tableau, a moment frozen in time.

Until Bomber let out a guffaw that came straight from his belly.

'Come on, you bad-tempered bastard!' he boomed. 'Buy us all a drink!'

Oz was sitting up in bed when Dennis arrived with the obligatory bunch of flowers and the sheepish grin. He had a pair of earphones stretched over his dark thatch of hair and was frowning to himself as he attempted to decipher the German radio programmes they piped into his room. He tore off the 'phones the moment he saw Dennis and beamed.

'Dennis! Good to see you, man!'

'How you doing, kidda?'

Oz shrugged. 'I'm all right – just a bit bored with this hospital radio. The German language is like interference in its own right, you know. All crackles and gungs and pzangs . . .'

Dennis sidled up to the bed, proferred the bunch. 'Bought you a little something.'

'Flowers?' asked Oz, puzzled.

'Look inside, man,' Dennis hissed, glancing furtively over his shoulder to make sure there were no doctors or nurses in sight.

Oz peered into the bunch. In the middle was a bottle of Pils. Oddly, Oz didn't look too thrilled, though he obviously appreciated the thought.

'I had to smuggle it in,' Dennis explained, '"cos I think that lady doctor's got a bit of a down on drink.'

'So have I after what happened last night,' Oz confessed ruefully. 'Speaking of which – what did happen last night?'

Dennis sat down and looked at him carefully. 'How much do you remember?'

'Well, I'm clear about that Eric with the glass, and I'm all right to the ambulance, but the rest is a blank. When I woke up here this morning, I thought they'd painted the hut again.'

Dennis nodded. 'You passed out in the ambulance. Loss of blood.' He paused. 'You're a lucky lad.'

'Lucky? Me?' Oz scoffed. 'The way I look at it, if I fell into a bag full of tits I'd come out suckin' me thumb . . . I'm gonna lose pay *and* get a hospital bill over this, aren't I?'

There was a flash of anger which Dennis chose to interpret as accusation.

'Don't worry about that, bonny lad,' he said quickly. 'I'll take care of it. Least I can do in the circumstances.'

'Ah, bollocks,' said Oz, chastened. 'I'm not gettin' at you,

238

Den. You'd have done the same for me. That's what mates are for, aren't they? Money doesn't come into it.'

They shook hands, each a little shamefaced.

Dennis relaxed after that. 'Anyway,' he told Oz, 'one good thing *did* come out of last night, apart from shakin' me up.'

'What's that?'

'Magowan's back behind bars,' Dennis said. 'He was dismemberin' those two Erics when the police arrived, so they've fingered him for the whole incident. You and me are down as innocent bystanders.'

Oz's thumb shot into his mouth. 'I think I've found a tit!'

They both laughed, a healing gust of humour.

'Aye, you'll do, Oz,' chortled Dennis. 'Not bad for a man who's not long had a blood transfusion.'

The laughter died on Oz's face so quickly that for a moment Dennis thought he'd had some sort of attack.

'Blood transfusion?'

'Aye,' Dennis said, nonplussed. 'They had to give you nearly four pints ...'

'You mean,' Oz cut in savagely, 'you mean to tell me there's four pints of German blood swillin' around inside me?'

Too late Dennis realised the terrible mistake he had made. He tried a desperate ploy to save the situation.

'Well, we can only surmise that it was German ...'

'But that means I'm half bloody Jerry!' moaned Oz.

'Look, they may have a special supply of English stuff put by in emergencies, Oz ...'

Neville was standing in the doorway, obviously wondering what was going on. He wore a short-sleeved shirt that showed a large plaster on his arm where the notorious tattoo was situated. It had been agreed that he would wear it at home as an interim measure, so to speak. Until he'd chatted up Brenda sufficiently to soften the blow.

'All right, Oz? How are you feeling?' he asked, tossing a bundle of English papers onto the bed.

'Bloody suicidal, man,' answered Oz grimly.

Neville's good-natured young face expressed confusion. Dennis, meanwhile, had spotted the plaster and was intent on seizing his chance while he could.

'Neville,' he said severely. 'I thought you were under strict orders to cover that up!'

'Cover up what?' said the lad.

Dennis sighed in well-feigned exasperation. 'It's no use playing dumb now – he's noticed the plaster!'

It was working: Oz was staring curiously at Neville's arm. Dennis turned to Oz and smiled as if embarrassed.

'According to medical ethics, donors are supposed to remain anonymous, but there's no point now, is there?' he explained. Then he rounded on Neville. 'You might have worn a small plaster, Neville!'

Oz was touched and impressed. 'You mean, Neville . . . ?'

'Aye – it was Neville.'

The man under discussion continued to look utterly baffled by the conversation. 'It was Neville what?' he asked.

Dennis took a deep breath. 'All right, Nev. If you won't tell Oz, I will. But I want you to know I'm proud of you.' He faced Oz again. 'Neville gave you four pints of his blood. Didn't you, Nev?'

Complete, agonised confusion.

'DIDN'T YOU, NEV?'

'Aye, I did,' the lad blurted, finally falling in with Dennis's ruse.

'Well, what a relief!' said Oz, glowing with pleasure and relief. 'How can I thank you, man?'

'It was nothing,' Neville said with a barbed glance at Dennis.

'You're a canny lad, Neville,' Oz continued. Then a thought struck him. He squirmed excitedly in his bed. 'Hey! You know what this means, don't you? Neville and I are blood brothers!'

Neville looked horrified. Dennis gave him a warning look. Neville nodded obediently, agreed they might be that.

'Give your blood brother the English papers, then,' Dennis said.

Neville shoved them over towards Oz, who thanked him warmly.

'Ah well,' said Dennis, looking at his watch. 'I'll have to be going. I've got to see young Dagmar.'

The new, reformed Dennis had done a number of things this morning, and the main one had been to fix to meet Dagmar for a drink. Heavy duty, and the lads knew it.

'Oh aye,' Oz said. 'Made your decision, then?'

'I have – but I think I ought to tell her first, if you don't mind.'

'I understand that,' Oz told him straight. 'And I can make my decision about stayin' without you, too, so don't feel any pressure from me, man.'

'Thanks Oz,' Dennis answered, realising the other man meant it.

Oz got stuck into the papers, still muttering about blood brotherhood. Dennis and Neville conferred briefly at the door.

'I'll see you back at the Club later, Dennis,' Neville hissed angrily.

'Aye. But I'll tell you. If he ever finds out, we're dead.'

The lad had to recognise that. Dennis turned and called out a farewell to Oz, then left. Neville wandered back and pulled up a chair by Oz's bed. Suddenly Oz seemed to undergo a palpitation. He was staring fixedly at the back page of the *Mirror*. His eyes were widening. His mouth was moving but it was a while before any sound came out.

'I ... don't ... believe it ...' he said slowly.

Neville leaned forward, concerned. 'What's up?'

'It's a sign,' Oz whispered. 'It must be! First you 'an me get related by blood, and now this! It's a message from above. I've got to get back home with you, Nev. I've got to!'

With great care and deliberation, as if it were a precious object, he turned the paper round to show Neville the headline on the Sports Page. There it was, a Geordie's dream:

KEEGAN SIGNS FOR NEWCASTLE!

They were half way across the Rhine Bridge when they stopped discussing Oz's condition and got down to theirs. As a couple, or singly? It came up when Dagmar commented how beautiful the bridge and the river were today.

'Aye – no doubt about that,' Dennis admitted. 'We've got a bridge much like this over the Tyne, mind. Well, not exactly like this, but beautiful in its own way.'

Dagmar smiled distantly. 'Sounds to me that you are homesick.' No reaction, so she forced the issue. 'So which is it to be, Dennis – the Tyne or the Rhine?'

Dennis chuckled drily, lit a cigarette, still staring out over the river.

'Well I'll tell you something, bonny lass,' he said gently. 'These last few days have been among the worst in my life. I don't imagine they've been a picnic for you, either.' A glance at her face told him he was correct in that. He pressed on anyway. 'But the way I see it now is this . . . if I was Dennis the bold, I'd be starting a new life for meself in a new country with a lovely young lass for me companion. Unfortunately,' he sighed, 'Dennis the bold is also a selfish sod, who gets his mates carved up when he tries to act big. So now he goes back to being Dennis the realistic. This Dennis knows that his role is to be a rock for other people to lean on. And if three of those people happen to be his wife and kids, he'll put realism before bravery every time.'

She understood what he was trying to say. The tears weren't too far away as she said: 'Would you have stayed if Vera had not come out the other weekend?'

Dennis nodded. In a way it was better to be honest. 'Probably.'

'Well, don't you think that I need you to lean on as much as she does?' There was suddenly bitterness in Dagmar's voice.

'It hadn't occured to me that way, no,' Dennis confessed unhappily.

'And why not? I am the one who's still trapped in a flat, living with my mother!'

It was almost unbearable. Dennis couldn't look at her at that moment.

'But Vera's got kids, Dagmar. Don't you see?' he said haltingly. 'It's the kids who make the difference. Because of the way I am, I'll always get pulled towards the area of greatest need. And that's back home. I'm sorry, pet. I really am.'

He'd had to say it. He'd meant every word of it. But that didn't make it any easier . . .

The back wheel of a bike suddenly appeared through the door of the hut that final night of their last working week. Wayne looked up from his bed.

'Anyone expecting a telegram?' he quipped.

The lads waited and within a few moments Barry appeared, manhandling his motorbike into the room with much panting and wheezing and groaning. He paused for breath.

'It's all right,' the Brummie lad gasped. 'Don't bother to give us a hand. I'll just rupture meself!'

Moxey got up but made no attempt to intervene. 'What's the score, Barry? Indoor moto-cross?'

Barry hauled the machine the last few feet, set it up on its parking tripod.

'Well,' he said, 'Old Faithful has got to get me to Jeddah next week, so I thought I'd give her a bit of a service before I set off.'

Neville looked at the bike and at Barry in dismay. 'You're not riding that thing all the way to Saudi Arabia?'

'No, I'm goin' to run alongside it, nurk!' said Barry irritably.

Wayne got up and surveyed the machine with obvious disapproval.

'Now look here, Barry,' he said. 'This is a bit previous. It's all right for the others, 'cos, I mean, they're all goin' their separate ways at the weekend. But this is still going' to be my home. I know it's the pits, but I don't want it turned into the Pits, if you know what I mean . . .'

'I'll be tidy, Wayne. Don't worry,' Barry said firmly. 'I could build meccano sets on a tea tray when I was a kid, without even losing a piece.'

Wayne went solemnly over to the table, found a battered tin tray, took it to Barry and shoved it under his nose.

'All right. But if so much as one nut or bolt strays off this tray, it's you on your bike!'

Barry was still working on the bike the following lunchtime when Neville came in, clutching a bundle of

243

tickets and travel documents. The site administration had let them have their passports back today. It was the final sign they were going.

'How's it going?' the Geordie asked. 'Be ready in time?'

'I think so,' said Barry. 'I've got one or two minor adjustments to make to the seat, and she needs topping up with oil.'

'Going to the right place for that, aren't you?' Neville chuckled. This was their last working day, and he was in good humour.

Barry looked puzzled, then laughed along with him. 'Oh yes – oil, Saudi Arabia. Ho, ho, ho! You're very cheerful and bright, Nev.'

'Got all our travel stuff for us Geordie boys,' Neville agreed, nodding enthusiastically. 'I've got the lot here. And I've just spoken to Brenda. Guess what?'

'What?'

'She's organisin' a surprise party for me tomorrow night.'

Barry stared at him levelly. 'How can it be a surprise party if you already know about it?'

'Don't quibble, eh, Barry?' said Neville, put out. Then he walked over to his locker and ceremoniously placed the passports and the rest in his locker. 'Where's the other lads?' he asked then.

'Over at the Club. Getting the supplies in for this afternoon.'

'What's happening this afternoon?'

'We're having a topping-out ceremony over on your section.'

'Topping-out do? But that bit's not finished yet.'

Barry stayed poker-faced. 'Don't quibble, eh, Nev?'

It was during the topping-out ceremony that Oz appeared, descending on a pallet with a crate of beer, courtesy of an Eric crane driver. He had his arm in a sling but he was bigger, uglier and more alive than ever. With his arrival, the drinking really got going. Later it transferred over to the Club. As Oz said, he might be a bit off the beer, but he had a few pints to replace, didn't he? And he took his medicine seriously, did Oz.

The booze flowed, the talk rambled. The lads discussed past experiences, swapped insults, made brave statements about the future. After a while, only Dennis was missing. He had made his apologies and gone off to see Dagmar. She and he had decided after their conversation on the Rhine Bridge that they couldn't part so bleakly. The lads understood. Soon it would be back to Vera and the kids and the estate house and probably the dole queue. A feller could savour what he had until he lost it, couldn't he?

It was late when they straggled back, singing drunkenly and all pals together. They stopped to salute the threadbare Union Jack that Moxey had hung on the scaffolding after the topping-out that afternoon. Oz, resplendent in his sling and magnificently tired and emotional, wandered on, occasionally casting a glance at the building and pointing to it with his good arm.

'See all that!' he slurred. 'We built that! Our skill did that...' He turned dramatically to the others. 'No computers will ever take the place of us ... last a thousand years, this buildin' will. There'll always be a place for quality workmanship. There may not be an England, but there'll always be ...'

And so it went on, as he and the rest of them staggered on across the site towards the hut.

There was a slight bottleneck at the door as they all tried to crush in at once. Muffled curses and thumps in the darkness. No one could find the light switch. Suddenly Wayne paused.

'Here,' he said. 'Wossat funny smell?'

Barry giggled drunkenly. 'It's Moxey's vick rub, innit?'

'Or his socks?' someone suggested.

Wayne wrinkled his nose. 'Nah – that's not socks!'

'Stonger than socks,' Barry agreed.

'It's petrol,' Wayne said then. He turned on Barry. 'Your naffin' bike's been leakin' fuel all over my floor, Barry.'

With a disgusted gesture, Wayne tossed away his cigarette end. They all froze as they heard a soft but ominous 'whoomph' noise. Something had ignited. And with seconds they were backpedalling down the steps in even more disorder than they had come, because the flames were shooting right across the floor, slithering and snaking and jumping higher . . .

'I'm glad we could say goodbye like this,' Dagmar said. She was more composed than she had been on the bidge. Or perhaps just resigned.

Dennis smiled. 'Aye. It's better than tears and jumpin' off bridges.' He looked at her with real concern. 'Are you going to be all right, pet?'

'I think so.' Dagmar sat next to him on the sofa and handed him his gin and tonic. Just like their first night together. Their first, ill-fated night. 'Yes,' she said, 'I have got over relationships before, after all. You will write to me, won't you?' She had been all right up until that last bit. It had come out a bit despairing.

'Of course, pet. I'll have plenty of spare time on me hands when I'm back on the dole.'

'Yes. I shall send you my new address when I move.'

Dennis looked around her mother's flat. The old dear was away on a family visit for the weekend and so they were alone. The place was neat, tasteful – and stifling for a lively young woman.

'Aye. Getting out of here will be a boon,' he said.

There was an awkward hiatus.

'Have you told Vera yet?' Dagmar asked, obviously trying to sound matter-of-fact.

Dennis shook his head. 'No. The arrangement was that I call her tomorrow morning.'

'So we could have one last night together?' Dagmar said quickly.

Dennis was torn. She looked beautiful tonight, and she was such a great lass. God, but he was tempted . . .

Before he could answer, the door bell rang. Dagmar started with surprise.

'Not expecting anyone, are you?' Dennis asked, putting down his drink.

'No. No one.'

'Then I'll come to the door with you. Just in case.'

They walked out into the hall together. Dagmar opened the front door with Dennis standing slightly to one side but close to her. Close enough to see Neville standing out in the corridor of the apartment building.

'Neville?' murmured Dagmar, glancing round at Dennis.

The lad looked very uncomfortable. 'Sorry to disturb you,' he said shyly. 'There's been an accident.'

'Accident?' echoed Dennis, moving into the doorway.

'Aye. The hut burnt down!'

'Revenge for the other night, or what?'

'Nothin' like that. Barry's bike caught fire.' Neville shrugged. 'Anyway, we've lost everything. Passports, tickets, clothes, money . . .'

'Suffering Ada!'

Dagmar clucked and looked sympathetically at Neville. 'You'd better come in, then, Neville. Stay here for tonight, okay?'

'Aye. Thanks.' Another embarrassed grin. 'Er, thing is, there's one or two of the lads as well . . .'

Faces appeared, grinning. Uttering greetings.

Barry.

Wayne.

Moxey.

Bomber.

Oz.

The whole of Hut B had come spend its last night in Germany doing its usual thing – messing up Dennis's sex life . . .

And so it was three days before the trio got back onto the fatal cross-channel ferry. Three days, a Monday, before they stood together again at the rail of the boat, taking the air and looking for a sight of land. Maybe they were a little wiser than they'd been a few months earlier. Certainly, for all their problems – Oz's bandaged arm, Neville's unexplainable tattoo, Dennis's near-broken heart – they were not really sadder, for your Geordie does not sadden easy.

'I think I can see England!' said Neville hopefully,

247

nestling into his jacket against the sea wind.

Dennis nodded. 'Aye. That's England all right. Mist, rain-clouds, cliffs as grey as slate. Home.'

'Bloody depressing-lookin' place when you think about it,' Oz commented.

Minder

– back again

Anthony Masters

Terry McCann and Arthur Daley are the Laurel and Hardy of London's criminal fraternity. Arthur's the one with the silver tongue, he could talk his way past St. Peter at the pearly gates if he wanted to. They say he even charges his mum petrol money when he runs her home . . . And when Arthur's hot air finally blows cold, it's usually poor old Terry who's left to do the dirty work! If there's ever a fast buck to be made, they'll be there like a shot. The only trouble is, where Terry and Arthur are concerned, there's always a sting in the tale as well!

MINDER – BACK AGAIN is based on the smash hit Thames Television series created by Leon Griffiths, starring Dennis Waterman and George Cole.

TV TIE-IN/FICTION   0 7221 5823 8   £1.50

Also by Anthony Masters, available in Sphere paperback:

MINDER

BACHELOR BOYS

THE YOUNG ONES'

BOOK

BEN ELTON · LISE MAYER · RIK MAYALL

Call it bad karma or anarchy in the U.K., there's never been anything quite like the cult-hit T.V. series *The Young Ones* — totally bizarre, totally original, totally aggressive and . . . totally TOTAL. So, here are the Young Ones in their own write at last: Rick the Radical Poet, Vyvyan the Psychopathic Punk, Neil the Suicidal Hippy, and Mike, the Would-Be Spiv. Together they reveal The Ultimate Truth About Everything to their avid fans, including absolutely zillions of helpless hints on:

★ HOBBIES
Neil's 101 really interesting things to do with a tea-cup
★ FILTH
Some kissing hints from Vyvyan. Lesson one: Snog the Dog
★ LAUGHS
Including Rick's only joke: These are my pants and I'm sticking to them!!!
PLUS
a controversial statement from the Acne Liberation Front. The Young Ones say: WEAR YOUR SPOTS WITH PRIDE

NON-FICTION/HUMOUR   0 7221 5765 7   £2.95

A selection of bestsellers from SPHERE

FICTION

DEEP SIX	Clive Cussler	£2.25 ☐
MILLENNIUM	John Varley	£1.99 ☐
SMART WOMEN	Judy Blume	£2.25 ☐
INHERITORS OF THE STORM	Victor Sondheim	£2.95 ☐
HEADLINES	Bernard Weinraub	£2.75 ☐

FILM & TV TIE-INS

THE RIVER	Steven Bauer	£1.95 ☐
WATER	Gordon McGill	£1.75 ☐
THE DUNE STORYBOOK	Joan D. Vinge	£2.50 ☐
NO-ONE KNOWS WHERE GOBO GOES	Mark Saltzman	£1.50 ☐
BOOBER FRAGGLE'S CELERY SOUFFLÉ	Louise Gikow	£1.50 ☐

NON-FICTION

PAUL ERDMAN'S MONEY GUIDE	Paul Erdman	£2.95 ☐
THE 1985 FAMILY WELCOME GUIDE	Jill Foster and Malcolm Hamer	£3.95 ☐
THE OXFORD CHILDREN'S DICTIONARY	John Weston and Alan Spooner	£3.25 ☐
THE *WOMAN* BOOK OF LOVE AND SEX	Deidre Sanders	£1.95 ☐
INTO THE REMOTE PLACES	Ian Hibell with Clinton Trowbridge	£2.95 ☐

All Sphere books are available at your local bookshop or newsagent, or can be ordered direct from the publisher. Just tick the titles you want and fill in the form below.

Name_____

Address_____

_____

Write to Sphere Books, Cash Sales Department, P.O. Box 11, Falmouth, Cornwall TR10 9EN

Please enclose cheque or postal order to the value of the cover price plus:

UK: 55p for the first book, 22p for the second book and 14p per copy for each additional book ordered to a maximum charge of £1.75.

OVERSEAS: £1.00 for the first book and 25p per copy for each additional book.

BFPO & EIRE: 55p for the first book, 22p for the second book plus 14p per copy for the next 7 books, thereafter 8p per book.

Sphere Books reserve the right to show new retail prices on covers which may differ from those previously advertised in the text or elsewhere, and to increase postal rates in accordance with the PO.